I0738394

A SUMMER OF
FEVER
AND
FREEDOM

A SUMMER OF FEVER AND FREEDOM

A NOVEL

CHELSEY ENGEL

Copyright © 2019 Chelsey Engel.

All rights reserved. No part of this publication may be reproduced, distributed or transmitted in any form or by any means, including photocopying, recording, or other electronic or mechanical methods, without the prior written permission of the publisher, except in the case of brief quotations embodied in critical reviews and certain other noncommercial uses permitted by copyright law. For permission requests, write to the publisher, addressed "Attention: Permissions Coordinator," at the email address below.

chelseyengelwrites@gmail.com

Publisher's Note: This is a work of fiction. Names, characters, places, and incidents are a product of the author's imagination. Locales and public names are sometimes used for atmospheric purposes. Any resemblance to actual people, living or dead, or to businesses, companies, events, institutions, or locales is completely coincidental.

Book Layout ©2019 BookDesignTemplates.com

Ordering Information:
Quantity sales. Special discounts are available on quantity purchases by corporations, associations, and others. For details, contact the "Special Sales Department" at the address above.

A Summer of Fever and Freedom/ Chelsey Engel. -- 1st ed.
ISBN 978-0-578-52252-4

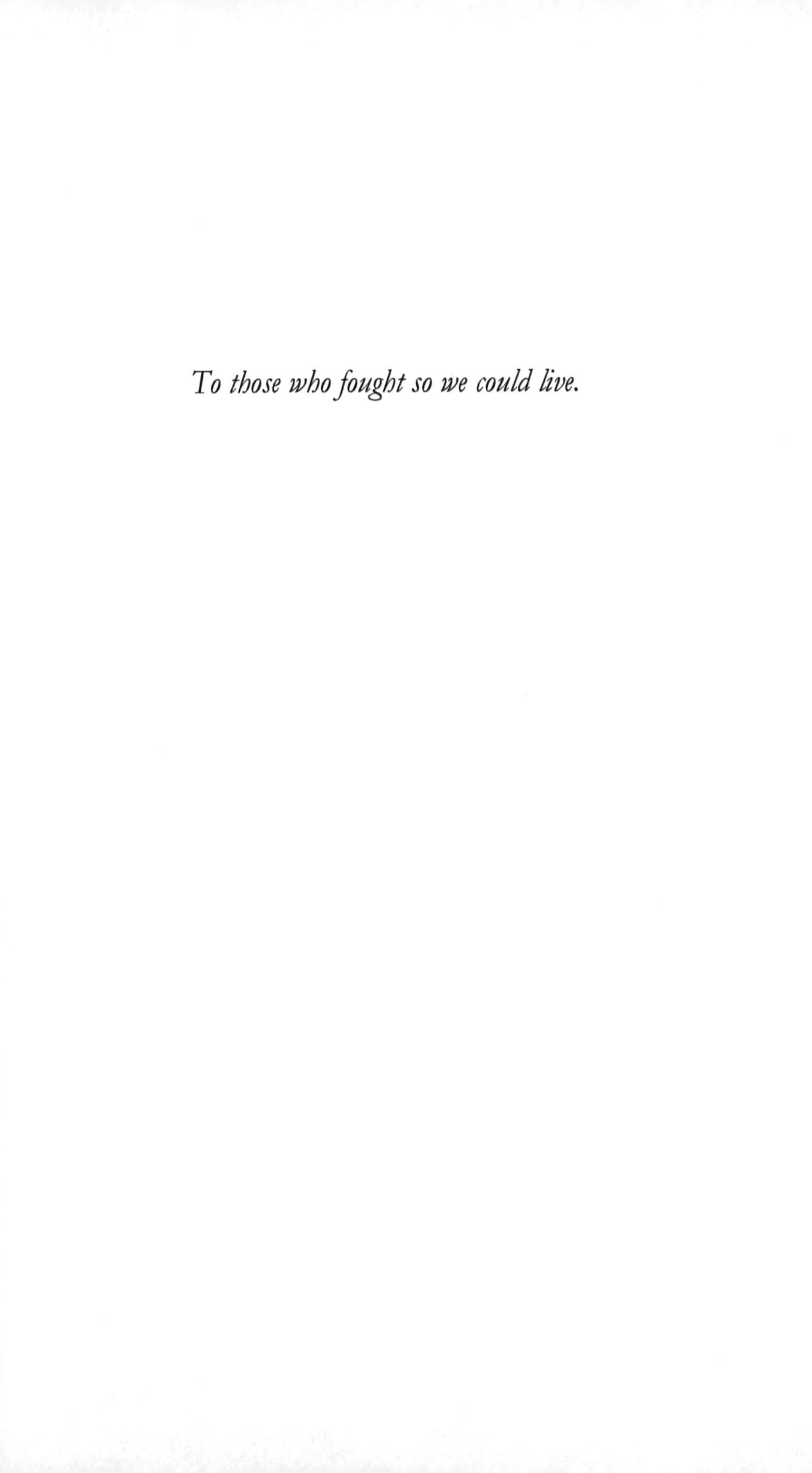

To those who fought so we could live.

ONE

••

TIME OF THE SEASON

Summer swept into the city with the ferocity of a plague, its heat weighted and wet like how Jane imagined Vietnam to be every day. The bookstore was on the first floor, but it did little to stave off the sudden suffocation. Even the covers of Steinbeck and Christie adopted faint layers of sweat, glistening like dewy windowpanes.

Jane tugged at the collar of her sleeveless blouse, her chest boiling as she wiped off the books on the front table with a handkerchief before using it to dab the pools of salt dripping down her neck. She cursed the humidity and wondered how her brother could stand it, then she reminded herself of gratitude. Then she cursed the war.

She tucked the kerchief into her back pocket as the door behind her swung open. She turned to find her best friend, Claire, bursting into the store, a smile of enticement plastered across her face.

"What now?" Jane teased with feigned exhaustion as Claire sauntered the rest of the way into the sun-soaked store swinging her beaded purse. She followed Jane to the checkout counter and leaned over it, lifting her feet slightly off the wood floor.

"Doug moved into his apartment in the Village with his NYU guys," she said. Claire loved many things; bringing up the fact that her older boyfriend was already in college was one of them. "They're having a party tomorrow night. You're coming."

Jane opened her mouth to protest, but Claire cut her off with a point of her finger. "No excuses!" She narrowed her cool blue eyes. "We're done with school. We're done with classes. You have nothing to study or read, not at least until August when you run off to Sarah Lawrence and leave me here in Brooklyn to die of boredom."

"You're never bored," Jane said with a smirk.

"Don't change the subject." Claire lowered her finger and softened her gaze. When she pouted her lips like a child, Jane laughed, but Claire pressed on, determined as always. "We only have three months left to hang out," she said.

"I'm not dying, I'm going to school!" Jane shouted with a chuckle. "In Yonkers!"

Claire released her pout and placed her hands on her hips hugged by her high-waist shorts. "Do you know how long it takes to get to Yonkers from Brooklyn?" Jane shook her head as Claire went on with her quest. "In any case, you need to get out and get your mind off your brother," she said. "You've got a whole month for me."

Stephen, her older and only brother, was finishing up his deployment in Vietnam and set to come home in early July, just weeks away. Both Jane and her mother, Rebecca, had been living on the edge of a knife for twelve months. And before that, things weren't much better. Jane's father died when she was four and Stephen was seven, leaving her mother to care for them alone while taking over his other pride and joy—his bookstore. She did her best, and she never complained. But Jane couldn't help notice the light that used to emit from her mother's eyes had faded. The emerald of her irises had turned to dying evergreens, and her dark red hair lost its sheen. When Stephen was drafted she'd practically disappeared into a cloud of gray. She dyed her hair now to hide the spray of silver, the fake auburn not nearly as vibrant, and her glasses had practically become a permanent fixture of her face. The world had taken so much from her it seemed to have nearly robbed her blind.

"That's right," Jane finally said with a sigh. "One month, then my mother will feel better. At least I hope she does."

"I hope she does, too," Claire said, stretching out a hand and placing it on top of Jane's resting on the counter. "I hope you both do." The two smiled until Claire pulled away dramatically, her big eyes returning. "One way you could feel better right *now*, though," she said with a wink, "is coming to a groovy party in the Village with a bunch of college guys with parents who have money."

Jane laughed and shook her head, looking up to the door when it opened again. Her mother walked in, returning from their apartment upstairs, and offered a smile upon seeing Claire. Before she could even close the door, Claire swiveled toward her. "Don't you agree, Mrs. Martin?"

Jane leered at her relentless friend. "Don't play dirty," she said before looking at her mother. "Mom, don't listen to her."

Her mother slid her eyebrows in toward each other, grinning. "What trouble are you trying to get my daughter into?" She fanned herself with a folded newspaper as she headed toward the office behind the counter.

"Doug is having a party at his new place tomorrow, and I think Jane has absolutely no reason not to come," Claire said. "We haven't had a chance to really celebrate graduation, anyway."

"She's right," Jane's mother said, to her daughter's surprise. She stopped at her office door and turned around. "You've worked so hard these past years both in school and here in the store. And it's summer. You should have fun."

Claire stuck out her hip and folded her arms, reveling in her victory. Jane's mouth hung open for a few moments before she threw her arms out. "Aren't you supposed to be telling me not to go out to parties and get pregnant?"

"I'm certainly not telling you to get pregnant, Jane," Rebecca said, her lips curving upward at the sides, her eyes glistening with the hint of a sense of humor returned, even if for just a moment. Claire chuckled, and Jane joined her. "We can certainly have that talk before you go," her mother went on. "You're heading to college soon, so I'd have to have it eventually. Might as well do it now."

Jane felt her face flushing as red as her hair. Claire's smile grew at the embarrassment. "*Mother*," Jane said through tight teeth.

"I'm just saying," Rebecca said, lifting her hands slightly, "you two should embrace the next few months you have. Things will certainly change after that, so take advantage of this. Listen to your friend, honey."

She nodded and ducked into the office, leaving Claire behind to taunt Jane for her win. Before a sneer could even form on her friend's face, Jane surrendered. "Fine," she said. "I'll come. Just don't leave me alone with people I don't know. You know I hate that."

"Yes, I know," she said, offering a hand. The two shook on it.

That night, Jane sat on her bed reading Stephen's latest letter, sent more than a week ago. She saw the footage coming from the fields of Vietnam, and she knew her brother hid the terror of it all behind his humor, behind his casual tone, his talk of drinking whiskey and playing chess with the men in his platoon. More than thirty-six thousand men just like them had died so far, sixteen thousand last year alone. Stephen could be next at any moment. He could have even been killed in the days since he wrote the letter. The reality blew through Jane's heart like a grenade.

She placed the letter in the box where she kept the rest, along with Stephen's camera he left behind for her to use while he was gone. She hadn't touched it once since the day he deployed. There was certainly nothing happening that Jane wanted to preserve in time. A chilled sweat had been brewing all over the country and all through her own apartment as the tension of the past few years swelled. Foundations were cracking, men were dying, and Jane didn't want to preserve any of it for later. She didn't even want it now.

She tucked the box back into her closet and fingered through her clothes. A shimmer from the dark depths of the rack caught her eye. She reached for the iridescent dress from her childhood, the one her mother made for her when she was around three years old, before the family was thrown into its first tragedy. She could remember Stephen telling her she looked like a princess when she put it on for the first time. The memory tugged at her already tender heart.

It had been years since Rebecca had even opened the door to her old sewing room. The door was permanently closed, like a haunted room no one dared enter. It appeared her hands had stopped working as the fatigue of widowhood wore on like the war.

Jane wondered for a moment what she might wear for the party the next day, one she very well could consider her first as an adult. Though she hardly felt like one. Crowds in small spaces made her dizzy and frightened like a child stuck in a maze. The idea of being trapped in an apartment full of drunken college students gnawed at that bashful, nervous part of her.

As she looked at her bedside clock, she reminded herself that whatever agony she felt over a little socializing was nothing. It was nine in the morning in Vietnam, and Stephen would be roasting under the morning sun once again, ducking between reeds to avoid gunfire and marching through rice paddies riddled with booby traps. She knew he would do anything to enjoy a relaxing evening in an apartment stocked with beer instead of jungles laced with land mines and the sounds of dying men screaming.

Jane turned off her light, crawled on top of the sheets, and collapsed onto her back with the window fan blowing in her face.

That night, her dreams were a haunting of army choppers circling over the apartment.

TWO

BROWN-EYED GIRL

Claire scurried up the subway steps ahead of Jane, who laughed at her friend's eager stride. "You act like you haven't seen Doug in weeks," she teased as they popped out and onto Second Avenue. Jane dodged a pack of giggling girls barreling down the sidewalk still steaming with the afternoon's rain. The scent of wet concrete followed them all the way to the apartment building where a handful of college kids lingered outside smoking.

"Hey, Clint," Claire said as they passed the stoop sitters, patting Doug's roommate on his shaggy head. He playfully knocked her hand away, grunting with a cigarette sticking out of his mouth. Jane was happy to slide by the strangers unnoticed, following Claire up the dim stairwell to the apartment engulfed in marijuana smoke. Claire rushed through it and into the kitchen, snatching Doug around the neck and kissing him like he was a sailor back from the sea. Jane couldn't help but shake her head. Claire noticed the silent teasing and hung on her boyfriend's shoulder as she drilled her eyes into Jane's. "You joke now, but wait until you meet someone. You'll be all over him."

Doug, silent as always, merely grinned and took a swig of beer, his plaid shirt untucked from his jeans. He sat down at the table in the center of the kitchen packed with bodies, and Claire collapsed into his lap after grabbing two Ballantines from the fridge and handing one to Jane. She edged the tab open, knowing she would be nursing the single can all night. Beer settled into her body like lead, making her feel heavier than she already did. The weight of her brother's deployment was heavy enough.

The night began with a flurry of heated debates on Nietzsche, on The Beatles, on the recent fascination with eastern religion. Jane settled into the conversation, offering only mild agreements and nods as she leaned against the counter that she was certain had never been washed. She kept checking the back of her jeans, certain they were stained with some unknown substance. The grunge of rock music joined the evening, too, pumping from the stereo in the living room. She was bobbing inside the languid rhythm when the mention of Vietnam snapped her focus back to the kitchen table.

"We're not meant to be the world police," Doug grunted, leaning back with exasperation. "We can't fight everyone's wars."

"What about the Nazis?" a woman with a long braid asked, leaning onto the table. "What if we hadn't fought them?"

"The Holocaust was a far different matter than what we're seeing in Vietnam," Doug said. "America is just fucking terrified of the 'C' word. Big, scary communism! We're not over there to help people. We're over there to inflict our idea of democracy because our egos are more fragile than glass."

Claire glanced up at Jane with nervous eyes. She knew the topic of the war shut Jane down, the idea of her brother being used as political ammunition gnawing at her each time a debate ensued. Jane merely smiled and sipped her beer, keeping her arms folded to hide the sweat she could feel pooling underneath them.

The heat of the moment and of the third-floor apartment was unleashing its wrath on her. She sensed her skin flushing and placed the beer on her neck, catching sight of the open window in the living room leading to the fire escape. She turned back to Claire with a smile, fake and bright. "I'm just going to step out for a minute," she said, pointing to the window.

Claire bounced up and tapped Jane's arm. "You want me to come with you?"

Jane shook her head. "Stay here with your man." She leaned in and gave Claire a gentle nudge, the smitten blonde chuckling and returning to Doug's embrace.

Jane weaved her way through the crowded living room, the array of mismatched rugs covered in bodies, some lying on their backs and staring at the ceiling, others huddled in the corner sharing joints and laughing at nothing. She stepped over a crate of magazines and records and onto the windowsill, crawling out into the humid yet slightly less stifling nighttime air. She let out a hefty sigh as she took the few steps forward to the railing and leaned over it. A single laugh sounded off from her left, and she turned to find the figure of a woman sitting on the fire escape steps leading to the floor above them.

Jane jumped slightly as the stranger stood and walked around to the front of the landing. Her onyx black hair settling at her shoulders would have disappeared within the sky if not for the subtle glow of the street lamp nearby.

"I didn't mean to scare you," she said with a slight grin, a cigarette nestled between her fingers. "I don't bite." Her grin stretched a little sumore as her dark brown eyes narrowed.

Jane tried to chuckle through her awkwardness. "Oh, no, I'm sorry," she stuttered, placing a hand on her chest. "I just didn't know anyone else was out here."

The olive-skinned woman pulled out a pack of cigarettes from her back pocket and extended them. "Need one?"

"No, thank you," Jane said, waving her hand. "I really just needed air." She pulled her hair up off her back, holding the tresses in a bunch on top of her head.

"I can see that." The woman nodded and raised her brows, her sly smile unmoved.

Jane peered down and noticed the circles of sweat staining the underarms of her mustard yellow shirt. She flung her arms down and turned toward the street. "Oh, my god," she said, certain her face had turned a blazing red.

The woman chuckled as she joined Jane's side. "You're fine," she said. "I'm just messing with you." Jane smiled but still couldn't brush off her humiliation. "And you're right," the jokester went on. "It's hot as hell. I'm glad I wore this." She shrugged one of her shoulders, both of her arms bare thanks to her cut-off black tee.

"I'm Maria, by the way," she said before taking a hit of her Lucky Strike. Jane offered up her own name, and Maria grinned again. "Yeah, you look like a Jane."

"What does that mean?" Jane scrunched her eyebrows and turned to Maria, who looked more than amused with herself.

"Jane has a sort of…innocent ring to it," she said, blowing a plume up to the hazy stars. "It's tame. Pure."

"Is that how I come across?" Jane's eyes widened.

Maria's smile softened. "You're offended," she both stated and questioned.

Jane started to speak but found herself biting her tongue. She had to admit her studious nature and general introversion could register as innocence or weakness to people who knew her; she just didn't realize she was so transparent as to attract the notice of strangers. She let out a slight breath and leaned further over the railing. "I guess I don't like to think of myself as some feeble little lamb, that's all," she finally said.

Maria barked out another single bright laugh. "Hey, I didn't say feeble," she said, arching her stark brows high behind her bangs. "I just meant…" She swayed her head from side to side and clicked her tongue. "Sweet," she said, shooting Jane a look she could only perceive as being born of mischief. Or, worse, mockery.

Jane rolled her eyes, prompting Maria to wave a hand in the air, the charred butt of her cigarette leaking ash as it swayed. "What? There's nothing wrong with sweet. It could be so much worse."

"I guess you're right," Jane said. Maria nodded and settled back into the railing.

The two strangers stood in silence for a few moments, peering out into the Manhattan madness. The Village teemed with cabs beeping and barreling down the street, with drunken graduates staggering and cackling along the sidewalk toward their next party, with the initial fever of summer's freedom. The hum of it all seemed to lull Jane into a foreign moment of relaxation, something she hadn't experienced in at least twelve months.

The sound of Maria flicking her cigarette snatched her out of the daze. Jane cleared her throat. "So, who do you know here?" she asked.

"Here?" Maria looked over her shoulder briefly before shaking her head. "No one." She jutted her chin upward. "I'm visiting a friend upstairs."

"Oh!" Jane looked up, catching sight of the open window above them. She turned back to Maria, frozen with shame again. "I really didn't mean to steal you away."

"You didn't?" Maria tucked in her chin, jokingly offended, then shook her head as if in defeat. "Damn," she said, turning back to the street.

Jane felt her eyes swell and thought she sensed a heat rise within her, though it was hard to tell with the already roasting air. A man's shout from the upstairs apartment rattled her out of the bizarre moment. "Maria! You ready?"

Maria stubbed out her cigarette on the railing and dumped it into what appeared to be a community ashtray resting on the metal steps. She reached into her back pocket, this time pulling out a small sheet of paper. "Here," she said, handing it to Jane. It was a flyer for an anti-war rally in Washington Square the following day. "I helped organize it. If you're down, you should come."

"Oh." Jane didn't have the nerve to say she had never been to any sort of protest before, and certainly not one against the war her brother fought in for the past year. "Thanks," she said with a smile.

Maria grinned that mischievous grin she seemed to have perfected. "It will be tame," she said. "Not that you're feeble and can't handle it."

With a wink she vanished into the sky, leaving Jane to stare at the flyer she held in her clammy hands.

....

THREE

ANOTHER SATURDAY NIGHT

Maria tossed her apartment keys on the coffee table and took off her shirt, parting her way through the beads dangling from the threshold leading to the dark kitchen. She pulled a beer from the fridge, the light nearly blinding her, and swiped the cold bottle across her forehead, using her tank to wipe off her drenched back. She shuffled into her room and collapsed onto her bed by the window overlooking Hudson Street. The Virgin Mary stared back at her from the unlit prayer candle on her desk, that virtuous namesake, the one she could never live up to.

She bought the candle five years ago, just a few days after her brother, Lucas, called to tell her their mother died, and she had yet to take a match to the wick. Tonight was no different. She lit a cigarette instead and rolled onto her back, peeling off her jeans and tossing them to the floor as the apartment door clicked open.

"Kay?" Maria yelled out for her roommate.

"Yes, baby!" Kay yelped in his lively, flirtatious tone. He sauntered into Maria's room, all bulging muscles and shining teeth. His black skin glistened with the glow of the season.

"How do you make sweat look stunning?" Maria asked, prompting Kay to fan himself in dramatic fashion as he flopped onto her bed at her feet.

"Girl, you know I look best wet." He slapped her knee before running a hand across his gleaming bald head. His rich, deep-set eyes widened as he seemed to suddenly notice Maria's state of dress. He peered out into the hallway toward the bathroom before swiveling back with pursed lips. "I hope I wasn't interrupting something," he whispered, bringing a hand to his chest visible through his sleeveless suede vest.

Maria blew a cloud of smoke in his face. "Only me trying to cool down," she said, giving him a light kick. "And stop staring at my boobs. I'm a lady, for God's sake."

Kay lowered his head and raised one of his perfectly sculpted brows. "Well, that's news to me," he said, his voice low and smooth. He slapped Maria's leg and stood up, heading for the door. "Plus, I've seen way more of you than this. Remember New Year's Eve 1966?"

Maria flung one hand across her face, hiding herself as if it would block the memory. "I haven't touched tequila ever since," she moaned.

Kay let out his giant laugh and spun out of the room. "How was Side City?" he yelled out as he began clanking around in the kitchen. Side City was a regular dance party that vibrated inside a Village basement bar. She had attended that night with her friend Patrick, who was also a fellow writer at *The Torch*, an independent activist newspaper where Maria had worked for the past two years.

"It was the same as always," she finally answered, rolling onto her side.

"Well, you're here alone, so I would say it's slightly different," Kay teased.

"Ha-ha." Maria flicked her cigarette into the glass tray on the windowsill. "It's too hot for that," she said, sitting up and resting her back against the headboard.

Kay offered her a playful smile before changing the subject. "Any more word from Pat's friends out in San Francisco?"

Maria took another drag and shook her head, swiping her bangs from her sodden forehead. "Not yet," she said. Patrick had a group of friends who headed out west several years earlier when the first wave of Beatniks took to the Bay. They founded a bookstore, Half Moon Books, that grew quickly, and now they were in the process of launching a publishing company, appropriately titled Half Moon Publishing. The prospect of Maria joining the crew as their journal editor had been dangled in front of her for the past month. "Hopefully soon, though," she went on. "I'd sure love to find my way out there."

Kay folded his arms and sighed. "As much as I don't want you leaving, I know you'd kill it out there."

"How many times do I have to tell you to come with me?"

"Honey, this city is in my blood," Kay said. "Queens like me are meant for Manhattan."

"Sure, sure," Maria said, resigning. "How was tonight's show, by the way?"

"Fabulous," Kay said, returning to the bedroom doorway. "Everyone loved my new wig." He patted his invisible curls with one hand and sipped his beer with the other.

"I'm sure they did," Maria said with a smile, and she meant it. When Kay the man dressed as Kay the drag queen, patrons of the bars where she performed flocked to the woman's charm, her wit, her carefree candor. And when the dresses and wigs came off, Kay still drew people in to his light. "We're all just moths drawn to your flame," she would often tell him.

"Jenny wore her new one, too," Kay went on, shaking his head and puffing out his lips. "Red is not her color."

Maria chuckled at the sassy dig as Kay retreated into his bedroom. She glanced out the window and returned her attention to her cigarette. The image of red hair flashed through her brain then, but it wasn't that of Jenny the drag queen—it was Jane, the young, docile thing she had chatted with briefly on Patrick's fire escape earlier that night. A smile stretched across Maria's face at the memory of the girl's pale skin flushing at her teasing. She couldn't resist flirting with her. It was a vice she indulged in regardless of its futility; flirting with shy women, and with women straighter than a lamppost, was most definitely Maria's Kryptonite. Though it was all perfectly harmless as she would likely never see the reserved redhead again. She imagined Jane crumbling the flyer she had given her into a ball and burying it inside her purse, too reticent and delicate for anything as wild as an anti-war rally.

Maria chuckled to herself at the playful encounter and killed her cigarette before settling into her sweat-soaked sheets.

....

THERE'S SOMETHING
HAPPENING HERE

We are so going!"

Claire had snatched the flyer so hard out of Jane's hands the previous night at Doug's she nearly ripped it apart. Jane knew Claire would jump at the chance to throw herself into the action, to be in the middle of a crowd, to do all things loud and wild just to say she did it.

She tried to pretend she didn't feel a pinch at her gut, a fluttering inside her heart tempting her to dip her toes into the waters of revolution. But soon the feeling spread to nearly every limb itching for something Jane couldn't even name. She knew she couldn't ignore it.

The next morning she dug her brother's Canon out of its box, slinging the camera around her neck before taking to the subway. For once, she felt like she might experience something worth remembering.

She ascended from 8 Street Station and made her way to the park, grateful that the summer air had simmered to its usual tolerable warmth. The rumble and hum of the crowd leaked through the Washington Square Arch where she found Claire waiting near one of the two giant columns. She waved with brazen excitement through the throngs of hippies and students spilling into the park and huddling around the central fountain.

"You brought it!" Claire's face beamed when she spotted the camera Jane cradled in her hands. "Finally!"

Jane laughed as Claire pretended to brush dust off the black and silver Canon. "I figured this was as good a time as any."

"I agree," Claire said with a wide, childish grin. She grabbed Jane's arm and led the way into the chaos.

The duo wiggled through the swarm, ducking underneath signs mounted to sticks decorated with messages like "Drop acid, not bombs!" and "End the war before it ends you." Jane smiled at one giant board in particular, held by a petite young woman with flowers in her hair, that simply read, "War is not healthy for children and other living things."

Jane began clicking away, snapping a few photographs of the varied signage until a man with an impressive black beard leapt onto the fountain's ledge, megaphone in hand. "Brothers, sisters, and comrades!" he yelled, prompting a wave of cheers and applause from the mostly young crowd. "My name is Brian, and I'm with the Students for Peace Alliance."

Jane was surprised at how such a simple introduction produced such a loud, visceral response from the people around her. When they finally settled down, Brian went on.

"Right now, more than 500,000 American troops are in Vietnam, where they are being forced to slaughter and bomb entire villages under the guise of battling communism." A round of boos and hisses erupted from the audience. Brian nodded, then lifted his chin. "Now, with Nixon's reckless appetite for war, we're spreading our violence into Cambodia and Laos. We are becoming the same kind of monster we claim to be fighting! And we know it's not those born with silver spoons in their mouths whose blood is being shed across the rice patties and who are suffering through the monsoons and the land mines and the relentless gunfire. Boys from all across this country, from the cornfields of Iowa and the swamps of Louisiana to steel towns in Ohio and right here in the greatest city on earth, are the ones paying that price, along with our tax dollars!"

A sliver of space opened up in the pack of protesters, and just then, through the gap, Jane spotted a bob of black that gave her pause.

Maria stood just below the lively speaker, her hands guarding a clipboard, her vision locked on her fellow activist as he delivered his oracle. Her eyes were full of purpose, with pride, with passion. Jane lifted her camera, peering through the viewfinder and aligning Maria's face in the center. She took one photo before her subject turned and tucked a strand of hair behind her ear. Jane snapped the shutter again, capturing the candid moment just before the gap in the crowd closed.

Several more speakers took turns with the megaphone, railing against the American government and its campaign in Southeast Asia. Though nobody said anything Jane disagreed with, she still felt uneasy, like she was betraying her brother in some way. Yet each shout and cry against the war today came with a powerful declaration that not supporting the war didn't mean abandoning the troops forced to fight it. It was a small comfort to Jane, allowing her to lean into the excitement of the rally.

By the time the last speaker spoke his truth, Doug had arrived at Claire's side, and as the crowd dispersed around the park, the trio found a spot near a tree to lounge. They sat on the shaded grass exchanging pleasantries Jane was zoning in and out of as she scanned the park in search of the raven-haired activist. She eventually spotted her standing with a small pack of students, urging them to sign whatever she held in her clipboard.

Jane straightened her spine, suddenly aware of her own physical presence. She reached for her camera as Maria turned her way, but found herself self-conscious and pretending she was about to take a photograph of Claire and Doug instead. She snapped the scapegoat shot and glanced off toward the fountain. Out of the corner of her eye, she saw Maria walking toward her. She shifted her stature again as the bold woman strolled right up to the trio, resting her clipboard on her hip. "Glad to know my guerrilla marketing tactics work," she said with a friendly smirk.

"You're the flyer girl?" Claire said, her head lying in Doug's lap.

Maria shifted her smirk to Claire now and chuckled. "I've been called worse," she said. "Maria."

"Well, thank you for the invite, Maria" Claire said, her voice as bright as the sun feathering through the leaves above them. "This was far out."

"Far out is the goal," Maria said. "Well, that and using our constitutional right to freedom of assembly to speak out against the massive humanitarian crisis our military is creating."

The teasing slight seemed to blow right by Claire as she'd already returned to staring into Doug's stoned eyes. Jane chortled under her breath, capturing Maria's attention.

Maria jutted her chin up and softened her lips into a curious smile. "What'd you think?"

Jane nodded. "It was very invigorating," she said with a grin. "Everyone is so…passionate."

"It's hard not to be," Maria said, shrugging. "Soldiers are dropping like flies. But hey!" Her dusky eyes brightened. "I did just hear Nixon announced he's withdrawing 25,000 troops by August, so that's progress."

Jane felt a slap on her knee and turned to see Claire's perky face glowing. "Look at that! Your brother will be in good company."

Her stomach fluttered at the bit of good news, of the realization that maybe soon the war might all be over and no one would have to go through what her brother had endured, what she and her mother had endured. Her guts tossed again when Maria's face seemed to redden as she cocked her head. "Your brother's over there?"

Jane couldn't tell if Maria's darkened cheeks were rouged with anger or with pity. She sighed internally when the radical softened and sat down beside them, crossing her legs and placing her clipboard on her knee. "I'm so sorry," Maria said. "That sucks. Everything sucks."

"He's coming home soon, though," Jane said, partly as an encouraging reminder to herself. "July 3."

"That's great," Maria said, flashing a rare bright smile free of irony or mockery.

Jane merely nodded, silenced by both Maria's softness and by the ache of missing Stephen. Yet an ounce of hope filled her being for the first time since he left.

Claire sat up and gave Jane's shoulder a light nudge. "Jane's really needed to get out of the house, so today was perfect," she said with a teasing smile. Jane rolled her eyes.

"Is that so?" Maria's eyes swelled. "Well, I'm glad I could help." She winked, and Jane felt a strange tingling sensation biting at her fingertips and toes just as she had when Maria ribbed her on the fire escape.

Maria cleared her throat, switching her focus to the camera resting in Jane's lap. "Did you get anything good?"

Jane recalled snapping the photo of Maria through the mass of bodies and felt suddenly ashamed, as if she had been a spy hiding behind the Canonflex. "I hope so," she said, shoving the secret mortification away.

"Do you develop your own film?" Maria asked.

"Oh, no," Jane said, shaking her head. "I wouldn't even know how."

"You wanna learn?" Maria's usually low voice lifted. "I write for *The Torch*, not sure if you've heard of it. We operate out of the community center on Christopher Street, and we have a small darkroom. You could bring your film in tomorrow if you like and I'll have one of the guys show you how to develop it. And hey, if you got anything good, we can run it with the story I'll be writing about the rally."

"I dig *The Torch*," Doug chimed in, blowing a cloud of weed into the breeze. "There's always a big pile of them in the rec hall."

"Yeah, we work with the universities for distribution," Maria said, though Jane barely registered what they were saying. The prospect of her images appearing in the radical newspaper brought an unexpected wave of heat and hunger to her body. The thrill occupied her.

"So, what do you say?"

Jane shook herself out of her daze and found Maria staring at her with raised brows.

"I'd love that," she finally said, trying to remain as casual as possible. "Though I doubt I got anything that great."

"Well, I guess we'll find out, won't we?" Maria's mischievous grin returned, and Jane felt her cheeks twitch as she worked to keep them from turning to flames at the sight.

FIVE

....

TENDERLY

aria kicked her boots up onto the small desk in the office corner, lounging back into her chair as she edited her story on the previous day's rally. She tapped her red pen against her lips, focused on the harsh evaluation of her own words. The sound of her own name ringing into the air yanked her out of her editing.

She turned to the front door across the room and found Jane standing in the entryway chatting with one of the editors, her eyes scanning the room with apprehension. Maria waved her pen in the air, halting Jane's search. She smiled and nodded, gripping the camera hanging around her neck as she approached. Maria stood and extended her hands in feigned surprise. "You found us!"

"I did," Jane said with a smile. "Even we feeble people are capable of navigating this big city."

Maria's mouth fell open slightly, surprised at the normally reserved redhead's sudden spout of self-assured wit. "Let me remind you, once again, I did not say feeble," she said, crossing her arms. She gave Jane's shoulder a friendly tap and nodded toward the darkroom. "Come on," she said, leading the way. "Max is gonna show you the ropes today," she went on as she

23

knocked on the door. She opened it upon hearing Max give her the go-ahead and led Jane into the black closet aglow with the red hue of developing lights. Maria resisted the urge to laugh as she watched Jane's eyes water at the vinegar-like scent of the processing chemicals.

Max hung a completed image on a line strung across the small space before turning to face them. He pushed his thick glasses up the bridge of his nose and extended a hand to Jane. "Max," he said with his usual socially awkward bluntness.

Jane shook his hand and smiled. "Thank you for being willing to show me how this all works," she said. "I know next to nothing about photography, honestly. I kind of feel like a fraud."

"Oh, don't worry," Max said, waving a hand through the air before sticking it back into his pocket. "I was clueless when I started, but it becomes pretty intuitive."

Maria watched Jane sigh a breath of relief. "Well, I'll leave you to it," she said, stepping around her and opening the door. She pointed at Max. "You let me know if there's anything we can use with my story. We're running it tomorrow, so it has to get to the printer by ten tonight."

"You got it," Max said.

"Good luck." Maria winked at Jane, who smiled and turned back to Max, then shut the door behind her.

•••

Jane held her breath as Maria held the photograph at its ends with gentle fingers. She watched her examining it, judging it, considering it.

"Oh, this definitely will work," Maria finally said, allowing Jane to release her lungs. She had already sorted through a few of the images, now scattered on her desk, offering a few vague "hmms" and clicks of her tongue. Jane was relieved to get a clear, verbal seal of approval.

"Really?" She relaxed her shoulders and wiped her palms on her jeans.

"Absolutely," Maria said. As she began to sort through the rest of the pile, Jane's heart jumped at the realization that the images she had snapped of Maria lay among that pile. A sliver of shame weaved up her spine, the same feeling she sensed when taking the voyeuristic photos. She held her breath again as Maria fingered through the shots and landed on the ones reflecting her own face. Jane's pulse quickened as she watched Maria's lips twitch into a slight smile. The impromptu model lifted the two photographs of herself and chuckled. "Hey, you got my good side."

She turned to Jane and smiled just as Max strolled up to the desk. "You decide?" he asked.

Maria reached for the image she'd approved, one of Brian yelling through his megaphone, the veins on his neck bulging with passion, the spectators' heads and signs occupying the bottom half of the frame, giving him an air of command. She handed it to Max, who nodded. "Right on," he said, pivoting away into the bustle of the office humming with palpable energy now as the team hustled toward its deadline.

Jane admired the commitment all these young people had to running their own paper, one they used as a platform for change, for action. The phenomenon was one sweeping the country as her generation sought agency and independence in all aspects of their lives. Jane was thrilled at the idea that she now played a role in the movement.

Maria organized the images and placed them into a folder before handing it to Jane. "You got skills," she said.

"You sound as surprised as I am." Jane laughed.

"Hey, as random and chaotic as life is most of the time, it's good to know it can still throw us fun surprises every once in a while," Maria said.

Jane smiled at the idea more than she expected. She certainly never saw herself being a photographer. She was planning to major in literature at Sarah Lawrence, but suddenly she wondered if the college offered any classes that would help her explore the craft.

Maria sighed and placed her hands on her hips. "Well, my work here is done," she said. "The rest is on the editors."

"Oh! Okay," Jane said, readying to leave, afraid she was intruding by loitering. "Thank you for getting Max to help me. I really enjoyed that."

Maria snagged a set of keys and a wallet off her desk, placing both in her back pockets. Jane noted her simple outfit, similar to the one she wore the night they'd met—tight black jeans and a fitted white tee, this one with sleeves. She didn't realize until then how jealous she was of Maria's curves. When she found herself lingering on her body, she ripped her eyes away.

"My pleasure," Maria said. She pointed off to the side and arched her brows. "I'm heading next door to Drip. I work there part-time. My friends are playing a little acoustic gig tonight. If you don't need to get home, you should come over."

"Now?" Jane asked.

"You don't have to, obviously."

"No, I just…" Jade stumbled, then shook her head. "Sorry. Yes, I'd love to check it out."

Maria smiled her sly smile and nodded toward the door, leading them out of the hectic office and into the Sunday evening air. A few doors down they descended a set of stairs into the basement-level café, the calming scent of coffee hitting Jane's nostrils the second she stepped inside. Maria led them through the maze of small tables, most of them already full, and toward the counter.

"You want anything?" Maria turned over her shoulder as they landed at the register.

"Sure," she said. "A latte, if possible."

Maria leaned onto the counter and shouted, "Bonjour!" A young man appeared from behind the large coffee maker, his long hair tied into a low ponytail.

"How's it hanging, Maria?" he said. "What can I get you?"

Jane scanned the café as Maria placed their orders. She smiled at the room occupied mostly by college students, and she wondered if she would appear as carefree as they did when she would come to wander the Sarah Lawrence campus, when she would assert herself as a woman of the world on a path toward a career, toward maturation, toward all that encompassed real life.

She became distracted by watching the three musicians fiddling with their instruments at the microphones in the corner by the window. One young woman with a tempestuous blonde mane tuned an acoustic guitar while her two bandmates, both men with similar wild child hair, plucked away at their own instruments, an electric guitar and a bass.

Jane almost jumped when she felt a warm tap at her arm. She turned to find Maria holding the latte up with a grin. "Cheers," she said, passing it off.

"Thank you," Jane said, cupping the mug. "What do I owe you?"

"Absolutely nothing," Maria said. "You got me the photo for my story. I owe *you*."

She tapped her own cup against Jane's and nodded. Jane felt herself blushing at the gesture and turned back to the band.

"Come on," Maria said, piloting the journey toward a table in the back of the room, one of the few left available. They settled into their seats and sipped their drinks.

After a few moments blanketed in silence, Jane sensed a surge of anxiety swelling inside her belly, a new sensation she seemed to feel often around this new character in her life. The quiet isolation of their table heightened the intimacy of their nearness to each other. Jane eventually cleared her throat and dug around for a question to ask, for something to break the tension twisting inside her.

"So, how long have you worked at the paper?" she eventually managed to spit out.

Maria relaxed into her chair and folded her arms. "Since the Students for Peace Alliance started it two years ago," she said. "I had been involved with them for about a year by then. I was working here at Drip and was pretty lost at the time, and getting my hands dirty in the trenches of activism helped me get my shit together. I was twenty and had a lot of growing up to do."

Jane internally startled at Maria's age. She was twenty-three now, apparently, a woman with a period at the end instead of a question mark.

"Anyway, since I didn't go to college and only learned writing by doing it, I was damn lucky to get the gig," Maria went on. "They were just starting up and needed anyone willing to do the work." She smiled as she added, "And I was willing."

Jane returned her own grin, entranced by Maria's story. It was certainly far more fascinating than anything she herself had experienced in her mere eighteen years.

"How did you get involved with the alliance?" Jane asked, anxious to learn more. "I mean, if you weren't a student."

"Well." Maria lifted her mug to her lips, sipping it slowly as her brows drew toward each other. She set the coffee back down and leaned onto her forearms. "I was kind of seeing someone at the time who went to NYU," she said.

"Ah," Jane said with a single nod. "I see."

"Yeah," Maria said, shifting in her seat. She seemed to suddenly soften, melting like butter sliding across a hot pan, perhaps drifting in the past. Or perhaps she felt she spilled too much and regretted the sharing. She cleared her throat and sat up an inch or two taller. "So," she eventually said, clearly ready for a change of subject, "what about you? What's your deal?"

Jane's eyes burst open, and she nearly laughed. "My deal? I don't think I have much of one."

"Well, that's bullshit," Maria said bluntly before taking another sip of her black brew. "Everyone has a deal."

Jane sighed and joined Maria by leaning forward. "I'm going to Sarah Lawrence in the fall," she said. "For English literature. I grew up reading because my parents…Well, my mother, now, owns a bookstore. I've worked there for years, so it just makes sense." She hoped the band would start soon so she wouldn't be forced to feel uninteresting for much longer.

"What bookstore?" Maria asked.

"Martin Books," Jane said. "In Brooklyn. We live just above it."

Maria nodded and leaned in further. "And what do you enjoy reading?" Her eyes were sincerely curious as far as Jane could tell.

"That's a big question." Jane laughed. "I'm a wide reader, so the list is long. Right now, I'm reading a lot of Russian literature—Tolstoy, Bulgakov, Dostoevsky."

"Ah!" Maria's eyes lit up in the suddenly darkening café. "So, you do have a little revolutionary in you!"

Jane laughed quietly as she switched her gaze to the front of the room, the remaining light in the space focused on the musical trio as they introduced themselves. The Janis Joplin-esque woman boasting the big hair and big-bodied guitar took to the microphone. "How's it going, Drip?" A flurry of claps and hoots rang out in the dim coffee shop turned concert hall. "We are The Wicked Tender, and we're gonna play some tunes for you all tonight that we hope you dig." She turned to the ruggedly handsome guitarist beside her and nodded. "Come on, baby," she said.

They opened with a slightly edgier version of "Baby, It's You" by The Shirelles, one whose swaying grit nearly lulled Jane into a trance. The woman's voice was textured yet restrained, soulful yet sweet. Jane quickly realized how perfectly the band's name suited its vibe.

A few latecomers strolled into the café and settled into the back with the group of patrons sitting beside Jane and Maria. The shuffling of chairs amidst the tight room forced Maria to shift closer to Jane, the space between them dwindling nearly to none. Jane shifted in her own seat, crossing one leg over the other and settling back into place. She focused on the song's swaying grit, her face warming, her limbs loosening to the point where her arms relaxed outward, one elbow resting against Maria's. It took a few moments for Jane to register the lingering contact. She looked down at their touching arms then up at Maria, who met her eyes and simply smiled. Jane forced out a nonchalant grin before turning back to the band and bringing her elbows in, her inner thoughts anything but cool or collected like the mask she wore.

As the night pressed on, Jane realized she felt even more off balance than usual around Maria. She told herself it was mere admiration and intimidation as the result of idolization. She told herself that because the idea of it being anything other than innocent infatuation was one that would add one more stressor to her already cracking foundation.

Yet, somehow, in the past days since she met Maria, Jane had to admit she felt more alive than she had since Stephen's deployment. Wearing that camera around her neck, capturing a political movement in its most raw moments, watching it all come to life within the developer, and, soon, seeing it in print as a permanent mark in history…It was thrilling in a way she never expected. Everything was more thrilling than she expected.

And though she didn't quite understand most of it, she certainly wasn't going to complain.

....

THE TIMES THEY ARE A-CHANGIN'

Maria tore her eyes away from Jane's slender figure as she walked away from the café toward her subway station. She reminded herself Jane was only eighteen, a highly impressionable age especially for a woman. Maria also reminded herself she was likely to leave the city for the west coast at some point in the near future and should stay far away from vulnerable creatures who were also, very likely, straight as an arrow. She reminded herself of all these things as she journeyed back to her apartment a few blocks away, exhausted from the long day yet uncharacteristically light in her step.

She walked into her apartment, dim and quiet, to find Kay sitting on their bright red couch holding a bag of frozen vegetables to their friend Michel's head. They both looked up at Maria as she entered, and she caught the bruised swelling underneath the improvised ice pack.

"Jesus!" She edged further into the room, getting a closer look at the cranial egg. "What happened?"

"Another raid near the pier," Kay said, his voice empty as his eyes.

Maria sighed and sat beside him. She couldn't blame Kay for the sense of fatigue in his tone. This was becoming more of a regular occurrence for queer people in the city, this relentless harassment from police. Everyone was tired of the constant hiding, the constant arrests, the constant looking over shoulders.

"Fuck," she eventually found the strength to spit out.

"Yeah," Michel said, allowing himself a light chuckle as he took control of the ice and reclined back into the couch. His glasses were bent.

Maria shook her head and sighed again as Kay got up and slid past her toward the kitchen. "I need a drink," he said. "Anyone else?"

"You know my answer," Michel said.

"Mine, too," Maria yelled out, slipping off her boots and cozying up on the couch. She studied Michel, one of Kay's several occasional lovers, and ached at the sight of his broken state. She noted a few drops of blood on his shirt collar and winced.

Kay returned to the room with three full glasses in hand, passing them off and settling in beside Maria. He lifted his drink and took a breath. "To survival," he said.

Maria moaned slightly, tilting her head in despair as Michel raised his glass with a smirk of surrender. The three sipped their drinks, enjoying them as best as they could in a resigned cocoon of silence.

....

Jane wrestled with nerves as she walked the stairs to the apartment above the store. She had been so distracted and swept up in the evening she had forgotten to find a phone to tell her mother she was going to be later than she originally expected. She opened the door, entering the kitchen with wary steps and peeking into the living room to find her mother reading in the loveseat by the window. She looked up at Jane's arrival and lowered her book to her lap with a sigh. "Thank God," she said.

"I'm so sorry," Jane said, her face twisting and tightening. She rarely ever socialized to the point where she would come home late, so the guilt was a new and agonizing experience. "I got some film developed today at a community newspaper, and one of the writers invited me to the café next door for a show. I completely spaced and forgot to call."

Her mother relaxed a bit more into her chair and let out another breath. "It's okay," she said, shaking her head and tucking her legs underneath her. The subtle glow from the lamp nearby shed light on the darkness under her bottom lashes. Jane noted the heavy lids, the slight redness overtaking the whites of her eyes. Rebecca was only in her early forties, but Jane realized now how much older she was beginning to look, the stress of Stephen's dangerous deployment sapping her beauty and her energy. Jane knew it didn't help that her mother was widowed for fourteen years now. She was sure the loneliness contributed to the wilting.

"You're eighteen now, and I need to trust you," Rebecca added as Jane sat on the ottoman in front of her. "I just want you to be safe."

"I was," Jane said. "I am. I promise."

Rebecca smiled and glanced down at the camera and folder Jane had placed beside her lap. Her mother's face unwound itself from its tension as her eyes broadened. "Oh, I haven't seen this thing in ages." She picked up the camera, and her smile stretched a little wider. "What did you take photos of?" she asked while running her hands over the silver and black grooves and knobs.

Jane swallowed as she reached for the folder. She had no idea how her mother would respond, if she would think her participating in a protest against the war was a protest against

Stephen. After experiencing the rally and talking with Maria, she didn't necessarily think the two had to be linked. But Rebecca rarely talked about the war, likely avoiding the topic in the hopes of it disappearing completely, and Jane's stomach tensed in anticipation of the reaction. She slid the images out of the large manila envelope and handed them to her mother, who flipped them gently, slowly, studying each one with great focus just as she did with her beloved books. Jane bit her bottom lip, bracing for impact. She finally let her teeth relax when she watched the faint lines near her mother's eyes deepen with her smile.

"You took these?" she asked as she continued scanning the photographs. Jane noticed her halting at the two of Maria, and the ache in her low belly she'd felt earlier that night returned. "They're wonderful."

Jane let her lips twitch into a grin. "One of them is missing because it's going in *The Torch* tomorrow alongside an article about the rally."

"This was where you went yesterday with Claire?" Her mother looked up from the photos, her face ambiguous.

Jane nodded. "Yes."

Rebecca glanced back down at the pile of images, shaking her head gently. "Everything's changing and moving so fast," she said barely above a whisper. She looked up and smiled. "Look at you, even! Already a woman."

Jane laughed and blew out a sigh, looking out the window into the Brooklyn night. "I definitely don't feel like one."

Rebecca patted Jane's knee and handed back the photos. "It's a slow process, but you're in it now," she said. "It's scary how fast it's all moving. It's good to slow down and capture time like you did with these." She nodded toward the folder as Jane rested it back on the ottoman.

"You're not mad?"

"Mad?" Rebecca's amber brows scrunched. "At what?"

Jane hesitated before finding her words. "At me, protesting when Stephen…" She drifted off and waved a hand in the air. "When Stephen is over there," she finally finished.

"Honey." Rebecca leaned forward, placing her hand on Jane's knee again. "I don't want him there just as much as those protesters don't want him there. I can't wait for all of this to be over."

Jane stretched her lips into a strained grin. "Neither can I."

....

SEVEN

I CAN'T HELP MYSELF

Maria found out from a friend who lived in Park Slope that the bookstore sat in the center of Crown Heights. After her morning editorial meeting, she set off across the East River to Brooklyn with a freshly printed copy of *The Torch* in her hands. She smiled at the cutline under the front-page image: Story by Maria Valentino; Photo by Jane Martin.

She felt more excited than she thought she should as she exited Nostrand Avenue Station and strolled down the pedestrian boulevard slicing through the parkway, the path lined with giant silver maples and elms showing off their fresh vitality. When she eventually caught sight of the navy and white Martin Books storefront sign, a swift ripple of nausea seized her stomach. She fought off the alien sensation, shoving it away with a single shake of her head as she rolled the newspaper into a tube and slid it into her back pocket.

Maria approached the door and spotted Jane's flash of red through the glass. She stood behind the counter, bagging an elderly customer's books with an easy smile. Maria walked in, triggering the doorbell hanging above the frame, and watched

Jane's smile twitch when she spotted her new patron. She thanked the frail woman for coming as she ambled out past Maria, who offered her a nod.

Jane ran her hands down her sleeveless orange dress, smoothing out nonexistent creases. "Hi," she said, an invisible question mark punctuating the greeting.

Maria certainly couldn't blame her for being thrown off by the visit. She herself was startled at her impulse to act as personal paperboy for this girl she had just met.

"Hey." Maria strolled toward Jane and snatched the paper from her pocket, waving it in the air. "Fresh off the press!"

She tossed the weekly paper onto the counter and waited for Jane's reaction. The young photographer picked up her very first clip, soaking it in as a smile slowly unfurled across her faintly freckled face. After a few moments of quiet examination, she let out a light chuckle.

"It's so weird to see my name," she said, looking up with a giddy grin as her pale cheeks pinkened with what Maria was thrilled to assume was pride.

"You'll get used to that," Maria assured her, leaning into the counter.

Jane's light eyes grew even wider. "Does that mean I'm expected to take more photos?"

"You're not expected to do anything," Maria said, lifting her brows. "But you obviously have an eye for this. You should definitely keep exploring it."

Jane remained quiet as she gazed back down at her debut work, her face soft, her eyes shrinking back to their neutral size. She nodded and smiled. "I guess that won't hurt," she said with a shrug.

Maria nodded and straightened her spine. "So," she said, slapping her hands on the counter, "I hear you sell books here."

Jane scanned the store and scrunched her lips. "It appears we do," she said. "Are you looking for one?"

"I am," Maria said, then tilted her head. "Though I'm not sure which one."

Jane smiled and offered an assured nod. "What do you enjoy?"

"Well, it's not for me," Maria said. "My roommate's birthday is coming up, and I thought I would get him something fun. Something that suits him. Something that's as…fabulous as he is."

"Oh!" Jane stepped around the counter toward the dark wood shelves. "Well, what does *he* enjoy?"

Maria let out an involuntary chuckle. How could one describe someone as indescribable as Kay?

"He enjoys beautiful things," she finally said. "Big, grand things. And he's a warrior. Resilient. Unwavering."

Jane's smile sweetened. "He sounds lovely."

A few quiet moments edged by before Jane led them down the rows of books. "He's also a performer," Maria added, not wanting to leave out the most fabulous thing about Kay.

"Oh! What kind?" Jane asked as she turned around. Her wide doe eyes gave Maria pause, the innocence pouring out of them in all their green light. She certainly didn't seem like someone who would take for the hills at the thought of Kay and his nighttime ego. Maria chose to trust.

"A very special and vivacious kind," she said. "He's a drag queen. During the day he's Kay, and at night, when he's in his element, he is Kay with a Miss in front."

She watched Jane's expression drift like a slowly melting ice cap into a blank liquid canvas. Eventually she took a breath, a light gasp that revealed it finally hit her. "Oh," she said. "Well, that definitely *is* fabulous."

Maria rejoiced silently as Jane seemed to continue down the aisle without any discomfort. She watched her sift through the store's inventory in her mind, her fingers coming to her lips in contemplation as she scanned the shelves. Maria joined the hunt, meandering to the other aisles and finding herself at the history section. A slight glimmer from the top shelf caught her eye. She reached up and snatched the book with the metallic-engraved title from its place, admiring its cover embossed with the image of a crown. She skimmed the pages and didn't have to go very far before knowing she had stumbled on Kay's gift.

Maria walked to the aisle where Jane searched, lifting the book up when she pivoted toward her. "This is the one," she said.

"Queens Who Conquered." Jane read the title aloud, her eyes billowing once again. She stepped forward as Maria handed her the book, an examination of various military and political victories won by royal women throughout history. Jane's smile grew as she poked around the inside. "I think you're right," she said, snapping it shut. "This is a great choice."

The light pouring in from the large front windows bounced off Jane's smiling eyes, nearly blinding Maria, who found herself needing to push away the sensation of an elevator dropping inside her stomach, just as she had before entering the store.

The sound of a door clicking open near the counter shook away everything Maria was feeling. Jane seemed to jump, too, as she swiveled back in the direction of the noise.

"Jane?" a female voice called out, prompting the beautiful redhead to walk toward the front of the store. Maria followed and saw a woman with auburn hair behind the counter.

"Mom, this is Maria," Jane said.

Maria hoped her gulp wasn't as loud as it felt. She knew Jane mentioned her mother owning the store, so there was no reason for her to be surprised or nervous or whatever the hell she was feeling. She had the urge to shake the woman's hand for some reason. To impress her.

Jane's mother smiled, and Maria instantly saw the relation. It may not have been as bright as her daughter's, but the grin still had her name written all over it.

"Maria, nice to meet you. I'm Rebecca."

Maria nodded and turned to Jane, who was back to smoothing out her already smooth dress. She took solace in the fact that it appeared she wasn't the only one in the room who felt off balance.

Rebecca slung her purse over her shoulder as she seemed to study the stranger. Maria sensed a kind curiosity in the inspection, like she was searching for someone familiar. She turned back to her daughter and let out a quick sigh. "I'm running to the post office," she said. "I'll be right back." She looked at Maria again, offering a single nod and another smile. "I hope you found what you were looking for," she said.

"I did," Maria said, her voice bright. "Thank you."

As Rebecca left, Jane moved to the counter. Maria paid for the book and watched Jane wrap it neatly and delicately in tissue paper before placing it into a brown bag. She handed it over, her pale pink lips sliding into the beam Maria was finding more and more contagious. She resisted the urge to allow her fingers to brush against Jane's as she accepted the bag.

"I hope he likes it," Jane said.

"Oh, he will." Maria felt herself lingering, felt the question brewing inside her, bubbling like a witch's brew. She cursed whatever spell was at play as she asked, "Do you like dancing?"

Jane seemed to freeze, her body completely still for a few moments before she cocked her head. "Dancing?"

Maria laughed and gazed down for a moment, rubbing her thumb across her nose. "Yeah, there's this dance party in the

Village every Saturday. The music is always great, and they don't check I.D., so there's that." She shrugged and raised her brows.

Jane chuckled at the gesture of enticement and put her hands on her slender hips. "I'm not the best dancer, but I do love music."

Maria waved a hand in the air. "Girl, it's dark down there," she said. "No one can see anyone else, and it doesn't matter anyway. You don't need to impress anyone." She shrugged again as she swiveled toward the door and offered a wink. "Except maybe me."

She walked out of the store without stopping to catch the reaction, smiling to herself as she made her way back to the subway, her imagination running wild with all Jane might be feeling and thinking in that moment. She chuckled, then caught her breath, uncertain as to when she had become someone who cared about how she made women feel outside of the bedroom.

As she waited on the train platform, Maria wondered how much longer she would have to wait for her former self to return from wherever it had so clearly wandered.

....

EIGHT

DOWN IN THE BASEMENT

The record player near the bedroom window spun out the textured, booming Aretha Franklin as Jane stared dumbfounded at her closet. She flipped through every dress, every skirt, every blouse, irritated with herself that she had no idea what was appropriate for a dance party. The only other similar event she had attended was her senior prom two months ago, which she had done so reluctantly with her math partner, Joey, at the insistence of Claire. She knew she was supposed to have been thrilled with the social rite of passage that every other girl seemed to dream about for years, of finding a beautiful dress, of wearing a corsage, of making out with her date in his car when the night was over. But Jane had felt lukewarm about all of it, especially the backseat canoodling.

As she continued sorting through her prospective outfits for the evening, she recoiled at the memory of Joey shoving his hasty tongue down her throat when he dropped her off that night. It was her first kiss, and if the experience was any indication of what future ones would be like, she wanted nothing to do with it.

Jane blew out a hefty breath, frustrated over her indecision, and finally pulled out a white short-sleeved dress, casual and cool, loose enough to dance freely yet tight enough to not appear prudish. As she threw it on and wrapped a silver belt around her waist, she wondered why she suddenly cared about what her clothes said.

She stepped in front of the full-length mirror hanging over her bedroom door, inspecting her selection. She placed her hands on her hips and turned to the side, smoothing out the hem of the dress that rested at mid-thigh. Her knees began bobbing along with the catchy, stompy beat of "Chain of Fools," the rhythm working into her bones and spreading through her veins. Before she knew it, Jane's entire body was swaying and rocking as she watched herself in the mirror, curious as to how her movement would appear to others. She suddenly ceased her dancing and put a hand to her mouth, stifling a laugh of embarrassment and confusion over the realization she truly only cared about how she appeared to one person in particular.

Jane removed her own muzzle from her mouth and took a deep breath. She freed the needle from the record, snatched her brown leather purse off the dresser, and reminded herself she was merely going dancing with a new friend. There was no reason to feel like a fool.

....

Jane squeezed her purse tighter when she spotted Maria leaning against the gray brick building smoking a cigarette, a few others standing nearby doing the same. She wore her usual black jeans, her black sleeveless shirt exposing her lightly toned arms. Jane noted how the shadows cast by the streetlight made the contours of her subtle muscles even more apparent.

Maria looked up and nodded with a smile before stomping out her cigarette with her boot. Jane's eyes shot straight to her lips, which were rouged with a luscious, dark red wine stain. Her black eyeliner was slightly thicker than normal. Jane wondered if Maria had struggled just as much as she did with her fashion choice before coming out, though she highly doubted the cool, suave Italian fretted about such frivolous things.

"Glad you found it," Maria said as Jane finally landed in front of her. "Places like these aren't usually easy to spot the first time."

"Well, I'm honored to have disrupted the status quo," Jane said with a proud grin.

Maria narrowed her brown eyes and pursed her merlot lips. "You really are a radical," she said. "Don't even try to fight it." She turned and opened the unmarked door, leading Jane into a long, dim hallway with cement walls, its cold, creepy blandness reminding Jane of a morgue.

"Where exactly are you taking me?" She tried to laugh through her unease as she followed Maria down a narrow set of stairs.

"Do you not trust me?" Maria looked over her shoulder and smirked, her eyes lighting up the dusky stairwell. Something inside Jane made her knees wobble, threatening to make her tumble down the stairs. She kept her footing, but when they reached the bottom her legs nearly gave out again when she saw a mammoth of a man in a leather jacket standing in front of them. His eyes were hard and beady, his hands clasped around his robust belly. Maria's confident stroll toward him calmed Jane at least enough for her to keep moving. The giant lifted his chin as they approached. Maria returned the nod and said, "Apache."

For a moment, Jane thought Maria might have sneezed, but then the man opened the door behind him. Jane breathed out a sigh of relief and offered the giant a smile, though she wasn't sure why considering he didn't do the same. She followed Maria into a smaller room with red walls and yet another door, this one unmanned. Jane could hear the faint hum of music and feel its gentle vibration in her feet. Maria turned over her shoulder again and smiled as she clicked open the door.

A wave of steam and soul blasted Jane the second they entered the clandestine dance hall. The music blared from the speakers towering in the back corner, a DJ wedged between them controlling the sweaty room's pulse as he spun records on top of a small stage. Maria forged a path through the sea of glistening bodies like Moses parting the Red Sea, Jane following behind like a frightened yet loyal disciple. They eventually found their way to a packed bar, the two servers tending to the parched patrons, flinging bottles and exchanging cash so quickly Jane could barely capture their movements.

"You drink?" Maria asked as she burrowed them a space at the small counter to wait.

"Sometimes," Jane said, feeling as if she were screaming, the music pounding her eardrums.

"Do you want water instead?" Maria asked as one of the overworked servers looked their way. Jane nodded, and Maria ordered a water and a beer. As the bartender passed off their drinks, Jane noted how Maria hadn't pressed her about not really drinking, how she hadn't shoved it down her throat anyway. If only Joey had been as considerate with his own urges.

Maria tilted her bottle against Jane's clear glass. "Cheers!" she said, taking a quick sip of her beer. Jane gulped down half of the water, her body already boiling from the confined, sticky chaos.

They moved to the side of the bar, joining a line of their fellow underground companions chatting along a black wall. Jane leaned against it as Maria stood in front of her bobbing to the fiery pipes of Etta James. She couldn't help but move her hips slightly, too, though she realized she may need to order a drink after all if she was going to dance much more than that. In the enclosed space her nerves still found room to explode; she would need the encouragement.

"So," Maria said, leaning in for Jane to hear her over the blasting vinyl, "what did your mom think?"

Jane cocked her head and tightened her brows. "About what?" She willed her hands to dry as she waited for the response.

"About your print debut!" She gripped Jane's arm for a moment, drawing it back as her eyes widened.

"Oh! Right." Jane laughed and placed a hand on her head, embarrassed at her daftness once again. "She loved it. I wasn't sure she'd approve of me being at an anti-war protest with my brother being over there and all, so I was pleasantly surprised."

"Well, it's a great photo," Maria said, taking another swig.

Jane smiled and hoped the bar's lack of lighting would mask the red she was certain seeped through her cheeks. She took extra precaution and hid behind her cup.

"What did you think I said?" Maria asked, leaning in again, her head tipped a hair to one side. "When I asked what your mom thought? You seemed confused."

Jane froze at the question, digging around her muddled brain for a way around the truth. Before she could even respond, Maria's dark lips curved into her signature smirk that allowed a faint set of dimples to the surface. "Did you think I wanted to know what your mother thought of me?"

There was no way the dungeon darkness cloaked the crimson on Jane's face now, she was certain of it. She shook her head and forced out a laugh, praying it sounded even remotely nonchalant. "Oh, no," she said, wiping a hand in the air. "It's just hard to even hear myself think in here."

"Ah, yeah, I should have warned you about that," Maria said, her grin fading only slightly. Jane let her muscles relax and her lungs breathe as Maria turned away and focused on her beer again.

Her sudden swivel back to face her snapped Jane to attention. "But in any case, I'm good with moms, so I'm sure yours found me adorable," Maria said, lifting one brow. Jane managed to laugh despite the various species of butterflies overtaking her stomach. Maria's face dropped suddenly, and her eyes lost their light. "Well, I'm good with most moms. Not my own, though."

The insects all ceased their fluttering as Jane felt the pang of sympathy course through her. "You two have a tough relationship?"

"We did," Maria said, sipping her beer once again. "She died a few years ago."

Jane's stomach dropped to the wood floor, killing any and all remaining butterflies. "Oh, I'm so sorry. I…"

Maria waved her off. "Don't apologize," she insisted. "We actually hadn't talked since I lived with her."

"When was that?"

Maria tilted her head back slightly, remembering. "Six years ago," she said without much emotion.

"Wait," Jane said. "You moved out when you were…" She paused to count, certain she was getting it wrong. "Seventeen?"

Maria let out a laugh paired with a sigh. "It's a long story," she said. "It's not all terrible, though. I met Kay because of it. He saved me, and I wouldn't have it any other way."

Jane smiled at the resilience. She couldn't say she was surprised by it. Maria seemed like a warrior in her own right, just as she had described Kay to be.

Maria turned to watch the crowd twisting to Wilson Pickett, then reached a hand into the air and waved. "Speaking of!"

Jane followed her eyes to find a tall black man with a hairless skull that glowed like the sun. Every part of him, actually, seemed to exude light. His sculpted, butter-smooth arms showed themselves off underneath a buttoned, pale pink blouse.

"Maria!" he practically sang as he wrapped an arm around his roommate. "I once met a girl named Maria!" He was singing now, for sure, and Jane found herself wanting to bask in all the man's glory.

Maria pulled him closer and extended a hand out to Jane. "Kay, this is Jane," she said. "Jane, Kay."

"Hello, Miss Jane." Kay reached out and shook Jane's hand with the perfect combination of strength and reverence. He drilled his eyes into hers with softness and intrigue. "You are gorgeous," he said with conviction.

Jane chuckled and buried her head as Kay turned back to Maria. "Where did you find her?" Maria tightened her lips and gave Kay's ribs a friendly yet solid nudge. "What?" he yelled, bringing a chiseled hand to his equally chiseled chest. "By the way," he said, his entire demeanor and attention shifting as he moved his hand in order to give Maria a tap on her shoulder. "I hear T may be here tonight, just so you know." His beautiful eyes bulged before he slid past the duo toward the bar, bidding me farewell along the way.

Jane noticed Maria's knuckles grow a few shades lighter as she gripped her beer bottle a little tighter. "Who's T?" she asked, dying to know who was behind the mysterious pseudonym.

Maria shook her head and tucked her free hand into her pocket. "No one," she said. "Just someone I know from a while back."

"Just someone?" Jane felt the fascination rising in her own voice. She could tell Maria sensed it when she dropped her head to the side and narrowed her eyes.

"Yes, someone," she said firmly yet with a grin.

Jane laughed and sipped her drink, catching Maria doing the same out of the corner of her eye. She wiped the crease of her mouth, her red lipstick never smudging, and lifted her beer slightly toward Jane. "What about you?" she asked. "Do you have any someones?"

"Oh, no," Jane said, cursing the return of her flushing skin. "I went to prom with a guy this past spring, but we didn't date or anything."

"You've never dated?"

Jane couldn't tell what resided inside Maria's tone or her eyes. Her mask was completely neutral, open. She swallowed and hoped Maria would be just as generous as she had been with not harassing her about her lack of drinking experience.

"No," Jane said with a shake of her head. She wiped away a strand of hair trying to stick itself to her forehead. "I guess I've always been so busy studying and reading, especially these last two years. It just never was a priority for me."

Maria nodded and slowly grinned, following it with a shrug. "Well," she said, "you're probably better off. It's not worth the trouble, and I'm sure your focus on school will pay off."

"Mmm." Jane wasn't sure what else to say. She didn't want to pry, but she was certainly curious as to why Maria would try to steer her away from dating. Had her experiences with romance been that bad? Was this elusive "T" a part of that bitter history? The mass of questions floating around Jane's brain led to a more pressing one: Why did she seem to be so interested in learning about Maria's romantic past, as well as what else it may reveal about her?

"Anyway," Maria said, standing up straighter and nodding toward the dance floor, which basically encompassed the entire bar. "After all that studying, you could probably use some fun."

With that, Maria began weaving her way through the pack of perspiring bodies before Jane could stop her. As they slid among the sweat, Jane tried to pretend her water was vodka, attempting to give herself at least an artificial boost of confidence and ease.

Maria stopped when they reached the crowd's buzzing center and smiled as she started dancing without a speck of hesitation. Jane tucked her hair behind her ear, anxious to do something with her free hand as she eased into her own movement. The small space tightened more and more as the crowd grew, yet somehow she managed to settle into the cramped camaraderie and let her limbs surrender to the music. Maria's carefree twirling and shaking helped, her coolness acting as a buoy for Jane to cling to among the sizzling sea of sweaty students and hippies. She wasn't sure how long they had been dancing when she was finally able to catch a breath, the music slowing to a languid, saxophone-soaked tune whose dirty rhythm brought quite a few pairs of dancers closer to each other. She wiped her forehead for the umpteenth time, scanning the scene frantically as she decided how to react to the suddenly sultry turn the night had taken.

It was easy to see in the way Maria danced that the edgy woman was confident with herself, with her body, with everything one could do with it. Again, Jane struggled to make sense of why she noticed any of this, why it mattered to her, why she felt the return of butterflies when she and Maria were forced to dance so close together that their bodies touched with every single dip and spin. She could smell Maria's sweat mixed with her earthy yet sweet perfume.

Jane wondered if all of this was normal, if all friends noticed these things about each other, if women dancing so intimately was so commonplace. She scanned the room and, lo and behold, spotted two girls around her age dancing near the DJ with even less space between them than she and Maria. And not far away she found Kay grooving with equal intimacy with a handsome, thin man slightly younger than him, his black glasses fogging over like a bathroom window during a hot shower. Maria must have noticed Jane's drifting as she placed a hand on her arm and leaned in toward her. "You okay?"

Jane suddenly felt lightheaded, the sensation of Maria's hot breath adding to the disorientation. She closed her eyes for a second and nodded. "Yeah, I think I'm just overheated," she said. "I probably just need to splash some water on my face."

Maria squeezed Jane's arm even tighter and jutted her chin toward the DJ. "Come on," she said. "The bathroom's back here." She slid her hand down to Jane's, grabbing it as she led them through the maze of melting bodies. By the time they reached a dim hallway behind the stage, Jane felt dizzier than before, her stomach still occupied by the flapping of a thousand wings. She attempted to steady herself by focusing on the drawings and etchings on the walls, years of inside jokes and declarations of love carved into existence with pocket knives and pens, as they waited in the short line for the single-stall bathroom.

"You sure you're okay?"

Jane was yanked out of her mural inspection by Maria's concerned voice. "Yes," she said, pushing out a chuckle and swiping her forehead again. "I already feel better being here and not in there. How do you do it?"

Maria laughed and put her hands in her pockets. "I guess I'm just used to it now," she said with a shrug. "I kind of enjoy the heat. In certain situations, anyway."

Jane felt flames blow through her again as Maria's brows lifted toward the ceiling. The innuendo settled into her skin like a sunburn. Her lips parted slightly as if she was going to speak, but she certainly had no idea how to respond. The sound of a woman's bright voice behind her calling Maria's name snatched her out of the internal inferno.

"Maria!"

Jane looked over her shoulder and saw a blonde woman exiting the bathroom, her eyes alight and locked on Maria.

"It's been so long," she said, her arms reaching out to embrace Maria in a hug. She accepted it, but barely, and she looked at Jane with a wary expression unusual for the normally self-assured activist. The woman pulled back and sighed as she folded her arms. Her blue eyes lit up the grungy hallway, and her metallic dress sparkled just the same. "How have you been?"

Maria hid her hands in her pockets again and gave the woman a single nod. "I've been okay, Theresa. How are you?"

"I'm alright," she said. "Busy, but good." She put a hand on Maria's arm.

Maria shifted her stance and cleared her throat. "Theresa, this is my friend Jane."

Theresa's eyes beamed as she removed her creamy hand from Maria's arm. Jane shook it and smiled, though she kept her teeth to herself. "Nice to meet you, Jane."

"You, too," Jane said, not certain if it was true considering Maria seemed to shrink in the woman's presence.

The bathroom door swung open again, granting Jane's entry, and she excused herself inside as quickly as possible, resting her back against the wall for a few seconds. She had hoped once contained in the bathroom alone she might have been offered at least some relief, but the heat only swelled. The tingling in her fingers and toes had returned, joining the twist in her stomach. She leaned her clammy hands against the tiny rusted sink, ignoring the grime certainly coating its every inch. She turned on the cold water and splashed a few handfuls over her face, letting it drip from her chin and jaw. She dried off with a paper towel from the dwindling roll resting on top of the smudged and spotted mirror.

Though the disorientation began to fade, the sinking suspicion that it stemmed from something other than merely an overcrowded basement did not.

Jane looked in the mirror, as best as she could given the cloudy film that coated it. She wondered if she bore the look of a woman who liked women, if there even was such a silly thing. Did she even wear the clothes for it? And what were those, exactly? The striped shirt of the lady-loving dancer near the DJ? The pastel button-up blouse Kay wore so well? Neither of those outfits seemed particularly gay to Jane. Then again, it was obvious she knew nothing about the word itself, and certainly not the world it encompassed and where within its walls Maria resided, if at all.

She suddenly felt out of her depth, cast into a roaring sea she had never learned to navigate. She hadn't even known it existed days ago, and now she yearned to explore it?

She cleared her throat and assured herself, once again, that curiosity was a virtue worth stoking. It was always wise to learn about new things, after all.

As she opened the door, her eyes immediately found Maria leaning against the wall near the threshold into the bar, her right cheek cupped by Theresa's hand. Maria shot her own gaze up and met Jane's in an instant. When Theresa backed away and disappeared to the dance floor, Maria gave her a nod and a tight smile. Jane already knew the difference between her many grins; she could discern this one's forced, broken nature even within a hallway that was nearly all shadow.

Maria looked up again as she approached, her dark eyes searching Jane's for something. A reaction, perhaps, or a question. A judgment. Jane's guts turned once more as Maria's placement within this new world seemed to come into clearer view.

"You okay?" Maria asked, her eyes now silently begging for a yes.

Jane was willing to give it. "Yes," she said, smiling. "Of course."

A silence underscored by the thrumming of the speakers in the next room stretched itself between them for a few moments as a grin worked across Maria's softening face. "Good," she said, blunt and confident, her self-possessed nod returning. "Make sure to tell me if that changes."

The wink. The smirk. The swivel.

Jane blew out a sigh, her chest feeling slightly tender, and followed Maria back into the bar.

·····································

When Jane settled into bed that night after peeling off her dress clinging to her soaked skin, she stared up at the ceiling with hard brows, her teeth clenched. She fell asleep after a few stubborn hours with her muscles tense and dreamed she watched Theresa kiss Maria on a fire escape as Jane's teeth crumbled and fell out of her mouth.

NINE

· ·

THE SAME OLD SONG

Maria's eyes kept finding their way back to her desk phone as she edited her latest story, the cap of her pen shriveled to nothing after she had been unknowingly chewing it all day. It wasn't until she finally worked up the nerve to put the pen down and pick up the phone that she'd seen her anxious handiwork.

In truth, she had been gnawing on more than pens over the past four days since she noted Jane's shadowed demeanor after the run-in with Theresa. She couldn't pull her teeth out of the feeling that Jane felt distressed or at least disrupted by the encounter, by what it possibly revealed about Maria. The part of her that found Jane more attractive and luminous than any woman she had ever met made her want to believe the feeling was a result of mutual lure. But the part of her that had already been a curious girl's experiment, one that had led to Maria's mother shunning her with great conviction and evicting her from their Philadelphia home, told her to cut it out. Move on. Don't do it again. The fact that she had run into that curious girl in front of Jane added a palpable sense of foreboding Maria felt she shouldn't ignore.

Despite it all, she found the number for Martin Books in the newspaper's giant phonebook and dialed it with hesitant fingers, not exactly certain what she planned to say. Or even why.

The surprisingly quick answer just after the first ring startled her.

"Martin Books, how can I help you?"

Maria smiled at the sound of Jane's voice. "Hey, it's Maria."

"Oh," Jane said, seemingly just as rattled. "Hi. How are you?"

"Great," she lied. "Sorry, I found your number and just wanted to check in to make sure you had a good time the other night. I mean…" Maria suddenly stumbled, throwing a hand up to her forehead. "I know you weren't feeling all that hot, being all…hot and everything." She closed her eyes and recoiled at herself, tightening her raised hand into a fist. She couldn't say a damn thing right. She chose to laugh, hoping to lighten this horrid weight. It at least worked enough to elicit a chuckle from Jane.

"I just wanted to check in and see how you were, that's all," Maria recovered, no matter how sloppily. She let out a breath and cursed herself in her flustered head.

"I'm good," Jane said, relaxed and maybe even slightly amused. "And I had a good time. I told you, it was just…overwhelming." A pause held steady through the line, broken eventually by Jane's voice cracking. "The heat, I mean," she shot out. "The heat was overwhelming."

"Yes," Maria said, shaking her head. "Yes, you said that."

An even more excruciating silence dangled between them until Maria finally cleared her throat and got down to business. "So," she said, straightening up in her desk chair, "you take any more photos lately? Anything good to share?"

"I haven't," Jane said. "I was thinking about going to Central Park tomorrow to explore and shoot around, though. As cliché as that is."

"What's cliché about it?"

Jane clicked her tongue. "It's so touristy," she said. Maria could hear her elegant nose scrunching on the other end of the line. She imagined her standing behind the bookstore counter, the light pouring in from the massive windows highlighting her freckles. She had to pinch her arm to snap herself out of the vision.

"Who the hell cares if there are tourists there?" Maria was proud of her resurgence. "This is our home. It's ours to document, it's ours to make art out of and make art for. You should absolutely go and take photos."

Jane sighed and paired it with a delightful laugh. "You're right, you're right," she said. "Okay, I'll go. You win."

"Great!" Maria lounged back into her chair, folding her arms and tucking the phone under her ear. "What's my prize?"

"What?"

"My prize!" Maria said. "I won. What do I get?"

"You get me going to the park and taking more photos!" Jane laughed.

"Well, that's great for you, but how do I benefit?" Maria asked. "The least I can do is join you. I need to be writing more for myself, and walking around always inspires me. What do you say? Can I explore with you?"

She caught the involuntary innuendo too late but decided to let it stand. She couldn't resist the barely-there flirtation. A little bit surely wouldn't hurt. The pause on the other end told her Jane had picked up the subtle allusion. Maria smiled and bit her pen again.

Jane's voice returned to the line. "Sure," she said. "I'd like that."

Maria waited just long enough to give Jane time to change her mind, then sealed it closed. "Okay, it's done," she said. "What time tomorrow?"

"Well, I'm done here at five, so it wouldn't be until the evening. Is that okay?"

"Absolutely," Maria said. "I happen to be more of a night owl."

Jane chuckled, and it sent a gentle shiver through Maria's arms. "I'm not surprised," she said. "Okay, so how about six o'clock, Columbus Circle entrance?"

"Perfect. See you then, Red."

Maria swore she could feel Jane's entire body flush through the phone. She laughed to herself before hanging up, then wondered if it was actually her own flesh that was blushing. She wiped away a bead of sweat forming underneath her bangs as she tossed her pen in the garbage and grabbed a new, uneaten one from the desk drawer.

TEN

....

SHIFTING SANDS

The sun just beginning to dip behind the steel giants of Manhattan turned Jane's waves a blazing red as she sat on a bench just outside the park's southwestern mouth. Her short emerald dress accentuated the green of her eyes, the tangerine sky's rays adding to their vibrancy. As Maria walked toward the bench, she felt her stomach tightening yet loosening all at once, the reality suddenly sinking in that she may never see this sight again if her planned confession pushed Jane away. She pulled herself out of the mental quicksand of her own making with her perfected unperturbed grin and nod as she approached the human band of light.

"Hi," Jane said, her voice weaker than usual, her smile taut.

"Hey." Maria widened her own smile in an attempt to alleviate the subtle bubble of tension that surrounded them. "How was your day?"

Jane hesitated for a moment, clearly shaken by the casual greeting of gray pleasantries. "Fine," she said. "Good. How was yours?"

Maria shrugged. "Slightly boring," she said. "I'm glad that's about to change."

Jane ducked her chin as she let out an airy laugh. "Don't speak too soon," she said as she lifted her head back up, the rose on her pale cheeks turning Maria's stomach into a storm once again.

She shoved her hands into her pockets and took a recuperating breath. "So," Maria said, looking off toward the park's pathways. "Shall we?

They set off on the urban trails peppered with after-work joggers and dog walkers, the steady rhythm of passersby serving as a much appreciated buffer between the duo. Jane focused on the exploration of her craft, remaining mostly silent as she clicked and zoomed and knelt to capture the gigantic park's endless subject matter. She halted before the Greyshot Arch, and Maria smiled as the budding photographer waved by a mother pushing a stroller, allowing her to pass before she settled into position and snapped a shot of the heavily trafficked bridge and its brick underbelly. They passed through the shadowed arch to the other side where an older man with tired eyes but lively lungs blew into his saxophone with such passion and vigor Maria wondered if he was going to end up pulling a muscle.

Her original plan was to write as they walked, to scribble her observations, to create impromptu poems. But the words she knew she needed to eventually deliver to Jane occupied all space in her brain, so instead she observed the studious artist in action, hoping to work up the courage at some point during the evening to clear the stifling air engulfing them.

They eventually found themselves in Sheep Meadow, the sprawling lawn dotted with evening loungers and with students throwing Frisbees, both with their two-legged and four-legged friends. Maria followed Jane as she meandered through the grass, the occasional click of the camera's shutter sounding like the hands of a clock, a reminder of the inevitable. She wiped her hands on her jeans as Jane turned to capture a wide view of the city sprouting behind the rows of trees on the western edge of the park, the buildings glowing bronze as the encroaching sunset reigned supreme. She hoped the picturesque scene would soften at least some of the blow she was about to deal.

"Do you want to sit for a while?" she asked, prompting Jane to turn back from the skyline. "This view is amazing."

Jane swiped a bundle of hair from her face and smiled. "Sure." She joined Maria down on the crisp lawn, tucking her legs to one side and blowing out a light sigh. "It really is amazing," she said, setting her camera beside her and glancing out at the melting horizon.

Maria smiled and admired the scene along with her. "Philly is a great city, but it definitely doesn't compare to this."

"Is that where you're from?"

Maria nodded. "I haven't been there since I first left," she said, "which is crazy considering it's basically right across the river."

"What happened? Why haven't you gone back?"

A stretch of silence seized the moment as Maria worked to weave a delicate transition. She could feel Jane's gaze on her, curious yet patient. Finally, she let out a breath. It was now or never.

"Family problems," she said. "My mother and I had a…falling out." She turned to face Jane, who looked on with narrowed yet tender and attentive eyes. She prayed the news wouldn't steal that softness away.

Maria cleared her throat and adjusted her seat on the grass. "On that note," she said, "I actually wanted to tell you something." She paused again, studying Jane's inquisitive face. "About me," she added. "It also might help explain something about the other night."

"Oh." Jane's voice rang light and surprised, and her eyes swelled slightly as she straightened her spine.

Maria forced her limbs to loosen despite the tension gripping her entire body. "So," she started, glancing to the dark orange sky for a moment to calm her nerves, "I told you I moved here when I was seventeen, but the only reason I did is because my mother kicked me out." She paused as she watched Jane's mouth open slightly, her amber brows lifting. "It's not what you think," she said, almost chuckling. "I wasn't out of control. I wasn't shoplifting or partying. I wasn't misbehaving." She stopped again and tilted her head. "I was just…My mother couldn't handle certain things."

"What things?" Jane asked.

Maria's pulse quickened, a million horses trampling through her veins. Revealing her sexuality to someone never triggered this swirling storm inside her; that's what scared her the most.

She drew another breath as she relived the traumatizing memory. "I always knew I was different growing up," she said, starting as softly as she could. "Most of the time I couldn't explain it, but I met Theresa when her family moved to town and she started going to my school. We became best friends almost instantly, and it didn't take long for me to realize what it was I had been feeling for a while."

She tried to block out the ever-increasing strain working itself onto Jane's face as she went on. "One day after school, we were in my bedroom listening to music, and she blindsided me when she told me she had been curious about certain things, too," Maria said, locking her eyes on Jane's now. "Things for girls."

A pained silence grabbed hold of the night, with even the laughs and barks that had been echoing around the lawn seeming to halt all at once. Jane's face worked through various stages of recognition, blank at first followed by a cocked head and an open mouth. After a few moments to herself, she finally popped her head back to neutral and simply said, "Okay."

Maria bit her bottom lip and nodded. "It was certainly all a shock to me," she said. "My mother drilled Catholicism into me and my brother growing up. I think because she was a single mother she felt she needed to do everything she could to raise us right, make sure we turned out healthy and sane despite not having much of a family structure. I surely didn't think I would end up…this way. And I definitely didn't expect my best friend to be feeling the same way."

Jane seemed to be working hard to steady her breath, though her face remained smooth and open. Maria was desperate to finish the story so she could hear what thoughts rattled inside her head.

"Anyways, after Theresa told me about her…curiosities," she went on, "she kissed me. Or I kissed her. Maybe we both did, I don't even remember. All I remember is my mother's face when she came home early and opened my bedroom door to find me with my lips on another girl's." Maria chuckled, shaking her head. "She gasped and cried, 'Oh, Maria!' I'm still not sure if she was referring to me or if she was praying to the Virgin Mary," she said, making Jane smile. "All I know is a few nights of arguing and cursing and forced prayer turned into me coming home from school the following Monday to an empty suitcase on my bed."

She heard Jane's light gasp and turned to find her eyes blown wide.

"I've made peace with all that now, honestly," Maria said. "I'm just telling you this since we ran into Theresa, and I wasn't sure if it seemed strange or confusing. Plus, I figured it would be the right thing to tell you, just in case…"

Jane shook her head as her eyebrows sunk closer together. "Just in case what?"

"Well," Maria said, "just in case it made you uncomfortable. Me being a lesbian."

Maria couldn't blame the twitch that seemed to jerk Jane's body. The word had a way of sounding blunt to outsiders.

Despite waiting for Jane's full reaction, Maria felt the weight at last release from her shoulders. The deed was done.

"It's okay if you are," Maria said, knowing full well she was lying.

"No," Jane said, waving a hand in the air. "Of course it's fine," she said. "I'm not uncomfortable. I actually thought…"

"What?"

Jane blushed again and bobbed her head from one side to the other. "I actually maybe thought that you were."

Maria couldn't help but laugh. "Aw, yeah? Am I that opaque?"

"No! No." Jane placed her hand on her forehead. "It's just, with what happened at the bar," she said. "With Theresa. I guess I sensed something there. You definitely seemed rattled."

"I didn't realize she would be there until Kay mentioned it, not that it matters," Maria said. "I don't have any negative feelings toward her anymore. I just mostly wasn't sure how you would react. I didn't want it thrown at you like that."

"Oh." Jane's face fell, and she reached for her thin gold necklace, playing with it in her fingers that Maria thought she could see trembling. "You didn't need to worry about that."

"Yeah, well, you seemed like you were going to pass out all night," Maria said. "I didn't want to be the reason you finally collapsed."

Jane covered her face with her hands for a moment before bringing them back down to reveal a shy smile. She shook her head and scrunched her lips. "I always find a way to embarrass myself."

"Oh, you didn't embarrass yourself," Maria said, slapping Jane's knee. She pulled away quickly, not wanting her tactile gesture to be seen as suggestive, even if her belly flamed at the touch. Jane lowered her eyes to the spot where Maria's hand had just been before lifting them again. "I was just worried," Maria added with a smile. "I certainly didn't want to have to drag your ass outta there."

"Well," Jane said, tucking a lock behind her now pink ears, "thank you for the concern."

The two sat in a surprisingly comfortable silence for a few moments until Jane's curiosity emerged. "What happened with you and Theresa? After you were kicked out, I mean."

"I went to her house at first, hoping to stay there at least for the night," Maria said. "She wouldn't let me in. Her parents were just as conservative as my mother, and she was scared. She didn't want to tell them why I was there, why I got kicked out."

"That's awful," Jane said, her voice just above a broken whisper. "She just left you standing there out on the street?"

Maria nodded, then shrugged. "Pretty much," she said. "I can't blame her, really. If I had a choice I wouldn't have had my mother find out either, at least not in the way she did. Plus, Theresa wasn't even sure if she was gay. As it turns out, she's not."

"Oh," Jane said, shaking her head. "That's…I don't know what that is except sad."

"It's okay," Maria assured her. "It was hard at first, but like I said, it all eventually worked out. Luckily, for me, I was already pretty independent and had taken the bus into the city here alone a few times, so I walked to the station after leaving Theresa's and slept there on a bench until the morning, bought a one-way ticket, and ended up on Christopher Street."

Maria's heart swelled at the sound of Jane's sympathetic moan. "Then what did you do?"

"I met Kay," Maria said, her voice lifting at the vivid memory. "He was sitting on a stoop with a few other guys, all just as magnetic, and I bummed a cigarette from him. They saw right away what happened to me because it had all happened to them, too, in one way or another. The next thing I know, I'm moving in with all of them into their studio apartment."

"How many people lived there?"

"I made number nine," she said, causing a gasp to flee Jane's pale pink mouth. The innocent shock made Maria giggle. "Honestly, it wasn't all that bad. There was a sense of solidarity among all of us, a sense of family I had never even felt back home."

"Did you ever talk to your mother again?"

"I tried," Maria said. "I called her a few times, but if she answered the phone, she hung up as soon as she realized it was me. And when my brother Lucas answered and tried to get her to talk to me, she refused. About a year after I moved here, my brother called and told me she died of a brain aneurysm."

"My God, I'm so sorry."

"Like I said before, don't be. The past is best left where it is."

"No," Jane resisted. "I mean, for there to be that broken bond between you and to never get a chance to speak your peace or to mend..." She shook her head, and Maria noted a thin veil of water forming on her eyes. "It's not fair."

Maria wanted to comfort her, but Jane wasn't wrong. There seemed to be very little in the way of fairness in this world, at least not in recent times. "I won't argue with you there," she said, her voice low.

Another brief round of quiet pervaded their private lot of lawn as the hum of nighttime traffic reverberated in the distance. Jane blew out a light sigh, breaking the sound of silence. "I grew up without a father, too."

The confession drew Maria's eyes to hers. She felt silly and ashamed for not asking Jane more about her own upbringing. "I remember you mentioning your mother running the store," she said. "I should've asked. I'm sorry."

Jane shook her head. "I'm like you in the sense I've moved on from it, in a way," she said. "I was only four when he died of a heart attack, so I only remember him in bits and pieces. It's more my mother I worry about, especially these past two years Stephen's been gone."

"I can't imagine," Maria said.

Jane shrugged. "She focuses everything on the store, and she reads a lot," she said. "We both do. When I was young she used to make clothes for friends and family, but she stopped not long after my father passed. I used to hope she would get back to it, but she never did. I think it could help her."

Maria smiled as she admired Jane's palpable love for her mother. The proud daughter sighed again and shook her red mane. "Anyways," she said, clearing her throat, "I hope you still talk to your brother?"

"Sometimes," Maria said. "Lucas worked at a car shop for a while after he graduated, then he took off to Canada to avoid the draft."

"Oh, wow." Jane's brows flew to the purpling sky. "Really?"

Maria prayed Jane wouldn't be upset at the dodger considering her brother didn't get to escape the war like Lucas. "I don't talk about it much," she said. "Being a draft dodger isn't exactly a noble or brave title to have, even if most people understand the war is fucked up."

"I certainly don't think it's cowardly," Jane said to Maria's surprise. "I didn't want Stephen to accept his draft notice as easily as he did. I think he didn't fight it because our father served in World War II. I think he felt like it was his responsibility, carrying on his service."

"I hate the position we've put so many boys in," Maria said, shaking her head. "Well, hey, just a few more weeks, right?"

Jane smiled. "Just in time for the holiday."

"That's perfect," Maria said, her own grin budding.

"I hope so," Jane said. "He's been gone so long, and he's seen so much, I'm sure. He never writes about it, though. I have no idea what he'll be like, how much he's changed. I can't believe he's twenty-one now."

Maria leaned back onto her hands and shook her head again. "Time is strange."

"*Life* is strange," Jane said, offering an exasperated smirk.

Maria glanced at Jane staring off into the last bloom of the evening blaze. "I agree wholeheartedly."

....

By the time they wandered out of the meadow and hit 72 Street Station, the street lights had simmered to life, coating Central Park West in a hazy glow against the impending indigo sky. The serenity added to the relief Maria felt washing through her, grateful for the evening going much better than it could have.

Yet a subtle tide churned within her stomach still, washing her onto some unknown shore that, for some even more nameless reason, she didn't feel quite like leaving.

As they stood outside the station, Jane cleared her throat. "You have to take the Blue Line, right?"

"Yeah, usually," Maria said, her hands secure inside her pockets. "I could take the Red with you and get off on Christopher?"

Jane's full lips tightened briefly before she nodded and smiled. "Sure."

The train was packed with late-night workers heading home with baggy eyes and Upper East Siders venturing down to the Village for jazz and drag. Maria and Jane stood beside each other, bodies gently swaying with the rocking of the rail, hips forced close, sharing a single pole they gripped for balance. Every few moments they shared a glance, a friendly smile. Behind her own grins, Maria wondered if her offer to escort Jane halfway home came across as chivalrous, as the action of a suitor. Suddenly her hands began to sweat. She prayed Jane couldn't see the slickness seeping from underneath them.

As they neared Christopher Street, Jane turned to Maria and broke their silence among the chatty herd surrounding them. "Would I be able to come in again to the darkroom sometime to try to develop these?" she asked. "I think I remember how to do it all, but if I can't be there without Max or your other photographer, or if I need to pitch in to help pay for supplies, I am totally fine with—"

"You can come in whenever," Maria said, cutting Jane off, softening the slice with a smile. She thought her entire body would melt when Jane flashed her own and looked down at her feet as the train began to slow.

"How about Friday?"

Maria smiled again, happy for Jane's casual tone, her shrugging shoulders. "That's perfect," she said. "Actually, it's better than perfect." She felt a rush pouring through her, that tingling ignition of hope. "That's Kay's birthday. He's celebrating at Stonewall right down the street from the office after his show. It's a shit bar with shit beer, but he, we take what we can get. I was going to work on some edits until then, so I can make sure you have the darkroom."

"Oh!" Though the word came out as apprehension, a light seemed to flicker behind Jane's eyes. Her answer sealed the beam. "That's great. I'd love to see how he likes your gift."

"Well, I have you to thank for that," Maria said.

Jane's smile brightened, and as the doors opened she shifted back, allowing Maria and her fellow exiting passengers to pass by her. "I'll see you Friday. Eight-ish?"

Maria nodded on her way out. "I'll be there."

Jane slipped her hands off the pole, pivoting around it, and as Maria turned over her shoulder to offer a wave, her eyes landed on the delicate pair of sweaty handprints just above where her own had been.

ELEVEN

··

THE WEIGHT

J ane sat at the kitchen table facing the window, stirring her
coffee the morning light turned into a glossy pool of rich
brown. She realized how similar its milky, mesmerizing color
was to that of Maria's eyes. She shuddered and clanked her spoon
on the rim of her mug before placing it on the table and taking a
sip.

She let out a sigh and rested the cup back in front of her,
thankful for the strong brew. She certainly needed it. She barely
slept the night before as a whirlpool of emotions threatened to
sink her deep into the bed, grounding her motionless yet full of
energy. Her mind leapt from rock to rock, from thought to
thought, too restless to remain on one for too long. She felt
empathy for Maria, for all that she suffered, for her exile, for Kay,
for all the wandering souls on Christopher Street. She felt anger
toward those who sent them there, toward the government and
its appetite for war both abroad and right here at home. She felt
grateful for her family, no matter how small it was.

The one emotion that appeared to rule above them all, however, the force that pinned her down in her sheets, pressing against her chest, was fear.

It was that fear that told her she was close to something. It was that fear that sank the stone, dropping her into the sea at last, no longer dangling her above its wild current. She knew, then, as she flailed in the uncharted waters, that she felt something for Maria, something ten times more powerful than she ever felt for friends like Claire or Joey. People were only ever scared of what they can't control, and if Jane knew one thing for certain, it was that she had zero power over this foreign yet eerily comfortable pull toward Maria.

It was a line the fierce Italian woman seemed to have cast into Jane's boiling flesh just two weeks prior, its hook digging into her deepest parts, ones she had never even thought to inspect before. She never had a reason, never had a muse, never had a hunger. She felt that hunger eating away at her now after learning her inklings about Maria's preferences had been correct.

As she took another sip of her coffee, her eyes glazed over in wistful yet frenzied thought, the shuffling of feet moved in behind her. Jane still did not stir, a heavy tingling holding her in a daze.

"Honey?"

She heard the sound of her mother's voice beside her and glanced up.

"Honey, are you okay?"

Jane shook her head and set the mug onto the table. "Yes, sorry. I zoned out."

Rebecca narrowed her eyes. "Hmm. You've been doing that a lot lately." She turned away toward the sink, placing her own mug inside.

"Have I really?"

Her mother nodded as she joined her at the table. "Yes," she said with a smile. "In a good way, though. You seem…happy."

"I've always been happy, Mom," Jane said, knowing perfectly well what she meant.

"No, I know that." Rebecca waved a hand in the air. "You just seem lighter. Maybe it's the photography, or maybe it's that new friend you're spending time with. Whatever it is, I'm glad it's happening."

Jane felt her chest tighten and burn, her internal signal letting her know her skin was set to blush. "Oh," she said. "Yeah, I've been getting out more and taking photos. You and Claire were right. I guess it turns out I needed it."

She hoped the oversimplification would suffice, perhaps conceal the obvious pink on her face. She smiled and hid behind another sip as her mother tilted her head, studying, excavating silently as all mothers do.

"Plus," Jane said abruptly, "it's only two more weeks until we get Stephen back."

Rebecca sighed and closed her eyes for a moment. "Goodness, yes. I will be so relieved when he's home."

Jane reached out her hand and placed it on top of her mother's. "I hope so," she said. "Maybe then you'll be lighter, too."

Rebecca's mouth edged into a pained smile as she shook her head and lowered her chin. "I'm so sorry, honey," she said. "I know I've been a bit…off since Stephen left. It's hard to live in the present when any day the ground can be ripped out right from under you, especially when it's already happened once before. It all feels so…heavy."

Although she had never experienced exactly what her mother had in her life, Jane absolutely knew what it felt like to be groundless yet frozen solid. But she wouldn't offer the solidarity aloud. She wouldn't offer any of these new feelings to anyone outside of her own muddled mind. To do so would make it real, and all she could manage right now, while her raw, vulnerable skin itched and tingled, was to dwell inside the unknown fantasy.

"I know," she said, simple yet true, giving her mother's hand a squeeze. "I know."

....

TWELVE

IT'S JUST A SHOT AWAY

Jane found herself humming and singing quietly along with the radio the photographers kept inside the darkroom, the music helping carry her along in an easy flow as she moved her images from the developing tub to the stop bath, to the fixer, all the way to the line above the tanks where she clipped them to dry. She settled into a comfortable rhythm, the scent of the chemicals fading away as the night stretched on, each photograph she pulled out of the bath bringing another smile to her face. It didn't matter if some of them didn't turn out, if some of them had a pinch too much contrast or not enough. All that mattered was the process, the creation, the doing.

As the swirly, dreamy introduction to "Little Wing" by Jimi Hendrix flew out of the radio like dandelion seeds blowing through a breeze, Jane thought of Stephen and realized how excited she was to show him what she somehow managed to do with his camera, even if it happened to take her until the final month of his absence to get around to it.

A knock sounded behind her. She yelled over her shoulder to give Maria the okay to open the door.

"How goes it?"

Maria's voice somehow startled Jane even as she knew she was entering. She had felt raw and wound earlier in the evening as well when Maria escorted her into the darkroom. She had barely been able to look her in the eye. Now, the electric current humming through Jane's bones returned as Maria stood behind her, watching her hoist her images aloft.

"These look amazing," she said, coming to Jane's side to get a closer look. She reached toward one and placed her hands behind it, allowing the damp paper to rest on the backs of her fingers. Jane inhaled a deeper breath than usual as she took in Maria's scent, so close it seemed to become her own.

She smiled and reached up to drape another of her creations on the line. "I can definitely do better."

"Of course you can," Maria huffed. "Who can't? But you've had zero photography experience up until two weeks ago. Now look what you're doing!"

Jane nodded and pursed her lips. The compliment launched itself a bit deeper into her body, residing in her stomach in a massive lump. She eventually smiled. "Thank you," she said, still not meeting Maria's gaze.

Maria stepped around her to examine the photos on the other side of Jane, who felt the breeze of movement blow by her, the subtle sensation nearly making her knees buckle. She attempted to distract herself by humming along to the radio again.

Maria turned away suddenly and placed her hands on the counter behind her. "You like Hendrix?"

Jane chuckled. "Yes. Don't you?"

"Absolutely!" Maria folded her arms and grinned. "I don't know, I guess I wasn't expecting him to be your thing."

"Because I'm a square?" Jane hung the last image and swiveled toward Maria, who shook her head and laughed.

"You're so not a square," she said.

"You thought so when you met me, though. Didn't you?" Jane couldn't help but smirk, though she doubted she looked half as charming as Maria when she did the same.

"No." Maria smiled, soft and devoid of satire. "I said you were sweet. There's a difference."

Jane had never been more grateful for the darkroom's haunted lighting. Maybe the fresh layer of crimson coating her entire body would blend into the shroud. For a few moments, she gazed back at Maria, her arms folded over her plain black shirt, strong legs laced one over the other, dark eyes searching Jane's for a reaction. It wasn't until then that she studied Maria's figure fully, though she had to admit she had noticed it before. She was seeing it in a new light now, though, literally. The risqué shade of back alley red practically begged her to look deeper at her friend's subtle curves, at the slight bump on her nose Jane found adorable, at her perfectly sized breasts, full yet somehow still unassuming…

She cleared her throat as another heat wave threatened to swallow her, then looked at the radio. "Well, I know Jimi because of my brother," she said, shifting the conversation back to reality and out of that bewildering fantasyland. "He loves him, and I totally understand why."

Maria unraveled her beguiling grin. "You are full of surprises, Miss Martin."

A sudden distant shout ripped both Jane and Maria out of their frozen gazes. Maria swept across the tiny room and flung open the door, Jane following behind. A pack of bodies flew by the office windows, hurtling down Christopher Street.

"Another fucking raid?" Maria turned back to Jane and threw her head back.

"What are you talking about?" Jane craned her neck as she watched a few more people fly by the building.

Maria sighed. "Most of us can't congregate at a bar or in public without getting arrested or beaten. That's why we have places like Stonewall and like the place we went to for Side City. We have to hide, and we have no way to do that ourselves, so the mob owns and runs all of it."

Jane felt her eyes widening. She had heard of some of the discrimination gay people faced, but it always felt like a million miles away. Now, it was playing out just a few buildings down.

"Anyway," Maria said, lighting herself a cigarette, "the police use the organized crime as an excuse to raid us. The lights come on, you step away from whatever or whoever you're doing, and show your identification. Most people are just told to get the hell out, but if you're a man dressed as a woman or if you're someone well-known or if the cops had a bad day, you get arrested and you get booked and you get your name printed in the papers the next day."

"Jesus," Jane said, her brain feeling broken in half. "I didn't realize all of that."

"Most people don't," Maria said, walking to her desk and flicking her cigarette into the ashtray on top. "I certainly can't expect you to. There aren't enough of us to get our side of the story out there, to let people know what's really going on. So, we suck it up and we deal with the raids. Except…" Maria's voice drifted off as she cocked her head. "Stonewall just had one. The cops never do them this soon after."

Her eyes drew to the door just as police sirens blared through the streets. Without even turning to Jane, she said, "Grab your camera."

She killed her cigarette and swept across the office floor as Jane snatched her camera from underneath the desk. Her heart hammered inside her chest like a furious blacksmith, the fear and fascination propelling her forward. As she and Maria burst out the door, a wave of clustered panic smacked her in the face. Hundreds of people, mostly young men, surrounded a group of police cars outside the Stonewall Inn as the cops struggled to place a woman into one of the vehicles. Her resistance was fueled by the frenzied crowd all around her, with the drunken gang shouting, "Gay power!"

Maria grabbed Jane's arm as they approached the scene. "This never happens," she said, eyes glued on the chaos. "They always scatter and go home. They never hang around."

Jane snapped a shot of the scene, praying the darkness wouldn't ruin her chances of getting at least one decent photograph. The fact that she was witnessing this at all blew her already rattled mind.

The boiling scene exploded within seconds when a cop hit the handcuffed woman's head with his club. The men nearest the abuse banned together, pummeling the police with their fists and fighting to free the beaten woman. Jane snapped as quickly as she could, avoiding getting knocked to the ground as the crowd grew larger and angrier. More shouts of "Gay power!" and "We've had enough!" ricocheted among the brewing pack, and when the obvious sound of a brick smashing through a window shot out like a gun, Jane knew there was no going back. The wild kingdom had been unleashed.

Soon flames crawled up the outside of the Stonewall, and men crawled up to the sky, breaking streetlights and tossing bottles at their oppressors. The assault forced the officers to retreat into the bar, slamming the door shut and blocking it from the inside. The crowd cheered and hollered, high on their own hunger. They continued breaking windows and burning trash cans, tossing their remnants onto the empty cop cars, offering them quite the clear message of what they thought of their kind.

As Jane captured what she could while dodging shrapnel, Maria stayed at her side, occasionally tossing a bottle and joining the various chants and songs that echoed into the night.

A police force bus suddenly slid into the street, freezing the scene as the ravenous swarm felt out their next move. Officers streamed out of the massive black bus, their riot gear locked and loaded, armor out, ready for battle. They stood still in their battle line, using their shields to block the trash the crowd began to throw at them—bottles, pennies, charred cigarette butts. The police began to march forward, batons raised to the black sky, but their intimidation was futile. In fact, its intended purpose led to the very opposite as the brave souls in the front of the line linked arms in solidarity, leading the crowd in a highly inappropriate song and dance number. They kicked their legs into the air, their own special kind of weapons.

The officers charged on, beating their shields with their batons, forcing the crowd back, a starving crowd seeing every shade of red, the color they brought to life by crafting Molotov cocktails, a violent happy hour special, and launching them at their enemies. Men and women leapt onto cars, both to avoid being crushed and to seize a better angle to fire projectiles at the police.

The animalistic energy invaded Jane's body like a virus. Her heart roared like flames, and somehow, even amidst the violent chaos, her eyes smiled at the explosion of history playing out right before them. She was witnessing true rebellion, capturing it all with her Canon she snatched tighter than ever.

A fire truck flew onto the scene, the Stonewall still burning in the night. Over their piercing sirens, Jane was still able to hear Maria cry out, "Kay!" She then took off running toward a group of men fleeing two police and their wicked batons. Jane snapped a few frenzied shots until she saw the bloodied face of one of the runaways. Her heart dropped to the trash-riddled ground when Kay's rich eyes looked up at Maria as she came to his side. Jane ran to him, helping Maria hoist him off the ground and onto the sidewalk.

"I'm fine! I'm fine!" he yelled, though the fresh patch of blood caked to his temple said otherwise. "Let's get the fuck home."

The trio fled down the hectic street, away from the battle and toward some unknown destination, Kay hanging between Jane's and Maria's shoulders and stumbling over his own two feet.

Jane managed to sneak one look back at the flaming scene before they turned a corner. Hell was burning in Greenwich Village.

....

They fumbled into the dark apartment and lowered Kay onto the couch, the beaten birthday boy leaning back with a moan. Maria ran to the bathroom for a wet washcloth while Jane dug into the fridge and grabbed a frozen bag of vegetables, making her way back to the living room with Maria right behind her. They each settled beside Kay and set to tending his wounds.

"What the hell was that, Kay?" Maria nearly gasped as she held onto Kay's chin and wiped away the blood oozing down his chin and onto his blue velvet blouse. His eyes seemed frozen wide open, staring straight ahead at the blank television.

"I don't even know," he said. "It was just another raid, at first. But those bastards are doing this more and more, and they're getting more violent, and I think we just…snapped." A light chuckle escaped his mouth. "I mean, how can we keep dealing with this shit, Maria?" He looked into her eyes now, his own back to life. "We have nowhere to go, nowhere to drink, nowhere to fuck, nowhere to love."

Jane's heart winced as Kay's exhausted ache spilled out along with his blood. While Stephen was thousands of miles away, he and his brethren fighting a vicious war, people had been fighting one right here, in her own city.

"We're not even legally allowed to have sex inside our own homes!" he shouted. "Then people have the fucking nerve to wonder why we do what we do, why we trick, why we use, why we live in dumps, sleeping on top of each other. Why we let another faggot beat us up in a shady apartment in exchange for next month's rent. Why we have to meet up in alleys and underground bars and in the trucks down at the docks."

The images rushed through Jane's mind like a flashflood. She could feel her heart throbbing inside her throat as her mind attempted to make sense of it all.

"We have no fucking options because they took them all from us." Kay's eyes bubbled now, and Jane even thought she saw the same glistening inside Maria's.

"I know," she said barely above a whisper. "I know, baby. We only have each other."

"Damn right," Kay said. He slid one hip up off the couch and snatched a pack of cigarettes from his back pocket. He took one out, passing the rest to Maria, and as he lit it, a grin worked itself across his face. "But you felt it, too, didn't you?" he said. "Tonight was different. We're not going back."

Maria smiled and lit herself a cigarette. "This is the Kay I like to see."

He then turned to Jane for the first time and narrowed his eyes. "What about you, baby girl?" He took a drag and blew it behind him. "You caught it all with that camera of yours. What did you see?"

Jane's heart froze at the request. Her mouth fell open as Kay put his hand over hers, holding the frozen vegetables to his head, relieving her duty. She sat with both hands in her lap now and bit her lip. She cleared her throat and looked him in his beautiful eyes.

"I saw resilience," Jane said, her throat suddenly parched. The image of the street burning as the crowd forced the police into hiding surged through her veins. That sensation of life being truly lived and fought for took hold of her again. "I saw patriots. I saw warriors."

Kay gazed at her, thoughtful and silent.

"And many queens," Maria added, giving Kay's leg a squeeze.

"Yes, I am a queen!" He stood up and twirled around, his open blouse flapping around him like wings. Maria cackled and relaxed back into the couch. "And happy birthday to me!"

"Aw, Kay!" Maria leapt from her seat and ran out of the living room, returning in mere seconds with a package that looked familiar to Jane.

"I guess it's good I forgot this here," she said, handing Kay his gift as he paused from his spinning. "It would've ended up as ashes in the street tonight."

"Maria, Maria," he said, shaking his head. "What do we have here?"

Maria sat beside Jane as he dug into the bag. His eyes blew open when he reached the treasure inside. "Oh!" He instantly began flipping through the pages, gasping.

Maria laughed. "They're almost as fabulous as you."

"Almost," he snickered, eyes locked on his book of royalty.

Maria rose again and gave Kay a kiss on his cheek, wrapping her arms around him. "You're my life," she said.

Jane's lips quivered at the quiet moment after all the chaos, at Maria's tender love. She smiled at the duo leaning on each other in their living room, a pair of fighters who so clearly knew the value of the lives they had to claw their way through for so long.

She hoped that Kay was right and that the time had finally come for that to change.

....

Jane hung up the kitchen phone after telling her mother she was staying the night at Maria's to avoid the chaotic streets. As she turned, she found Maria walking out of her bedroom. She leaned against the kitchen doorway and folded her arms. "She okay?"

"Yeah," Jane said. "As long as I'm safe, she's fine."

"Good." Maria smiled and turned back to her bedroom. "I just put fresh sheets on the bed. I insist you get to enjoy their virgin touch."

Jane choked out a laugh and knew she couldn't hide her flushed skin even if she tried. "No, no. It's your bed. I have no problem sleeping on the couch."

"You're my guest," Maria said, her eyebrows tightening though her smile remained. "Get your ass in there."

Jane sighed and surrendered, reluctantly making her way past Maria to the bedroom behind her. Kay was already passed out in his own, his snoring funneling through the door. Maria followed behind her and swept across the room's wood floor, closing the curtains. "It gets crazy bright in here in the morning," she said.

Jane tried to listen, but she couldn't concentrate as the scent of Maria engulfed her, the earthy aroma floating off every surface inside the cozy bedroom. The plush white duvet caught her eye first, its softness and lightness a stark contrast to the dark edges of Maria. Though the supple side of her had shown its face tonight, and Jane realized there was even more to Maria than she had realized.

"If you need anything, just come out and let me know." The nearness of the voice startled Jane out of her daze. She looked up and found Maria alternating between smiling and biting her lip in the doorway just beside her. Maria cleared her throat. "I left a shirt and pair of shorts there on the bed for you if you want to change," she said. "Feel free to wake me in the morning if you get up before me. I'll make us all breakfast." She leaned forward and winked. "I make a mean omelet."

Jane chuckled and nodded. "I can't wait."

Maria swiveled away and closed the door, leaving Jane alone in her bedroom aglow with the gentle gold of a nightlight near the window. She edged further into the room, cautiously as if her mere presence might break something. She made her way to the bed and sat by the clothes Maria laid out for her. Jane lifted them, folding them over in her hands, enjoying the soft cotton against her skin before setting them back down, afraid of what emotions might stir inside her if she dared to wear them.

Instead, she curled onto her side still wearing her jeans and blouse, collapsing into an exhausted sleep as images of the insane evening dissipated in the calming cloud of Maria's fragrance.

THIRTEEN

DAZED AND CONFUSED

Maria flipped the omelet inside the pan, the sizzling reminding her of the buzz of the streetlights as rioters climbed their posts and clipped their wires. She sighed and shook her head while the memories coursed through her like the flames fanning up the Stonewall. It had been merely hours since the spontaneous yet long overdue revolt, but the disconnect so common after such a startling experience seemed to place her years ahead of the chaos.

The patter of bare feet on hard floor yanked Maria back to the present. She spun from the stovetop and found Jane standing in the doorway, her waves wild and blazing in the harsh morning sun drenching the small kitchen. The sight clawed at Maria's throat, its foreign, captivating nature catching her off guard. She realized then that no woman ever sauntered out of her bedroom unless it was in the midnight darkness and she was navigating to the bathroom after a few hours of casual sex.

"What?" Jane ran her fingers through her mane, eyes frantic. "Does my hair look ridiculous?"

"No!" Maria shook her head, snapping herself out of the daze. "Sorry," she said, swiveling back to the stove. "I'm just still so disoriented from everything. I barely slept."

It wasn't a lie. As she lay on the couch the night before, Maria found herself unable to close her eyes. The chaos of the evening sank its claws into her, but so did the image of Jane's skin caressing her sheets just two rooms away. The relentless picture mauled at her defenses, the ones she erected when she was thrust out into the world at seventeen, the ones she had strengthened to avoid these thoughts because she knew a breach was indeed possible. She knew it the second she spotted Jane under the tree at the protest in Washington Square, her scarlet hair blowing in the balmy breeze, her skin flushing at every grin Maria unabashedly threw her way. And if she were to be even more honest with herself, she could say the flame was stoked that very first night on the fire escape.

Now, with Jane settling into a seat at her kitchen table, molding into every nook and shadow of the apartment as if it had been made for her, the force hit Maria in a massive surge, the levees breaking for the very first time with such might she had to lean forward against the counter to catch her breath.

"Are you okay?"

Despite the bizarre storm inside her, the sound of Jane's sweet voice calmed Maria in an instant.

"Yeah," Maria said, shuddering out the squall through her shoulders. "I just can't get last night out of my head." She turned from the oven and walked the fresh omelet to the table, placing the full plate in front of Jane's bulging eyes.

"Maria, I can't eat all of this!" She laughed as she gazed up, openmouthed.

Maria smiled as she walked back to the counter and poured two cups of coffee from the pot. She returned to the table, taking a seat and sliding Jane a steaming mug. "I believe in you," she said with a wink.

Jane shook her head and noted Maria's empty place setting. "Are you not eating?"

"No," Maria said, taking a sip of the coffee she held with both hands. "I normally don't eat breakfast."

"Oh." Jane looked down at her teeming plate. "You didn't need to make something just for me."

"Well," Maria said, setting her cup down and wiggling herself into a smirk, "don't worry too much. I made one for Kay, too."

Jane smiled, her mood instantly lifting.

"Good!" Kay's voice abruptly boomed from the hallway as he shuffled into the kitchen, a kimono draped over his naked body. "Because I'm ravenous."

"And you're bruised!" Maria winced as she caught the purple knob sticking out of Kay's temple. Jane turned from her breakfast and sighed at the sight.

"It's fine," Kay said with a wave. "As long as it goes away for the gala."

"What gala?" Jane asked after a bite of spinach and tomatoes.

"It's more of a gay-la," Maria said, lifting her brows.

"It's a drag show in August," Kay said, ignoring Maria's quip and snatching the plate she made for him from the counter. He hopped up onto it, swinging his long, muscular legs, his toes brushing the linoleum floor. "After everything that went down last night, I imagine it's going to be quite the affair." He took a bite and moaned, chewing dramatically. "Girl, if you make me fat, I won't be able to find a dress that fits."

"Oh, we'll find you one," Maria said, eyes narrowed. She turned suddenly to Jane. "What about your mom?"

Jane paused her eating, her fork suspended in the air. "What about her?"

"She should totally make Kay a dress." Maria took a deep breath and tilted her head. "What do you think?"

"Your mother's a designer?" The intrigue in Kay's voice stroked Maria's optimism.

Jane chuckled, covering her mouth with her hand. "Hardly," she said. "She used to make clothes sometimes, but that was a long time ago. I hoped she'd get around to it again eventually, but—"

"But what?" Kay hopped off the counter. "Ain't no time like the present." He sauntered through the kitchen, halting in the doorway. "If she can make something as gorgeous as you, she can certainly make a dress fit for all of this." He slid a hand down his silk robe before disappearing into his bedroom.

Maria's mouth tightened into a childlike smile as she held her coffee in front of her face. Jane drilled her eyes into her, lips pursed into an ornery grin. "What if my mother says no?"

"Tell her the dress is for a queen," Maria said with another wink. "She won't be able to resist."

She prayed her own resolve wouldn't buckle so easily as Jane shook her head and returned to her omelet.

•••

The night's mayhem came back to Jane in broken flashes as she leaned her foggy head against the subway window on her way home, a journey spent floating in a haze of disconnect. It all felt like years behind her now, the Stonewall hundreds of miles away. Soon she would have photographic evidence of the riot, one she knew she had been lucky and privileged to have captured. As she reached Brooklyn and exited the train, Jane wondered if the feelings that had taken up residence inside her since the night she met Maria meant that she was part of the community that stoked it. Or, at least, might be. The idea clung to the corners of her mind while she walked down the parkway to the store, where she knew her mother would already be either in the office or stocking shelves.

When she opened the door, Jane found her mother at the counter emptying a box of books, her face collapsing with relief. "Thank goodness," she said, her shoulders relaxing down her back. "I was worried it still would've been crazy out there and you wouldn't be able to get here."

"It is still crazy," Jane said, placing her camera bag on the counter.

"What even happened?" Rebecca stood with one hand on her hip, the other still hanging onto a book she draped over the box, her eyes looking as lost as Jane felt.

"I don't even think I know," she said, shaking her head. "Maria thought it was just another raid on the Stonewall." Her mother's empty face told Jane of the innocence she should have suspected. "It's a…gay bar, just down from the office."

Jane waited for her mother's open-mouthed, brow-arched nod to complete itself before she went on. "Apparently they were raided recently, and people were fed up. A cop smacked a woman on the head with his baton, and the scene just…exploded."

She explained the chaos that unfolded as best as she could—the fires, the trash cans, the police shields, the blood. And she did her best to articulate what Kay and Maria divulged to her—the firings and arrests, the names dragged through the mud and through the papers, the clandestine confines of queerness. Her mother's face softened along the way, her eyes intense as she soaked in the wave Jane thrust upon her shore. Every few moments, Rebecca shook her head slowly, an aching sigh or moan escaping her pursed mouth.

When Jane had talked herself spent, she let out her own sigh and collapsed onto her elbows on the counter. "I guess I've heard a few of these things before," she said. "On the news, in passing. And there was that ridiculous video they showed at school once that made it seem like being a homosexual was like being made by the devil himself."

Her mother let out another breath and shook her head. "This is what happens when people don't read. They become ignorant."

Jane felt her eyes about to burst out of her skull as she choked out a laugh. She glanced up at her mother who looked at her as if she were insane. "What?" Rebecca said, shrugging. "It's true."

Jane was thankful for the brief moment of lightness among the pile of ashes all around her.

"I feel like everything I've been told is a lie," Jane said after she and her mother settled from their laughter. "We have entire communities living underground all because of what? Ignorance? Fear?"

"Probably both," Rebecca said simply, tilting her head slightly to one side. "People are afraid of what they don't know."

"But how can you be afraid of people?" Jane stood straighter now, her brows tense. "People who just want to be able to go to restaurants and have jobs and hold someone's hand on the sidewalk without being beaten?" She hadn't realized how heated her tone had become until her mother placed a hand on hers.

"I don't understand it, either," she said with a pained smile of solidarity. "There's nothing logical about it. Some things about this world will probably never be understood. That's one of the hardest things we have to come to terms with."

Jane certainly knew about the unexplainable, the confusing, the illogical. Her attraction to Maria proved to be anything but easy to grasp. Her brewing feelings about the nation's irresponsibly waged war, while her brother fought in its trenches, certainly didn't help with the disorientation.

She shook her head and closed her eyes for a moment, the image of Kay bloodied and beaten on his couch and on his birthday stamping itself into her bruised brain. "I don't think I can come to terms with people getting kicked out to the streets and thrown into jail and ripped apart by land mines."

Rebecca's eyes glistened as she squeezed Jane's hand. "I don't expect you to," she said softly. "One of the things I love most about you is that heart of yours. The only bad thing about it is how often it will likely feel like it's breaking because of how much it's capable of feeling."

Jane grunted. "Maybe I can learn how to feel less."

Her mother smiled and released her hand. "Think of something else," she said, returning to her box of books. "In the meantime, I'm glad you're safe. And what about your friends? How are they this morning?"

"Good, I think." Jane pictured Kay in his peach Japanese robe and a smile swept across her face. The image stirred up his request, and she glanced at her mother as she continued sorting through the books.

"Speaking of my friends," Jane said, "one of them, Kay, has a show coming up in August, and they need a dress." Rebecca barely flinched at Jane using the ambiguous "they," her eyes remaining focused on her organizing.

Jane cleared her throat. "I know it's been years since you made anything, but I feel like you would really like them and I'm sure whatever they want will be fun, to say the least, so I was wondering if you might want to help?"

"Help?" Rebecca's brows pulled inward, though her sight never left her books.

Jane swallowed and finally spit it out. "I was hoping you could make them a dress. Like you used to do."

Her mother paused her sorting, stopping with a book in each hand. She looked at Jane, amused. "Really?"

Jane nodded and leaked out a cautious smile. She knew this wasn't going to work.

"Huh." Rebecca's lips puckered in thought. She said nothing else for a few moments as she got back to her books. Finally, she said, "Can your friend come over sometime so I can see what they need and if I can even do what they want?"

Jane's eyes swelled as her wary grin strengthened to a pleasantly surprised one. "Of course," she said.

Rebecca carried on as if nothing had happened, but Jane couldn't ignore it. "I have to say, Mom, I wasn't expecting you to even consider it. It's been so long."

"Yes, well, it seems these new friends of yours are making you very happy," her mother said, placing a hand on her hip and offering her daughter a friendly smirk. "And if that's the case, I would love to help them."

Yes, Jane thought. She was very happy, though it was someone other than Kay who was responsible for the majority of it.

"Plus," Rebecca said, nodding down toward the camera bag, "you've picked up a new hobby. Perhaps I can get my old one back."

Jane wanted to throw her arms around her mother and scream with joy. Instead, she smiled and started helping her unpack their new stock, grateful for the normalcy of routine.

....

FOURTEEN

GOIN' OUT OF MY HEAD

Maria returned to her apartment after she and Kay wandered around the Stonewall block, a battlefield burned in black and ash gray. The police cars had been hollowed out, their windows turned to glassy dust on the ground, their tires punctured and deflated. She watched Kay and a few others spray paint "Drag power" onto the walls of the inn and its surrounding buildings.

Despite the violence and darkness of the previous night, Maria couldn't help the grin that plastered itself on her face while she watched people feast their eyes upon the wreckage for the first time. Tourists nearby stopped to stare while fellow gays who hadn't participated in the riot descended onto its aftermath, hungry for a taste themselves. Kay and the others assured those who missed out that they would get their chance that evening as calls for another riot had already spread around the Village before the cloud of smoke even had time to dissipate.

The news instantly gave Maria her own craving, a craving to call her new favorite photographer to make sure she didn't miss out on the action. And as she walked into her apartment and picked up the phone, she told herself that was all she was doing—informing a colleague of an opportunity. Nothing more.

The beat her heart skipped when Jane's voice sounded from the line challenged that belief.

"Martin Books, how can I help you?"

"You can help me by coming back into the city tonight and taking more photos," Maria said with no introduction.

A slight pause ended with Jane's light gasp. "What do you mean? Are the riots still going on?"

"Sort of," Maria said, leaning against the kitchen wall and twirling the phone cord in her hand. "It's relatively calm right now, but people are planning to come back out tonight."

"Oh, wow," Jane said. "So, Kay was right. This wasn't just a one-time thing."

"You sound disappointed…"

"No!" Even Jane's defiant tone sounded pure, a command cloaked with kindness, like the call of Sunday church bells. "I think it's amazing," she said. "And I can't believe I got to see what I did and capture all of it."

"So, does that mean you want to capture more of it?" Maria asked.

Jane chuckled. "Yes," she said. "Yes, I absolutely do."

Maria smiled. "Good," she said. "Meet at my place around eight?"

"Store closes at seven, so that's perfect."

"Perfect," Maria reiterated, knowing full well the situation she was continuously cornering herself into was anything but perfect.

When she hung up, ten seconds had barely passed when the phone rang, startling her in her tracks back toward her bedroom. She answered to Patrick hooting and hollering so loud she had to move the handset away from her ear.

"Patrick, what the hell?" Maria couldn't help but laugh through her faux anger.

"Were you there?" he yelled. "Have you seen it?"

"I was there last night," Maria said. "So was Kay. It was crazy."

"I hear it's happening again tonight," Patrick said, the excitement in his voice like that of a child on Christmas Eve.

"It is," Maria said. "I'm running to the office soon to try and make some flyers. I want to do some leafleting while people are out."

"Of course you do."

Maria tilted her head, sighing. "Is there a reason you called, my dear Patrick?"

"Well, the riots, for one," he said. "This shit is crazy. But also, I've got great news on the San Francisco front." Maria held through the pause that followed, waiting for Patrick to go on. "The job?" he reminded her. "At Half Moon?"

Maria caught her breath, startled at her forgetfulness. How could that have slipped her mind so quickly?

"Right," she said, shaking her head. "What's the news?"

"They want to give you a call and do a phone interview," Patrick said, his voice filled with excitement. "If they feel like you'd be a good fit, they said you could start in September!"

Maria's eyes swelled, and her throat cracked. "Wow, that's…fast."

"That's not a bad thing, is it?"

"No," Maria said, not entirely certain if that were true. "Just…fast, that's all. Am I supposed to call them or will they call me?"

"I'll let them know you're interested and they'll reach out to you," Patrick said.

"Sounds good," Maria said. "Thanks, man. I owe you drinks."

"Make it a joint and we're set."

As she hung up, Maria thought she caught a whiff of Jane's sweet, fresh scent coming from the table where she had sat just hours earlier. A brick suddenly seemed to settle into her stomach, that sinking feeling of regret.

Though she wasn't completely convinced of its source quite yet, Maria had a pretty good sense, and it had her seeing red. In more ways than one.

She pushed the inconvenient truth down by snatching a bottle of whiskey from the kitchen cabinet and shooting a quick shot. The rest could be dealt with later, in the night when most seeds could be further buried.

....

FIFTEEN

LIGHT MY FIRE

The second night of riots drew just as many protesters to the streets, the crowd spilling into the surrounding blocks of the Stonewall as they danced a fiery dance with police. Maria kept an eye on Jane throughout the chaos, making sure no one threatened her safety, while she and a few other activists handed out leaflets calling to get both the cops and the mob bosses out of their businesses and out of their bedrooms. Most people accepted them enthusiastically, walking or running away with fists in the air. When she had run empty and Kay had run out of steam, Maria snatched Jane away from the dwindling madness and the three set off to a nearby diner where a group had gathered to gorge after their ravenous evening brawl. They walked in and were immediately met by the jukebox blaring Judy Garland's "I Happen to Like New York." The singer had just died a week earlier, and the emotions were still raw. Maria smiled and Kay brought a hand to his chest at the glorious yet heart-wrenching sound of the gay men in the corner singing at their tops of their lungs along to their late songbird's jazzy, powerful vocals. They had lost the icon who became their godmother in some odd yet pure way, and they lost her at such a tender time, and they grieved in the beautiful, performative, magnetic fashion Maria so admired.

She nodded to an open booth among the cluster of hungry rioters, leading the way for Kay and Jane. They settled in and all ordered coffee from the young waitress who bustled about the hectic tables with admirable ease. Maria had seen her before, a few times out at bars and protests. Her sexuality was unknown, but Maria found her attractive either way. Objectively, at least. Tonight she forced herself to see the petite blonde as something more than simply aesthetically pleasing. She needed the distraction, the reminder to stay on the track that led out west.

Maria wiggled into the back of the booth, sprawling her arms out along its corner. Kay had spun around, his back toward her and Jane as he chatted with Michel, who sat just behind him, so she was forced to focus on the one person on whom she wanted to avoid placing any extra attention.

Jane, luckily, was distracted herself, seemingly captivated by the passionate dialogue circulating throughout the group.

"Did you see Marsha up on that pole?" one man hollered, turning from the jukebox. He grinned so wide Maria thought she might go blind. He placed his hands on his narrow hips and shook his head. "When she dropped that big ass bag onto the hood of the cop car? Smashed that motherfucker to pieces!"

Marsha P. Johnson, the queen of them all. Maria had seen her many times and swore she and Kay could be related. Their magnetism, their charm, their honesty. They were in a class of their own, Maria was sure of it. And she wondered if that was precisely why the world feared them. Why it haunted and hunted them. Envy could be a sinister thing.

The diner swelled with pride, the rambunctious hooting and hollering punctuated with anger and determination. An older man, Gerald, a well-known elder within the gay community, sat at the counter alone, his face hardening as the lively conversation went on. It was easy to see he didn't share the group's celebratory energy. During a lull in the ruckus, he used the break to express just that.

"Excuse me?" he asked, swiveling in his chair. "How much damage do you think you caused? You ever think about how much that will cost the city and piss them off even more?"

Maria wasn't surprised. The Geralds of the community, those lucky enough to have reliable income and stable housing could never relate to the younger gay people, to the queens on the street, to the vagabonds who used casual lovers as ways to have a place to sleep at night. Rioting certainly wasn't something Geralds felt they needed to consider. The privilege often made Maria sick, even if she was happy for them and wanted what they had.

"Money talks, honey," Kay finally said, speaking for the crowd who apparently agreed, offering nods and mumbles of agreement. "Why do you think boycotts work?"

"What y'all did out there wasn't a boycott," he said. "It's tacky, it's cheap, and it makes us look like animals. We've worked so hard to present ourselves as normal, and—"

"Yeah, and where has that gotten us?" Kay asked, his voice strengthening. Maria watched the crowd tense, including Jane. "We're still shoved into rot-filled basements and into hospitals where they shock us and slice into our brains to try to fix us. For Christ's sake, we can't legally suck dick in our own apartments, Gerald."

The older, traditional man tightened his lips, unable to argue.

"We've got nothing left to lose," the slender man who mentioned Marsha added. He folded his arms and leaned against the booth beside the jukebox.

Gerald shook his head, his eyes dark. "If you fight back, they'll fight back harder," he said. "They'll make it worse."

"How can it get worse?" Kay choked out a laugh. "We're dying, Gerald."

Maria pinched her eyes shut. The number of stories she'd been having to write about her fellow community members being found dead throughout the city had been growing steadily in recent months. Whether at the hands of cops, at the hands of pimps, or the hands of their tortured selves, her people were indeed dying.

"I say if you're gonna go down, you might as well go down swinging," Maria said, giving Kay a nod. "The worst that will happen is you make even a little bit of fucking progress."

"Amen, sister," Kay said.

"And you get to scare the shit out of them every now and then," Michel added, tapping Kay's arm with a smile. "Since we're scared shitless most of the time just walking down the street, I'd say that's a fair exchange."

Gerald shook his head, his eyes slightly lighter. The waitress returned to take food orders, breaking up the tense energy and helping spread focus. After Maria, Kay, and Jane ordered, the volume of the jukebox rose again, bringing with it yet another Garland number that distracted most of the diner. As the waitress, Peggy, according to the nametag she wore on her short-sleeved, pale blue shirt, stopped at their table to drop off napkins and silverware, Maria caught her gaze, holding it only for a moment before shifting away toward the crowd. Peggy cleared her throat as she walked off, her gold ponytail swinging like her hips. Yes, she was attractive. Yes, Maria could return to herself by hiding under the current of those blonde waves. She had to, or else she might lose herself for good.

Maria zoned back into the table and wondered how long Jane had been looking at her, studying her with those open eyes. She felt her pulse jump and decided to reassign its focus. She tapped

Jane's shoulder, forcing herself past the electric shock she sensed purring through her body as she did it. "Gonna hit the ladies' room," she said. "Can I squeeze out?"

"Of course." Jane smiled, never batting a lash.

Maria made her way down the row of booths toward the restrooms in the back of the fluorescent diner, catching Peggy's gaze once again as she passed off a cup of coffee to Gerald. She smiled and Maria offered a grin back, slipping into the bathroom with forced nonchalance. She hovered over the sink, hands gripping the edges of the ceramic bowl. She turned the faucet and splashed water onto her face, drying off with a paper towel that felt as abrasive as whatever was scratching at her chest and throat. The mirror revealed a tight face, stressed and uncertain.

"Get your shit together," Maria said aloud, staring into her own eyes. She took a deep breath and spun out of the bathroom, her swiftness nearly causing her to crash right into Peggy as she made her way down the hallway.

Maria grabbed her chest and gasped. "I'm so sorry."

Peggy placed a hand on her arm and smiled. "No, I'm sorry," she said, removing her touch. "I'm never paying attention to what's in front of me."

"Right," Maria said, clenching her teeth beneath her smile, ignoring the visceral force longing to pull her eyes to Jane. "I'm the same way."

Peggy smiled even brighter, and her cheeks flushed. "I'm Peggy, by the way." She pointed at her nametag. "I think I've seen you around. With a lot of these guys, I think?" She moved her finger toward the boisterous group behind her.

"Yeah, probably," Maria said. "I think I've seen you around, too. I'm Maria."

Peggy nodded. "Sorry for almost running you over, Maria."

The distraction would have been welcome, Maria thought. "No problem," she said. "I won't hold it against you."

"Can I buy you a drink, then?" Peggy asked, surprisingly bold. "I mean, to make amends."

Maria took a breath. This time she surrendered to the magnet drawing her toward Jane, who sat patiently in the booth, smiling at Kay and Michel as they teased each other. The rush of impulsivity and the therapy it offered swept through Maria.

"Yes," she blurted out, dragging her eyes back to Peggy. "What time do you get off?"

"Midnight," Peggy said, her eyes lighting up. "Meet me next door at Frankie's?"

"I can't wait." Maria said with a wink.

As she walked away, she felt a pang of guilt gnaw at her guts. She added it to the list of conflicting emotions swirling inside her and returned to the booth.

....

SIXTEEN

THE UNKNOWN SOLDIER

Jane and her mother had swept and polished every surface of their apartment over the past few days, so there were few tasks left they could use for distraction. Rebecca busied herself with the store, preparing to close the second her son walked through the door. Jane paced her bedroom while making a mental list of all the things she wanted to do with her brother over the next two months before school. After the brainstorming began to actually hurt her brain, she walked downstairs to the living room and sat in one of the chairs by the large windows overlooking the parkway. She looked down at the telephone sitting on the sill, longing to turn to the only thing, the only person she could count on to settle her nerves.

"Hello?" The husky sound of Maria's voice sent a shiver up Jane's spine before she crumbled, realizing she might have woken her.

"Hey, it's Jane. I'm so sorry if you were sleeping, I've just been so worked up all morning waiting for Stephen, and I—"

"Hey, it's okay," Maria cut her off, huffing out a barely audible laugh. Jane smiled at the reassurance, feeling lighter already. "I was awake, just not for very long."

"Oh," Jane said. "Still, I hope I'm not bothering you."

"Of course you aren't."

Jane wanted to believe her, but Maria sounded distracted, and her voice was softer than usual. Perhaps she was just trying not to wake Kay. Or perhaps someone had spent the night with her and it was she Maria was trying not to disturb.

Jane felt her face suddenly slacken.

"So, Stephen is due back this afternoon, right?" Maria said, pulling her back into the present.

"Yes," Jane said, clearing her throat. "We're a nervous wreck."

Maria chuckled again. "Your mother is going to freak out, isn't she?"

"Probably," Jane said with a laugh.

"What about you?"

"I have no idea what I'll do, honestly," Jane said. "Hopefully breathe. I feel like I've been holding my breath since he went over there."

"Well, I hope you can finally let it out," Maria said. "I know what that can feel like, how heavy a secret or a fear can be…" Her voice drifted off like dust in the wind.

Jane's stomach abruptly dropped. Was she talking about her mother?

"I know you do," she finally said, her voice soft as the story of Maria being kicked out at seventeen stamped itself into her mind.

"All I'm saying is," Maria went on, sliding by the somber moment, "you and your mother both deserve to breathe."

"Thank you, Maria."

Another pause stretched between them until Jane broke it with the news. "Oh, I meant to tell you this the other night when I came back into the city, but the chaos of it all kind of made me forget."

"Oh! What?" The life had found its way back to Maria's voice.

"My mother said she would meet Kay to do measurements and see if she's able to make him what he wants."

"Really?"

Jane laughed. "I couldn't believe it either. I think she sees me taking photos and it reminds her a bit of her own creative side."

"That's great," Maria said. "And she knows what it's for?"

"Well." Jane bit her lip.

"Jane?" Maria's voice took on the tone of a mother about to scold a child.

"I didn't necessarily say Kay was a man. Or a woman."

"Mm-hmm."

"I really don't think it will be a problem," Jane said, fumbling through the promise she knew she couldn't truly make. "She seemed genuinely upset when I told her about the riots, about what triggered them. She's not closed-minded."

"Well, I guess I have no reason to doubt that," Maria said with a lighthearted sigh. "I know her daughter, and she seems to be pretty open-hearted and minded. It probably runs in the family."

Jane's cheeks burned, heating the handset she held to her ear. "Thanks, Maria," she said, hoping her voice didn't crack too hard. "And make sure to thank Kay for me, for trusting me and my mother with this."

"I'll tell him," Maria said. "Just let us know when he should come. He'll likely want me to come with him, too."

"Of course. I'll let you know once Stephen gets settled and my mother gets down from her high."

"You guys doing anything tomorrow for the Fourth?" Maria asked.

"We're doing whatever Stephen wants," Jane said. "Maybe Rockaway. Maybe nothing. What about you?"

"I might go with Kay down to the docks for a little thing on the pier," Maria said. "It should be pretty rowdy this year."

Despite the chances of a raid or more violence, Jane wished she could join in the rebellious fun. But she also couldn't wait to spend time with her brother, to see him in the flesh. The image of Stephen's face tugged her back to reality.

"I'm sure you'll have a blast," Jane said.

"If for some reason your celebrations end early, come on down," Maria said.

"Okay," Jane said, smiling yet again.

"And good luck with your brother," Maria said. "I'm sure everything will go great."

"Thank you," Jane said. "Me, too."

Despite the odd breaks in the call, Jane hung up the phone filled with a new sense of optimism. She decided to head down to the store and wait out the rest of the sentence with her mother. She descended their stairwell and opened the door to summer's thick, floating blanket of heat. A cab had pulled up just down the sidewalk, and it took her a moment to recognize the face of the man who slid out of it. His eyes had deepened, and his muscles had grown, almost bulging through his plain white shirt. It wasn't until he fully lifted his head that she truly believed he was home.

"Stephen!"

Jane darted toward her brother as he made his way to the store. He smiled slightly, swinging his bag off his shoulder and placing it on the cement just in time for Jane to jump into his arms, squealing like a child.

"Hey, sis," he said, lowering her to the ground almost instantly with a fake grunt. "I can't do that like I used to now that you're a grown woman."

Jane slapped one of his large arms as she tried to catch her breath. "Are you kidding? You could lift a car!"

Behind her the door of the bookstore swung open. Jane turned around and beamed at her mother, who stood in the entrance with both hands covering her mouth. "My God," she said, shaking her head. She walked closer, Stephen meeting her in the middle.

"Mom," he simply said as she nearly collapsed into his chest. She wrapped her arms around him, sobbing out happy tears that drenched his sleeve. Jane cried her own as she looked on. Eventually she grabbed Stephen's bag for him and slung it over her back.

Rebecca finally pulled away from her son, grabbing him by the shoulders, soaking all of him in. "Are you okay?" she asked barely above a whisper. She moved her hands to his face now, patting Stephen's cheeks. He took them into his own, sliding them off his skin.

"I'm fine, Mom," he said, leaking out a slight grin.

Jane was expecting a bigger affair, a brighter smile, a livelier embrace. But Stephen appeared drained, probably exhausted from the long journey. She also reminded herself that he had just endured a year in hell on earth. It would obviously take time for his energy to replenish itself.

"Well," Rebecca said, wiping her tears, "I am more than fine. I am so happy you're home."

She stood in front of him, eyes still blazing. Jane wondered if she, too, sensed Stephen's internal shrinkage masked behind his new bulkier physique. "Come in, come in," she insisted, ushering her son into the apartment as she popped her head inside the store to lock the door.

Jane followed behind her brother up the stairs. Stephen turned over his shoulder along the way and said, "You know, you didn't have to carry that." He nodded at the bag Jane had strapped onto her back. "I had to carry way more than that over there."

"And now, you don't have to!" Jane said as they reached the landing. They entered the kitchen and Stephen inhaled a massive breath. Letting it out, he looked around and placed his hands on his hips. Jane slid around him and tossed his bag on the floor as their mother entered the room just behind them. She shut the door and gave Stephen's back a light tap.

"How does it feel?" she asked, folding her arms and walking to the fridge.

Stephen nodded a few times. "Clean."

Jane laughed, taking a seat at the kitchen table. "I'd hope so," she said. "We've been scrubbing like crazy for days."

"You didn't need to do that," Stephen said, sinking into the chair beside her. Rebecca came to the table with a glass of iced tea.

"When was the last time you had sun tea?" she asked, crossing her arms.

"Ha!" Stephen chuckled and took a giant gulp. "Since I left," he said, wiping his mouth.

Rebecca rubbed his back again. Jane couldn't blame her mother's relentless affection. She probably needed to keep touching him to convince herself he was here, with them, in the flesh.

"But actually," Stephen said, "I would really love a beer." He turned to face her, his hazel eyes hopeful. "If you have any?"

"Oh." Rebecca's face fell slightly. "I think there are a few in there. You know I'm not a big drinker." She walked back to the fridge, opening it and digging deep. She found an old brew and handed it to Stephen, who cracked it open with a desperate sigh. Rebecca's brows flung to the ceiling. "I guess I can't really be upset about this, can I? You're clearly a man, now." She chuckled and looked at Jane, who offered a shrug and a smile. She certainly had no place to disagree considering she'd had several beers already at eighteen.

"I'm twenty-one now, Mom."

"Oh, I know," Rebecca said, swiping the air with her still trembling hands. "It still feels new to me. We didn't get to celebrate it." She sat down in the chair beside him and across from Jane, placing her elbows on the table and her chin in her palms, admiring her child who had managed to escape the jungle's jaws of death in one piece. Jane wanted to run up to her room and grab the camera so she could capture this moment she had been aching to witness. Her body refused to budge, however, as she took it all in.

"You're really back," she said, her eyes bulging.

Stephen grinned and placed a hand on hers. His skin was rough, but Jane cherished the touch. "I'm really back," he said with a nod.

He then returned to his beer, pounding what remained of it back in only two gulps. "I'm going to take a shower," he said, scooting his chair back. "You have no idea how badly I missed hot water. Or any running water, really."

"Yes, you do that," Rebecca said, standing with him. "What can I get started for dinner? I'll make whatever you want."

"Oh, anything will taste amazing," Stephen said with a light chuckle. "I can't remember the last time I didn't eat something out of a can."

Rebecca let out a moan.

"Don't, Mom," Stephen said, pausing in the doorway to the living room. "Really, it wasn't all that bad."

Rebecca sighed. "Okay," she said. "Wait, why aren't you in your uniform?"

Jane swiveled to face Stephen, shocked that she hadn't noticed the lack of fatigues until now.

"Oh," Stephen said, placing a hand on his stomach. "We took them off before we deplaned."

"Why?" Jane's brows tightened toward each other.

"The commanders told us to," he said nonchalantly. "The uniforms just attract more attention. It's easier this way, incognito."

A silence filled the kitchen as Jane's and Rebecca's faces both fell, the silence broken only by the gentle hum of the refrigerator.

"It's why I just took a cab here instead of having you meet me at the airport," Stephen said, running a hand through his light brown hair, slightly longer than when he left. "We don't need a scene."

He left the kitchen, making his way upstairs to the bathroom. Jane sank into her seat, wondering how Stephen could say all of this without barely batting an eye. She cleared her throat and looked at her mother, her green eyes somber, murky like a marsh. She shook her head and set to work on dinner. "They just got back from war, for Christ's sake," she said, her voice harder than usual as she opened the fridge. "They should be able to come home in uniform."

Jane knew of the hostility so many people aimed at the soldiers returning home. She had heard the names they called them, "baby killers" probably the worst of all. But like the protesters in Washington Square reiterated, it was possible to condemn the war while supporting those drafted to fight it. How could they possibly be spit at for what they were forced to do?

Like Kay and Maria, like Michel and Marsha, Stephen and his fellow soldiers were shunned and shoved, no matter what they did or how. The realization clawed at Jane's throat. She chased it away with a few sips of the tea Stephen barely touched before helping her mother with dinner.

SEVENTEEN

IN THE MIDNIGHT HOUR

Jane awoke in the middle of the night to use the bathroom, stepping quietly into the hall and creeping her way past Stephen's and her mother's rooms. When she finished, she heard a faint cough coming from downstairs. She turned to the bedroom doors and realized Stephen's was ajar. She slithered down the stairs and found him sitting in the chair by the window, a half-empty glass in one hand, a cigarette in the other, hard eyes locked on the evening sky.

"Can't sleep?" Jane asked, standing in the doorway at the bottom of the stairs. Her eyes ached from the glow of the lamp beside Stephen.

He looked over at her, his face appearing even more chiseled as the moonlight spilling in through the window cast deep shadows under his eyes and cheekbones. He shrugged. "I'm still on jungle time."

Jane sat in the chair beside him, tucking her legs up and off to her side. "When did you start smoking?"

"Since the men in my platoon carried cigarettes and handed them out like candy," he said. "I'm also an M&M addict now."

Jane leaked out a quiet laugh, not wanting to wake her mother. "If I would've known I could've had a whole box here waiting for you."

Stephen took a hit and blew out a puff of smoke, a sight so foreign to Jane she couldn't help but stare. He noticed her attention and smirked. "It bothers you," he said.

Jane shook her head. "No," she said. "I know people who smoke, Stephen. I'm not that naive." She tossed him her own smirk. "I guess it's just weird seeing you do it."

"I don't blame you," he said, killing the cigarette into a can perched on the windowsill, the moonbeams reflecting off the aluminum. "It's weird sometimes to think I'm a smoker now."

"Lots of things are weird now," Jane said.

"Like what?"

Jane sighed, not entirely sure of what she even meant. Then the scent of the charred cigarette drifted into her nose, bringing the image of Maria's face into her mind.

"Well," Jane said, deciding to go with the safe answer, "for one, I finally started taking photos with your camera."

"Yeah?"

Jane nodded. "I really enjoy it. I'm just mad it took me so long to start."

"Do you have any I could see?" Stephen's eyes glistened with the first hint of lightness since he stepped out of the cab that morning.

"Right now?"

"I'm not doing anything else," Stephen said. "I don't want to keep you up, though."

"Oh, please." Jane unwound her legs to stand. "I actually haven't been sleeping all that well lately, so no worries."

She ascended the stairs as quietly as she could, retrieving her folder from her room. Back in the living room, she handed it over to Stephen. "You've got a portfolio and everything!" he said with a smile. "Hot shot."

Jane slapped his arm and sat back down in her chair. She watched him flip through the images, her heart pumping in her throat as she waited for his reaction. Stephen's ambiguous face made her teeth dig even harder into her lip. He said nothing for a few moments, seemingly taking his time to peruse the work. Eventually, he shook his head and let out a light whistle. "These are good, Jane," he said, continuing toward the back of the folder.

Jane allowed her muscles to melt and freed her bottom lip from her teeth's grip. "You think?"

"I know," he said, looking up briefly.

She felt her cheeks twitch at the compliment, then they burned when she realized which images Stephen's eyes fell on now. She took a breath and sat up a hair straighter. "I wasn't really there to protest," she spit out. "Claire insisted we go, and I thought it would be a good opportunity to try out the camera—"

"Jane," Stephen cut her off, his gaze searing into her with great purpose, "even if you were, it's okay, you know. I don't think I met a single guy over there who wants to be there. Not anymore." He shifted his focus back to the photos.

Jane's heart slowed, and her hands unclenched themselves from the fists she didn't realize she'd been making. Stephen suddenly smiled, and Jane craned her neck to see why. "Well, she's cute," he said.

Once again, Jane's cheeks flushed. "That's Maria," she said. "She's the one who told me about the rally."

"She's a friend of yours?"

Jane could only nod. Stephen accepted it with yet another smirk. "You should invite her over sometime."

A single bark of a laugh flew out of Jane's mouth, which she covered instantly with her hand. She glanced over her shoulder and up the stairs, paranoid she had woken her mother.

"What?" Stephen's innocent face melted Jane's heart.

"No offense, but you're not really her type."

"How dare you?" Stephen joked. "I'm everyone's type."

Jane chuckled and relaxed into the wingback chair. "You're handsome and charming, and now you have those gigantic muscles. I get it. But that still won't work for Maria."

"Why not?"

"Because she's a lesbian."

Jane blurted it out without thinking. She was pretty certain it was the first time she ever said the word aloud. The feel of it slipping off her tongue sent a rush through her veins.

Stephen's eyes swelled like blood in water. "She's a what?" He looked back down at the photo of Maria, his eyebrows scrunched tight. "No way."

Jane couldn't help but laugh again. "Yes, way," she said. "Why do you sound so surprised?"

Stephen shook his head and moved on to the next image. "She doesn't look like a lesbian."

"What does a lesbian look like?" Jane pressed, teasingly folding her arms.

"Oh, I don't know," he said. "I guess I don't know what any lesbian looks like, really."

"Well, not every gay person looks the same," Jane said.

"Clearly," Stephen mumbled. "Where did you meet her?"

"At a party."

"A party?" Stephen lifted his head again. "Things really are weird, aren't they?"

Jane tightened her grip around her elbows like a stubborn child. "I'm cool now," she said with an uppity grin.

"Yeah, yeah," Stephen said. "Well, whatever you are, you're a good photographer, too. Who developed these?"

"I did," Jane said. "Maria works at *The Torch* and they have a darkroom, so I've used it a few times. They also printed a couple of my photos in the paper." She smiled as she remembered how much she loved seeing her name in the paper alongside her images, especially the grainy, chaotic ones of the riot.

"Wow." Stephen sat back, crossing one foot onto his knee. "A real Ansel Adams."

"Ha!" Jane laughed and threw her head back. "Not quite."

"Well, one day, maybe."

Jane nodded. "Right now I just enjoy shooting when I can."

"What are these ones?" Stephen asked. "Jesus, Jane. What kind of riot was this?"

"Oh," Jane said. "Yeah. Wow. Well, I was in the darkroom, and there was a raid at a gay bar down the street. Maria and I went outside, and it was just…chaos. The people just decided they had enough of the police and enough of the mob running their bars, and they fought back."

Stephen released a light chuckle. "I could see that," he said. "Were you safe? You really shouldn't have been out there."

"I was fine," Jane said, the excitement of that evening flooding her body again, causing her chest to pound. "I was more than fine, actually."

Stephen downed the last of his dark drink. "Well, I suppose you had Maria there to protect you," he said with a wink.

Jane rolled her eyes and rose from the chair. "On that note," she said, her slight humiliation making Stephen laugh, "I'm going back to bed." She paused in the doorway with one hand on the wall and looked over her shoulder. "I'm really happy you're home."

Stephen smiled, swirling his glass holding only the ghosts of ice now. "Me, too."

Jane took a breath, hesitating to leave her brother in his isolation. "You want to talk about anything?" she asked, the question drawing his eyes to hers. "I mean, what you went through over there…If you ever want to talk about it, I'll listen."

A blank filter swept across Stephen's face. After a few silent moments, he scrunched his lips and shook his head. "I'm fine, sis. I'm fine."

She didn't buy it—not completely anyway—but Jane shrugged it off knowing she had no room to judge. After all, Stephen wasn't the only one keeping things to himself.

....

EIGHTEEN

GIMME SHELTER

Jane had no idea what time Stephen eventually went to bed, and she didn't tell her mother about their impromptu midnight meeting. She didn't want her to know he couldn't sleep. Even if it was indeed just jet lag as her brother insisted, Jane wanted to preserve as perfect of an image for Rebecca as possible, the image of a peaceful return, of long-craved normalcy.

Stephen finally entered the light of day around noon, entering the living room where Jane and her mother had waited patiently for him. They sat in the same place where she and her brother lounged secretly just hours earlier.

Rebecca rose from her chair. "How did you sleep?"

The optimism in her voice made Jane's eye twitch. She didn't need to turn over her shoulder to know the vein on Stephen's forehead was doing the same, that involuntary quirk that revealed his stress.

"Just fine," he said, his voice slightly hoarse. Jane wondered how much more he had to drink after she went to bed. "Better than fine," he corrected, heading toward the kitchen.

"Do you want me to make you something to eat?" Rebecca asked, taking a few steps with him.

"No, I'll get something when I'm out," Stephen said, still moving with purpose. "I'm going to run a few errands."

"Oh." Rebecca halted her stride and brought her hands together at her navel. Jane could hear the disappointment in her hollow voice. "Did you want to do something later to celebrate? It's the Fourth of July, after all. This day should be about you."

Stephen was the one freezing his footsteps now. He swiveled back toward her and shrugged. "I'm still pretty tired," he said. "I wouldn't count on me for any special plans." He turned around, walked into the kitchen, and said over his shoulder, "I'll be back soon."

With the sound of the apartment door closing, Rebecca whipped her head back to Jane with wide eyes that did everything they could to hide the confused hurt swimming inside them.

Jane sighed and offered her best smile. "I think he just wants things to feel normal," she said. "Making a big fuss might not help with that, that's all."

Rebecca bit her bottom lip and looked away, nodding warily. "Right," she said, her voice fragile as glass. "That makes sense."

Jane watched with an ache in her chest as her mother smoothed out her pale blue dress even though there wasn't a single crease.

....

The sun had turned to red by the time Stephen came stumbling up the apartment stairs. Rebecca shot up from the couch while Jane sat frozen in her chair. She listened with scrunched brows as her brother struggled with the door handle.

When he finally made it through the kitchen, she stood and watched him wander in, adrift, his eyes glazed and glistening like the sweat spilling over his face.

Drunk.

"Hey," Stephen said. He swallowed and cleared his throat.

Rebecca took a step toward her inebriated son. "You've been gone quite a while," she said gently, cautious. "Where all did you go?"

Stephen shrugged. "Nowhere," he said. "Everywhere. It don't mean nothin'."

Jane swore every bit of air had been sucked out of the room. She watched her mother's face twist into pained confusion. "How drunk are you?" Rebecca asked, her voice far calmer than Jane thought it should be.

The drawn-out whistle of a holiday firecracker suddenly blew through the sky somewhere in the neighborhood before exploding.

"Get down!"

Jane's heart leapt toward her throat as Stephen hurled himself to the floor and rolled under the dining table. Rebecca's hand flung to her chest. Her eyes were frantic. "Stephen!"

Jane marched forward and placed a hand on her mother's arm. She froze at the sight of her older brother, all man and muscle, covering his head with his hands. Another firecracker went off, and he waved his arms. "What are you doing?" he shouted. "The fuckers are hitting us!"

Without thinking Jane rushed to him, crouching beside him and rubbing his back. "Hey, Stephen, it's okay. It's just fireworks," she said as casually as she could. "For the Fourth of July."

Stephen looked up at her with uncertainty, his brows taut, eyes still panicked. "July?"

Jane nodded. "Yeah, it's July here, in America. You're home now." She stopped rubbing his back as his breathing calmed. She sat on the floor, cross-legged, and leaned in. "And I am so glad about that."

Stephen nodded furiously. "Right," he said, his face still tight and pale. "Fucking firecrackers."

Jane shrugged. "Firecrackers," she said with a forced smile. She allowed herself to breathe normally again, to let her pulse rest. She turned slightly to check on her mother, who stood helplessly just behind her with her trembling hands resting on both sides of her slackened jaw. Jane tried to offer a reassuring look but wasn't so sure it helped. She turned back to Stephen, who began getting to his feet. Jane stood along with him.

"What do you need right now, honey?" Rebecca had finally found the strength to speak as she stepped toward Stephen. "What can I do?"

"Nothing, I'm fine," he said, his voice and face both stern. "I'm going upstairs."

He walked away before Jane could stop him, flying past their mother who stood seemingly paralyzed. She chewed on the inside of her cheek as she shook her head. "What am I doing wrong?"

Jane's eyes burst open. "Mom," she said, almost gasping. "You're not doing anything wrong."

Rebecca kept shaking and gnawing. She brought a hand to her forehead, as if trying to steady her brain. "I should've been prepared for this."

Jane went to her mother and wrapped her arms around her quivering body. She realized then how thin she had gotten while Stephen was away.

She wondered when he would truly come back.

NINETEEN

SPARKS

Jane didn't want to go, but her mother insisted. Stephen had taken shelter in his bedroom, showing no signs of leaving its comfort anytime soon. Rebecca demanded Jane enjoy the holiday evening. But enjoyment wasn't what Jane craved. She wanted reassurance. She wanted solidity.

She could hear music pumping and people laughing before she even hit the waterfront. She scanned the street for the flashing lights of police cars, for the blare of their sirens, for the screeching feedback of their megaphones, but the air sat hollow save for the exuberant ruckus coming from the pier.

She watched two young men climb the pathetic chain link fence, bouncing over to the party along the Hudson. Jane followed their lead, hoping her lack of grace wasn't terribly obvious, and landed with a light thud on the other side. When she straightened to her feet, brushing off her jean shorts, she searched the crowd spread out in clumps about the pier. Kay's booming yet balmy voice caught her ear, and she found him leaning against a stack of crates, cigarette in hand, surrounded by a small group of men all equally eye-catching. She approached warily, anxious to find Maria and talk to her about the disaster of a day.

"Look what we have here!" Kay yelled as Jane offered a weak wave. The men encircling him all turned, their eyes beaming wide.

"My goodness!" one yelped, bringing a hand to his chiseled chest. "You're stunning."

"Like Rita Hayworth," said another.

Jane laughed, the clenching of her stomach muscles easing the pain of Stephen's breakdown just a little. "I wish."

They fawned over her, running their hands through her locks and complimenting her pale skin. Perhaps she would normally shrink inside herself, blush from the flattery, swat their hands away. All she could do tonight, though, was continue perusing the pier for black bangs and a cutoff shirt. She needed comfort, and she didn't care anymore why Maria gave her that. Not right now. Not when she needed to get the sound of Stephen screaming out of her head.

She finally spotted Maria leaning against the pier's railing on the farthest end, a bottle in one hand, the other moving wildly as she chatted with a blonde woman standing in front of her. Jane's stomach leapt, and she chased the feeling by excusing herself from her admirers and heading toward the duo. As she got closer, she noticed the woman talking to Maria was the waitress from the diner they visited on that second night of the riots.

Maria looked up when Jane was merely a few steps away. She straightened her spine and cleared her throat. "Hi," she said, a hint of hesitation in her voice. "I really wasn't expecting you to show up."

"I wasn't either," Jane said. She was going to say more, but the waitress, now out of her uniform and in a short red dress, flung herself into view.

"Hi!" She extended a hand and flashed a broad smile. "I'm Peggy," she said.

Jane felt bombarded by her presence, by her prom queen beauty. She swallowed and shook the girl's hand. "Jane," she said, keeping it simple. She took a breath and focused on Maria, who she just now realized was quite drunk. Her eyes shone with the sparkle of intoxication, and her breath smelled like beer even from a distance.

"So, why aren't you celebrating with your brother?" Maria asked, the words slurring and sliding over each other.

Jane took a breath, wondering if she could divulge her brother's episode in front of Peggy. She shook her head and released her lungs. "He's still really tired," she said. "Jet lag and all. He just wanted to stay home." She felt her heart convulsing at the lie.

Maria nodded, though her eyes looked anything but attentive. "Well, you're here now! Grab a beer." She waved toward a blue cooler on the ground near Kay and his cohorts.

"It's surprisingly not that bad," Peggy said, lifting her bottle in the air with a wink.

Jane forced out a quick smile before focusing back on Maria, who turned away in an uncharacteristic display of something Jane couldn't quite name. She nodded and made her way to the cooler.

Normally Jane wasn't one to feel compelled to drink, but an awkward air engulfing the pier blended with the stress of Stephen's outburst, and suddenly all she wanted was to drown it all out with the Ballantine she snatched from the ice. When she turned around to head back, the desire became need. Her liver and her heart screamed out for the golden liquid as she watched Peggy eliminate the little space between her and Maria and plant her lips on hers.

Jane stood frozen yet burning, her beer lingering near her mouth that quivered at the kiss. She lowered the bottle, her hand shaking, as Maria placed a hand on Peggy's waist. The touch made

Jane turn away, seeking refuge in the sight of Kay and his friends dancing. She hoped the change of scenery would quell the fire swelling inside her belly, but the nauseating heat only grew. She chased the blaze away by pounding her beer and tossing it in the trash can as she walked toward the fence.

There was no thought, no warning, no contemplating. She simply leapt over the barrier, scratching her knee on the way, and headed toward the subway as the bright sound of sparklers and laughter exploded behind her.

....

Jane barely remembered the train ride home when she made it to the apartment door, her hands trembling and fumbling with the lock. Her brain felt as if it had been razed, along with every other part of her body, and holding still to reality, or to the keys she struggled with, had become impossible.

Before she could open the door, her mother did it for her from the other side. Jane jumped and grabbed her chest. "Mom!" she nearly shouted.

"Shhh." Rebecca ushered her inside and closed the door. "I think he's asleep."

"How was he?" Jane asked in a whisper as she and her mother crept through the living room and up the stairs.

"I heard him snoring a few minutes ago," she said when they reached the landing. "Otherwise, he was quiet. Never left his room." She crossed her arms as if trying to warm herself.

"It's good he's resting, at least," Jane said, exhausted in her own way. "He clearly needs it."

"Yes," Rebecca said with a sigh. She shook her head, as if trying to shake out the image of her crumbling son, and cocked her head. "Why are you home so early? You were barely gone."

Jane swallowed as the sinking feeling in her stomach returned. "I was just too worried about Stephen," she said, taking comfort in the fact that it wasn't a complete falsification.

"Oh, I'm so sorry, honey," Rebecca said, her eyes darkening. "I don't want any of this to cause you any stress."

"It's okay," Jane said, heading toward her bedroom. "I just wanted to be here and in bed, that's all."

She faked a smile, which her mother seemed to buy, and closed her door. She collapsed onto her bed, still fully clothed, where she lay awake for several stifling, confusing hours before finally joining her brother in sleep.

....

TWENTY

DO I HAVE TO COME RIGHT OUT
AND SAY IT?

Maria's hand froze on the telephone, gripping it but unable to remove the handset from the wall. She took a breath and closed her eyes, a pang of guilt clutching her guts.

Last night, when the celebrations dissipated and the pier emptied, she denied Peggy when she asked to come to Maria's place for the night again. That one evening they shared was supposed to be a one-time thing, a distraction from the relentless gnawing at Maria's heart that began and ended with Jane.

Jane…

Maria searched the pier for her after Peggy's unexpected public kiss, one that left her feeling empty and in need of light to shine upon the hollow pit inside her. But her ray was nowhere to be found. She had slipped away within seconds, making Maria wonder if Jane witnessed the display and felt awkward or…something else.

Pondering on that possible something else kept Maria awake that night, and this morning she shuffled her way to the phone, weary-eyed and nauseous. She wasn't entirely sure what she was going to say, but it wasn't her talking that mattered. All she knew for certain was that she wanted to hear Jane's voice.

When she got it, Maria's heart fluttered and fell at the same time. "Hey, it's me," she said, her forehead scrunched.

"Oh," Jane said with an air of sullen surprise. "Hi. I'm surprised you're awake already."

"Yeah." Maria sighed. "Well, I didn't really sleep much. Figured I'd might as well get up."

"Right."

Jane's blunt, lifeless response stuck to Maria's bones like sap. They felt heavy suddenly, packed down with lead. She sighed again and sank into the kitchen chair. "Is it busy at the store?"

"We just opened, so not yet," Jane said, her tone slightly more vibrant. "Maybe later."

"Hmm." Maria clenched her eyes shut, anxious over their unusual lack of easy conversation. She bit her lip, admitting to herself she knew exactly why that distance stretched out between them. She cleared her throat and shifted in her seat. "You disappeared last night," she said after what felt like minutes of silence. "I looked for you, thinking maybe you were with Kay, but he said you left."

"Yeah, I'm sorry about that," Jane said. Maria grew even more frustrated when she couldn't tell if the apology was genuine. Jane, who usually evoked every thought and feeling through her gestures or her vocal tones or the varying shades of pink that flushed her skin, was now a blank canvas of beige. "I just…" Jane stumbled. "We had a bad day here with Stephen yesterday, and I was feeling a lot of things…" Her voice drifted off, and Maria wanted to reach through the phone to find it. Instead, she closed her eyes and sighed.

"Jane, I'm such an asshole," she said. "I was drunk and thoughtless and didn't even ask how he was when you got there—"

"It's okay," Jane interrupted, her voice crisp now.

"No, it's not," Maria said, her face burning up.

"Maria, you were…having fun and trying to celebrate. You shouldn't have to defend that."

"Well, I want to," Maria insisted, her own voice hard, committed to being heard. "I was a bad friend. I want to hear about your brother, if you want to talk about it, of course."

A short silence was followed by Jane's light sigh. "Thank you," she said, her tone pleasant again but tired. "I'd like that. Not now, though. I really shouldn't linger on the phone in case someone comes in."

"Ugh, of course," Maria said with a grunt. "I'm sorry. Again." She let out an aching laugh and her muscles loosened when she heard a light, airy one from Jane. She smiled and asked, "Can we meet up soon, then? Coffee? A photo tour? Dancing?" She smirked at the last one, hoping Jane would hear the teasing tone.

"You choose," Jane said with a chuckle. "I'm too tired to think."

"Great," Maria said. "I love taking charge."

"I know you do," Jane said with another laugh. If Maria had any hangover left from the holiday festivities it was completely cured now from the bright sound, from the underlying innuendo they danced around that sent a rush from her belly to her bust.

After a few silent moments, Maria cleared her throat. "Meet me at my place. Tomorrow evening. Seven?"

"That works. The shop closes at five."

"I know," Maria said proudly. "I memorized the hours on your door."

"Resourceful," Jane said.

"See you then, Red."

....

Maria smiled when she saw the camera strapped around Jane's neck as she stood waiting on the doorstep. She hadn't told her to bring it, but she was hoping she would. She wanted to see her in action again.

"You ready?" Maria asked as she closed and locked the door.

"Sure," Jane said. "Even though I don't know what for."

Maria winked and spun around to reveal her stuffed leather backpack. "We're just going somewhere we can talk."

She led Jane to the subway, remaining tight-lipped and teasing for the short ride, and had them get off at 59 Street where Columbus Circle greeted them when they emerged from New York's metal and rubber belly. "This looks familiar," Jane said with a grin as they entered the park.

"Does it?" Maria scrunched her brows and turned to Jane with her devilish smile. Jane merely shook her head and followed her commander in silence all the way to Sheep Meadow where Maria swung her bag off and pulled a blanket out of it. She laid it out on the grass in almost the exact same spot where the duo sat during their last rendezvous in the field. She then whipped out a bottle of wine from the bag along with two cups. "Thirsty?"

They settled onto the plaid throw as Maria poured their reds. "To being a better friend," she said, lifting her glass.

Jane chuckled through a moan. "It's really okay, Maria," she said. "But thank you."

Maria smacked her lips together, savoring the wine. "Okay, so tell me," she said. "What's going on? How is Stephen?"

Jane sighed and lowered her eyes to her Merlot. "Not great," she said. "I thought he was okay. I mean, he was quiet when he got home, which I just assumed was because of the long plane ride." She sighed again and shook her head. "He left the apartment Friday afternoon and came back hours later completely drunk. Then firecrackers went off somewhere in the neighborhood, and he…lost it."

Maria winced, familiar with the stories of veterans coming home with shell shock, with crippling fears of loud noises and the depths of darkness. "Damn it," she said.

Jane took a deep breath, closing her eyes as she let it out. "He threw his body on the ground, yelling for us to get down. He eventually got up and locked himself in his room." She looked at Maria with glistening eyes. "He's like a completely different person, like a child my mother and I have to babysit, which is crazy because while he was over there, he had to be so strong. He had to do things most men never have to do, even though he was really just a boy. Of course, I don't know what all he actually did and saw. He won't tell me."

"He's just probably not ready," Maria said, placing a hand on Jane's knee. "It's only been a few days. Just being home is probably a shock to his system."

Jane closed her eyes again, a lone tear escaping from her thick lashes and rolling down her cheek. Maria removed her hand from her knee, wanting to catch the droplet. Instead, she returned her hand to her own lap. She noticed Jane flinch slightly at the sudden lack of touch.

"You're right," Jane said, taking a generous sip of her wine. "I'm just scared I'm not going to get my brother back."

"He can get help," Maria said, her voice soft. "They have services. Counseling, medication, group therapy. Though, he likely just needs to ride this out for a while before he will even consider it. Most guys do."

Jane collapsed her shoulders. "I don't want him to wait until he hits rock bottom. I'm worried it will be too late." She breathed out a resigning laugh. "Then again, it was probably too late the second he stepped foot over there."

"American exceptionalism," Maria scoffed. "We certainly are exceptional at ruining an entire generation of men."

Jane remained silent, then brought the wine to her lips. After a lengthy sip, she blew out a massive breath. "I appreciate you listening, but let's talk about something else, if you don't mind."

"Of course," Maria said, straightening her spine. "And again, I'm sorry for not being…present the other night when you really needed an ear."

"You were having a good time," Jane said, looking away. A few seconds of silence ended when she turned back, her jade eyes solemn yet still vivid as ever. "Peggy's cute."

Maria sucked in her breath. Without the calming rhythm of her lungs, all she could hear now was the beating of her own heart, its valves opening and closing, pumping itself into a frenzy. She eventually managed to shrug. "She's fine," she said, "but I don't think I'll be seeing her again."

"Oh. Why not?"

"She was just…a distraction," Maria said, taking her turn at peering off into the meadow.

"From what?"

Maria bit her lip, hoping to bleed out even some of the tension seizing her body. Telling the truth, at least in its entirety, would do nothing. If she confessed to Jane the feelings that kept her up at night, the ones she had never experienced before, the ones that made her feel insane yet alive at the same time, she would be risking the friendship the two had built over the past month. Because even if what she felt for Jane was reciprocated, it was likely mere curiosity, just like it had been with Theresa. The last thing she wanted was a repeat of that shame and humiliation, that heavy loneliness, that haunting regret. Plus, the phone interview she had yesterday with Half Moon went well. When they finished she was certain they would be calling her back to offer her the job and she would be off to California at the end of the summer. Letting her heart take the reins now would be pointless.

Yet she couldn't help notice the hint of grief she felt at the thought of being prairies and rivers and mountains away from Jane. She wanted her always as she was now, an arm's length away, the late-day sun bronzing her locks of red. She closed her eyes, took a breath, and turned back to Jane.

"From someone else," Maria finally said. She wouldn't go any further, but apparently it was enough.

Jane's porcelain face cracked, slowly like a stress fracture, undetected until it's too late. Her eyes softened through the collapse. "Oh," she said, her amber brows lifting gently, her lips remaining apart for a few moments. They then tightened abruptly as she swallowed.

Maria watched the evolution of Jane's reaction with bated breath until a rogue flying disc whirled over their heads. They ducked as the two players running by them shouted an apology over their shoulders. Maria laughed, grateful for the diversion, grateful for the smile that swept across Jane's face as they readjusted their seats after the near miss. They looked at each other briefly before focusing their attention on their wine. After a deep inhale of the red, Jane cleared her throat.

"Does Kay still need a dress?" she asked, her voice back to its pleasant, innocent tone. "I have a feeling my mother could use the distraction now."

"Well, Kay will certainly bring that." Maria winked, relaxing into the rhythm she and Jane always managed to create together. "Just let us know when she's free."

Jane smiled and nodded, her eyes sparkling as they so often did, and Maria felt her heart reach for the steering wheel once again. She turned away, focusing on the drab steel giants of Manhattan, before it managed to drive her off a cliff.

....

TWENTY-ONE

I KNOW WHAT I WANT TO DO,
BUT I DON'T KNOW WHAT FOR

The sewing room smelled stale from years of confinement. Rebecca opened the sole window in the small room and lit a candle, airing and burning out the dreariness and dust. Jane swept the wood floor, then sat on the windowsill and watched her mother prepare her workstation, lifting the cover from her sewing machine, a beautiful, pale green Singer, and digging out her large box of needles and thread from the closet. She hummed gently as she moved about the room, and Jane couldn't help but think her lightness was caused by the weight of Stephen being lifted off her shoulders as he had gone out, again, to the bar. Though the drinking wasn't appreciated, Rebecca undoubtedly enjoyed the brief reprieve from her duties of watching him like a hawk.

"Did your friend mention what kind of material she wanted?" Rebecca asked, standing at her sewing table with her hands on her hips.

"Um." Jane's lips tightened. "I don't think so," she said, her hands fidgeting with each other. "Also, there's something I didn't tell you about Kay, something I'm sure you'd like to know…"

Her voice drifted off as her mother's eyebrows crawled to the ceiling.

"Okay," she said, drawing it out with an air of curiosity. "What is it?"

Jane swallowed. "Well, Kay isn't a woman. At least, not during the day." She watched as her mother's forehead grew a garden of wrinkles. "He's a drag queen," Jane went on, spitting it out as fast and casually as she could.

At that moment, the apartment doorbell rang out, startling them both and turning their eyes river-wide. Rebecca suddenly shook her head and let out a chuckle, which surprised Jane as she jumped off the sill.

"I'll go get them," she said. Still nervous, she scurried into the hall with her eyes on the floor and bolted down the stairs.

She paused for a moment when she reached the bottom, standing in the entryway with her eyes closed. She took a breath and opened the door to Kay's broad shoulders and smile, Maria standing beside him, her hands buried in her pockets. Jane focused on Kay, suddenly unable to look Maria in the eye. "Come in," she said, ushering the duo inside.

She led them upstairs, through the kitchen and living room up to the third floor. Her mother stood just outside the sewing room, patting down the front of her black pants. She took a breath, standing a bit taller. "Hello," she said, offering her hand. "I'm—"

"Rebecca," Kay said with a light gasp. "You are beautiful!"

Jane couldn't remember ever seeing her mother blush before that moment. She smiled at the foreign pink color seeping through her cheeks.

"Well," Rebecca said, her eyes brightening, "I may need to keep you around all the time." She chuckled and glanced at Maria.

"Nice to see you again," she said. "You've been keeping my daughter very busy."

Maria tilted her chin down. "I hope that's okay," she said, flashing that sly smile.

"It's more than okay," Rebecca said. "We've certainly been needing some…entertainment lately. It's good for us."

"Hopefully I can provide some entertainment for you," Kay said, leaning forward and blessing her with his enchanting smile.

"Oh, I'm sure you will," Rebecca said with a subtle wink.

Jane beamed at her mother's rapport with Kay, someone opposite her in nearly every way. She suddenly felt silly and judgmental for believing he would receive any other welcome.

"Okay," Rebecca said, extending a hand toward the sewing room. "Let's get you measured."

Kay sauntered in just as Jane expected him to—with pride, with pageantry. Her mother shook her head and smiled before turning back to her daughter and Maria. She wagged a finger as she slid into the room. "Leave us to it, now."

She closed the door, leaving Jane and Maria alone in the hallway.

"I love her," Maria said.

Jane turned to her, still trying to process her mother's unwavering acceptance of Kay. "Yes," she said with a gentle nod. "She's pretty great."

Maria smiled and leaned back against the stairwell banister. "So," she said, crossing her arms and peering around the hall, its walls boasting their original baroque-style wallpaper, "this is where you live."

Jane glanced around with her, nodding. Eventually, Maria met her gaze and seized it. "Which one is your room?"

Though her hands immediately turned clammy, Jane didn't hesitate to nod toward her room at the farthest end of the hallway.

Maria looked over her shoulder, then turned back with raised brows. She escorted herself into the peach and white bedroom, Jane following just behind, hoping her footsteps overpowered the sound of her frantic heart.

She watched Maria from the doorway as she began to explore, beginning with the dresser and the picture frames on top. Photographs of Stephen resided in each, and Jane suddenly felt an ache in her chest when she realized he could stumble home any minute. He would meet Maria and Kay, and what kind of scene would that become? She snapped back to the moment when Maria bent down to skim through her box of records, her most intimate possessions.

Maria glanced at Jane over her shoulder. 'May I?"

Jane nodded. "Of course," she said. She finally entered her own bedroom and sat on the bed, more nervous than she could ever remember being in all her eighteen years. Claire was the only person other than her mother and Stephen who had ever been in that room. The intimacy of it made her stomach churn.

Maria pulled a Jefferson Airplane album from the collection and placed the record on the platter. She moved the needle and looked over at Jane. "You have great taste."

"Thanks." Jane couldn't find anything else within her to offer. Her brain was spinning too fast for her lips.

Maria stood and scanned the room again, her eyes landing on the vibrant tapestry hanging on the wall above Jane's bed. "That's beautiful," she said, walking forward a few steps until she stood right at Jane's side. "Where did you get that?"

"Stephen mailed it to me from Thailand," Jane said, hoping her breath didn't sound as shaky as it felt inside her throat. "He was there for R&R."

"Did he like it there?" Maria sat beside Jane now, one leg bent across her knee. Her casual confidence made Jane even more nauseous.

"He did," she said. "He said the food was amazing and the beaches were unreal."

"I bet." Maria's brown eyes widened, then they moved about the room again. "I like this. It's all very *you.*"

Jane laughed. "What does that mean?"

"It's just…" Her voice drifted like her hands that flew through the air in gentle strokes.

"Sweet?" Jane asked with her brows slightly lifted.

Maria looked at her with an even wider, mischievous gaze. She was quiet for a moment, then narrowed her eyes. Jane quivered at her naturally sultry features.

"Yes, exactly," Maria said, smiling. "But it's also very unique and bright. It suits you." She leaned back on her hands, apparently far more comfortable on the bed than Jane, who felt her body tightening as she fought off the throbbing in her chest.

She realized this was how she was supposed to feel when Joey leaned across his center console to kiss her. The thought made her heart pound even harder.

Maria tilted her head. "You okay? You seem distracted." She straightened up and sat cross-legged.

Jane shook her head. "Sorry," she said. "I guess it feels a bit strange seeing you in my room."

"Well, you've already been in mine," Maria reminded her. "Hell, you've slept in my bed!"

Jane managed a chuckle that she prayed pulled focus from her fiery face. "Yes, I suppose you're right."

Maria's lips pursed themselves into a coy grin. "Do you prefer we go downstairs?"

Jane considered it, but it wasn't discomfort that she felt. The heat blowing through her was a welcome one. "No, that's okay," she said, making sure she held Maria's gaze long enough for her to believe it.

Maria was quiet for a moment before she sighed and leaned back again. She closed her eyes. "I love this song," she said. It was "Today," Jefferson Airplane's plush folk ballad. "They're gonna be at Woodstock, that festival upstate," she added. "I'm thinking about going."

Jane had heard of the event on the radio, but she never even thought about making the trip.

"Would you want to go?" Maria asked, her eyes growing bigger.

"Really?"

"Why not?" Maria sat all the way up now. "Everyone's gonna be there—Janis, The Who, Jimi!" She gave Jane's shoulder a slap, her excitement seemingly uncontrollable now.

Jane laughed and shook her head, mostly at her own sudden sense of happy surrender. "Yeah," she said, shrugging. "Why not?"

Maria beamed. "You deserve one last hoorah before you start school," she said. "I mean, I'm just doing this for you."

She winked, and Jane thought she would melt right then.

Perhaps it was Jerry Garcia's intimate guitar weaving out of the record player. Perhaps it was the sparkle in Maria's eye. Perhaps it was the burning she felt building inside her ever since she met her. Perhaps it was the medley of all three that pulled her in toward Maria, that urged her to lean forward, bringing the two closer than they'd ever been. Whatever it was meant nothing the second Jane felt the soft heat of Maria's lips against her own.

Maria seemed to freeze but for only mere seconds until she pressed back. Before Jane could process what was happening, before she could process the sensation of her head filling with gasoline that someone had set on fire, the sound of the kitchen door opening tore her away from the moment, and away from Maria's lips.

Jane sprung back, covering her mouth with her hand. Maria sat red-faced, shell-shocked, silent as stone, as Stephen's footsteps through the kitchen and into the living room rang out beneath them.

"I'm so…" Jane began to speak, shaking her head. She stood up and glanced down at Maria, who met her gaze with her own stunned, glossy one.

"That's Stephen," Jane said, unable to keep her thoughts in order. She took a breath and smoothed out her green dress, a nervous habit she apparently shared with her mother. "Maria, I'm sorry. I didn't mean to—"

Maria waved a hand and offered an awkward smile. "It's okay," she said, sounding as if she ran out of breath.

"No, it's not," Jane whispered, worried Stephen might hear them as he worked his way up the stairs. "I shouldn't…I don't know what I was thinking."

Stephen reached the landing only two doors down from Jane's room. She stretched her neck, searching for his face. He looked up and spotted her, nodding with a lackluster smile. She offered her own false grin. "Stephen," she said, Maria rising from the bed and entering his view. A flash of familiarity swept across his face. "This is Maria." Jane reached a hand out to the friend she had just kissed.

Maria waved with an ease that made Jane's stomach twist. "Hi," she said, her teeth flashing. "I've heard so much about you."

Stephen stood outside the bedroom door, studying Maria. His lips curled more, and Jane knew he recognized her from the photographs. "Maria," he said, nodding.

He gave Jane a sly glance, one that tossed her guts and gave her the desire to punch him in the shoulder. But more than anything, it caused a true smile to form on her lips, ones that were still tingling. Stephen, at least, was enjoying himself, even if it was at her expense. And surprisingly, he didn't seem as drunk as he had been the other day. That's all that mattered to Jane.

"You and your sister have great taste in music," Maria said, slicing the quiet tension. She folded her arms and jutted her chin toward the record player. "You hear Hendrix is gonna be playing at Woodstock?"

"Is he?" Stephen lifted his brows. "That big hippie festival?"

Maria laughed. "Yeah, that one. I'm going, and I convinced your sister to come with me." She nudged Jane's shoulder, which electrified at the touch.

The realization that she would be sharing a tent with Maria for three days, sleeping only inches apart from her, suddenly hit Jane's already spinning brain. She hated how awkward she had made things with Maria, their friendship tainted by her impulsive act. Though she couldn't fully admit the kiss was a completely impromptu moment considering it was something she had thought about since they lingered under the red lights of the darkroom together. She wondered how it would feel, how Maria's lips would taste, how different it might be from her sloppy encounter with Joey. Now she knew, and she would pay the price.

Jane's internal panic spiraled, blocking out Maria and Stephen who chatted about music in the hallway. Before she knew it, all three of them had descended into the living room where Stephen handed Maria records from the shelf behind their small dining table. She watched from the couch as they chatted like old pals, not saying a word, lost in the sight of their casual conversation as she tried to get a grip on her humiliation. It appeared the kiss truly did mean nothing, with Maria moving on from it so easily.

Though that's what Jane thought she wanted, the ache in her stomach convinced her otherwise. It was the same pang that froze her solid as she watched Peggy do to Maria what she just did to her minutes earlier.

She was ripped out of her self-pity by the sound of her mother and Kay walking down the stairs.

Jane peered over her shoulder and watched Kay saunter into the living room, Rebecca just behind him with her measuring tape draped around her neck. Kay plucked his black t-shirt at his chest with his long fingers, his chin high in the air, cheeks plumped from his wide, child-like grin.

"Okay, Miss Valentino," he said, walking toward Maria. "Your highness is all ready to go."

Jane watched her mother bite the insides of her cheeks to keep from laughing. Then she quickly shifted all her focus to Stephen, realizing he was meeting Queen Kay for the first time. He didn't flinch.

Maria placed the records she was holding onto the dining table.

"You can borrow those if you want," Stephen said, turning back to sift through his collection.

Maria's eyes widened. She hesitated briefly before snatching up the records. "Thank you! I'll give them back to Jane as soon as I'm done."

Stephen shrugged. "No rush."

Jane sat stunned on the couch. She was relieved knowing Maria planned to keep her in her life despite what transpired between them, yet Jane would now have to face that humiliation every time she saw her. The realization gnawed at her stomach. She wanted to retch, but instead, she merely smiled.

She wondered how long she could keep up the act, how long until the mask would fall. Until then, she would cling to the cover like moss on peat.

145

TWENTY-TWO

WHEN YOU FIND OUT WHO YOU ARE

Jane lay on her bed reading, trying to enter a fantasy world, a different place and time in which she hadn't kissed Maria the day prior. In which she hadn't made a fool of herself. But trying proved fruitless; the memory was far too potent.

The phone rang in the kitchen below her, and Jane jumped as if it rattled inside her chest. Her mother answered it right away, then called out for Jane. It was exactly what she feared.

She crawled down the stairs, trying to find her breath along the way. She wasn't even close to being ready to talk to Maria. Luckily, she didn't have to. Jane was greeted instead by a familiar-sounding cheer.

"Oh, thank God! I thought you'd been kidnapped."

"Sorry, Claire," Jane said. "I know I've been a bit distracted."

"Well, let's fix that," Claire said. "I'm calling to invite you to Doug's to watch the moon landing. They're setting up a projector on the roof. You've gotta come."

Jane was so desperate for a distraction she didn't even think twice. Yes, she said. She would go and watch man do the impossible. She would watch people be brave and adventurous. She would watch them do what she wished she could.

After hanging up, Jane went back upstairs and heard her mother humming from the sewing room. She walked down the hallway and peered inside, finding Rebecca threading a needle at her table where a heap of shiny lavender fabric draped over it.

"Hey," Jane said, giving the doorframe a light tap. "You're not wasting any time, are you?"

Her mother looked up and smiled. "Well, we've only got just over a month," she said. "Gotta start now."

Jane couldn't help but smile, too. She walked into the room, leaning on the windowsill again. "Thank you for doing this," she said. "You certainly didn't have to."

"I wanted to," Rebecca said.

Jane didn't want to push, but she wanted to dissect what lay at the root of her mother's unquestioning acceptance of Kay. She marveled at it, and it made her sick knowing so many people weren't nearly as lucky as she was to have a parent like that. Then again, Kay wasn't her child. What would she think if she knew the things Jane felt about Maria? If she knew what she had done not even twenty-four hours earlier just down the hall? If she knew her daughter was certain she was falling for someone in a way she couldn't even understand?

Rebecca's voice snatched Jane from her anxious musing. "He reminds me of your late uncle," she said.

"Simon?"

Rebecca nodded, her face soft. "Always a character. Always charming, sometimes devilishly so." She placed the fabric on her lap. "When we would be home alone as kids, we would raid our parents' closet and try on their clothes to feel like grown-ups," she said. "After a while, I realized Simon only ever tried on your grandmother's clothes. He would slip into her heels and barely be able to move in them, but he'd look at himself in the mirror and it was clear on his face that it wasn't the walking that mattered, it was the wearing."

Jane hadn't known her uncle all that well before he died, so imagining him as a child was difficult. Imagining him as a child and dressed in the clothes of her grandmother she never met was even more challenging, but the vague picture itself, and the thought of her mother letting her brother be who he was, made her smile.

"I knew he was different," Rebecca said. "I knew he was special. But I don't think I realized how much it all meant to him until the night our parents came home from a party one night earlier than we expected." Her voice turned softer and brittle, and her eyes darkened. "I'd never seen that look in our father's eyes. He was usually such a vapid man. He showed nothing. I thought it was because he felt nothing, but he made it clear then exactly how he felt."

She shook her head and sighed. "He shouted things at Simon that I was certain he would come to regret later, but I don't think he ever did. Later that night, I heard Simon crying in his room. I put my head against his door and called for him, but he wouldn't answer. He wouldn't let me in…"

Jane felt nauseous, and the sun drenching her back didn't help. She stood and sat next to her mother on a stool, getting a closer look at her eyes as they glistened. "You never told me," she said.

Rebecca nodded, squeezing her eyes shut, her temples tightening. "I think I just pushed it all away because Simon never spoke of it," she said. "We never played dress-up again, and I never saw him smile the way he did in Mom's heels again. He never got married. He kept to himself after he moved out and went to college. I would ask him about dating, if he was seeing anyone, but he always told me his work at the ad agency was more important."

As her mother wiped away a tear dangling from her lashes, Jane fought back the burning behind her own eyes. Rebecca cleared her throat and returned to her needle and thread. "Kay has a chance to experience joy in who he is, even if just for a night," she said. "I think Simon would have loved knowing that was possible."

As awful as the suffering sounded for the Simons and Kays and Marias of the world, Jane felt a wave of jealousy swell within her. To experience joy in who one was, one must know who they are. Jane became less familiar to herself with every passing second since the summer began hot and quick. She wondered what it would feel like to be able to spot oneself in a lineup.

"Do you think Simon knew?" Jane asked. "Knew who he was, I mean."

Rebecca pivoted in her chair and tilted her head. "I think he knew, but perhaps didn't know how to communicate it. Maybe he didn't have the language. It was a different time then. There were no Stonewalls."

Jane cursed herself internally. Language wasn't her problem. Words and writing were her great loves. No, what she lacked was not a dictionary, yet she couldn't find the missing piece to the puzzle that revealed Maria's face. Perhaps there was none. Did everything have to be broken down?

She stood and paced a few steps before turning abruptly in her heels. "Would I be able to go to Woodstock?"

Rebecca looked up for only a moment before returning to her work. "Who would you go with?"

"Maria."

"That's it?" Rebecca removed her glasses, her habit of concern. "I don't know how I feel about two young women camping alone around thousands of strangers. That doesn't exactly sound safe."

Jane chuckled. "They're hippies, Mom. They wear flowers in their hair and play music. I don't think it's possible to be drum-circled to death."

Rebecca laughed, too, and rubbed her eyebrows. "How do you plan on getting there?"

Jane went to speak but realized she didn't have an answer. She bit her lip and couldn't help but laugh when her mother threw her hands in the air. "Please don't tell me you plan on hitch-hiking."

"No!" Jane said. "I don't know…"

"I can drive." Stephen suddenly appeared in the doorway eating an apple, the first solid food Jane had seen him eat in days. "I'll go with them."

Jane glanced at her mother, her forehead tight with anticipation. Rebecca wasn't as convinced. "Are you sure that's a good idea?" she asked, a large piece of fabric dangling from her hands. "There are going to be so many people, and lots of loud noises. Will you…be okay?"

Jane hadn't thought of that. Sleeping outside was probably something Stephen never wanted to do again after doing it for twelve months in the dense, damp jungle. And the massive crowds could certainly trigger an episode for him. His face didn't reveal any of these concerns as he stood chewing the last bits of his apple. "I can't miss Jimi," he said with a shrug and a grin. "I would never forgive myself."

Rebecca relaxed her shoulders, sighing out her surrender. "Okay," she said, nodding toward Jane. "That's my compromise. Your brother goes with you."

Jane beamed yet thought she might be sick at the same time, that unnerving, polaric sensation that had plagued her for weeks. She turned to Stephen and smiled as he offered a solitary nod and walked away.

She was happy she would have him at the festival as a buffer, something to sand the edges of Maria, to keep her from piercing through Jane any more than she already had.

....

TWENTY-THREE

FLYING

Maria bit her nails at the kitchen table, the phone cord dangling beside her ear, her eyes glazed over and glued numbly on the window. She'd hung up the phone quick and with shaky hands, her throat bone dry.

"We want you," the Half Moon founder said. "Can you get here right after Labor Day?"

She'd longed to take a train across the country for so long, to cut through the Blue Ridge Mountains and trace the prairies and stare into the pink deserts and inhale the scent of the west coast that she could then call home. This was what she wanted. This was her dream.

Yet Maria's dreams lately entailed only visions of Jane, her open mind and her bleeding heart. Her fragrant youth, her unpretentious wisdom. The idea of leaving New York suddenly made her nauseous, a feeling that made her head spin.

Then she remembered the kiss.

As she sat in the kitchen, elbows on the table, fingers covering her mouth, Maria recalled the moment on Jane's bed. It had only been a few seconds, hardly long enough for Maria to react. By the time she realized what was happening, it was too late. Her hesitant acceptance had taken too long, her chance ripped right from her hands when Jane backed away, ashamed.

She felt as if she had been kicked out of her house all over again.

Foolish, that's what she was. There was no reason for Maria to allow something as simple as a kiss to dampen the opportunity to expand and explore her career. Yet she knew there was never reason in anything as fluid and mind-numbing as matters of the wild heart.

With no reason in sight, Maria picked up the phone. She dialed and swallowed her guts edging their heavy way up her throat. Jane's voice, as always, sent her flying.

"Martin Books, how can I help you?"

"Hey, it's me."

"Hi," Jane said. "You."

Maria melted. "Do you have plans to watch the moon landing?" She let her stomach flutter as she asked, despite the pang of denial biting at her with fangs of steel. "Patrick told me about something on the roof of his building, if that seems enticing to you?"

"Actually," Jane said, laughing nervously, "Claire told me about that since her boyfriend lives right below him."

"Oh, that's right," Maria said. She pretended she hadn't remembered this and merely wanted an excuse to know for certain she would see Jane. She wanted to soak as much of her in before the flight she knew she needed to take, regardless of its now tainted ignition.

"Yeah," Jane said, "I was actually planning on asking if you were going."

"I am." Maria didn't hesitate. "I'll see you there. Oh, and do you think I could give you Stephen's records in exchange for a few more? I had my eye on that Coltrane album of his."

"Oh, that's actually mine," Jane said.

Maria smiled and leaned against the wall. "Of course it is."

Jane laughed. Maria wished she could see her then, her face undoubtedly flushing with abandon.

"Well, I'm glad you like it," Jane said. "You can certainly borrow it. No bartering necessary."

Maria twirled the phone cord between her fingers, no longer trembling. "Thank you," she said.

"Oh, also," Jane said, her voice quaking slightly again, "a minor hiccup with Woodstock. My mom is only okay with me going if Stephen goes with us. I'm not sure if that changes things for you or…"

"Absolutely not!" Maria said. "Of course he can come. I'm surprised he wants to go, though. It seems like it might be a lot to handle, no?"

"I was, too, but he's the one who offered."

"That's good," Maria said. "Right?"

"Yes." Jane sighed. "I hope it is, anyway. I think he likes you."

"Oh," Maria said, smiling and folding her arms. "I'm honored."

Jane sighed again, adorably exasperated. "Don't let it go to your head."

"Too late."

•••

That night, Maria lay in bed reading a book she had snagged from Jane's store back in June, *The Well of Loneliness*, a classic yet controversial lesbian novel from the 1920s. She poured over the pages, seeking a wild concoction of pity and refuge and vindication. It was okay to be reckless, she told herself. It was okay to fall, to flail, to flounder. She was lucky to be alive, after all, to be able to indulge in such things as star-crossed flings.

Not that this, whatever this was with Jane, was meaningless. It was anything but. However, she saw no ending other than one dusted with the ashes of charred hearts.

Maria couldn't help but walk through the fire anyway.

Her throat burned as she read, "To her it seemed an inevitable thing as much a part of herself as her breathing; and yet it appeared transcendent of self, and she looked up and onwards towards her love—for the eyes of the young are drawn to the stars and the spirit of youth is seldom earth-bound."

....

TWENTY-FOUR

INTERSTELLAR OVERDRIVE

It was a cooler than average evening for July, though the air still sizzled with anticipation. As Jane exited the stairwell and found herself on the roof overlooking the Village, she felt its pulse, its song, its fever. A group of guys, including Doug, huddled around the projector, adjusting its image shining on the rooftop's maintenance room wall. Music streamed from an invisible radio, gently underscoring the hum of the small crowd spread throughout the concrete theater in the sky. Her heart leapt, practically tumbling off the building, when she spotted Maria lounging at the ledge smoking a cigarette.

Jane smiled at the serene sight and began making her way over to enjoy it up close, but Claire jumped into her path, almost knocking the red cup out of her own hands. "You made it!"

"I told you I would," Jane said. She tried hard to focus on her friend who she hadn't seen much ever since Maria stole her away, but the unknown usurper had finally spotted Jane across the roof and was now staring in her direction, her brown eyes deep and sultry as she blew a plume into the cityscape.

Claire pulled Jane out of the fog with a light slap on the shoulder. "I miss you," she said, pretending to pout. The feigned petulance lasted all of one second. "Come get a drink!"

She tugged Jane's arm, dragging her to a rickety table near the projector where liquor bottles riddled the chipped surface already puddled with spilled Smirnoff and Jim Bean. Jane chuckled at the mess. "I think I'll pass tonight," she said, giving Claire a gentle shoulder nudge. "How have you been?"

"Great," Claire said with a shrug. "Except I've barely seen you all summer! What have you been up to? How's Stephen doing?"

Jane tried not to laugh at Claire's speed-talking, a drunk habit she could only find charming. Then again, there was a tangible magic draped over the night like a canopy. Everything seemed charming. Even the trouble with Stephen couldn't break through the invisible cloud of enchantment. "He's hanging in there," she said. "He's definitely different."

"What about your mom?" Claire asked before finishing off her drink.

Jane smiled as the image of her mother at her sewing table sparkled in her mind. "Better," she said, nodding. "Much better."

"Good!" Claire leaned forward, fishing and glowing. "And how about you? You look good, so you must be good."

Jane felt herself blush as Claire winked. She ran her fingers through her hair, suddenly conscious of her appearance. "I do?"

Claire puffed out a breath and rolled her eyes. "You know you do. Now, who is it?"

Jane cocked her head. "What?"

"Don't play coy," Claire said with a drunken giggle. "Maybe it's just because Stephen is home, but I have a feeling there's something else behind this glow of yours." She flipped a tendril of Jane's hair up and away from her face.

"You're crazy," Jane said, though she knew her friend's suspicion was far from lunacy.

Claire chuckled behind the empty cup she held to her lips. "Well, whatever or whoever it is," she said with raised brows, "it's clearly making you happy."

Jane shook her head and smiled tightly, using every muscle in her face to keep it from bursting into flames. She let out a sigh and turned over her shoulder, catching Maria stub out her cigarette under her boot.

"I'm going to say hi to Maria," Jane said, patting Claire's shoulder.

"That activist?"

"Yeah," Jane said, smiling. "That activist."

Claire nodded and narrowed her eyes. "She's cool," she said, spinning around and heading back to the makeshift bar for a refill.

Jane chuckled to herself. "Yes, she is."

She parted her way through the sea of people and their smoke, arriving at Maria's side along the roof's brick ledge convinced she was already high. Or maybe it was just the effect of Maria.

"Hey," Jane said, leaning into the barrier, using it for balance. The dizzy wave Maria always seemed to bring with her was pumping strong.

"Hey," Maria repeated, a foreign sense of wariness in her voice, of tenderness. Jane could feel the tide between them had shifted now that their lips had touched. They sized each other up now, searching, bracing. She glanced up at the moon, at its subtle crescent.

"Crazy, isn't it?" Maria said, drawing Jane back to the earth.

"What is?"

Maria folded her arms and tilted her head to the sky. "To think two people are up there right now," she said, pointing. "To think we'll be able to look up and practically see them do it in real time."

Jane smiled, marveling at the thought. "It's an incredible thing."

Maria sighed. "What's incredible is we're able to put man on the moon, but we can't get out of Vietnam," she said, shaking her head.

Jane couldn't contain the chuckle that leapt from her lungs. Maria, always organizing, always philosophizing, always fighting.

"Sorry," Maria said with a huff. "I don't know how to shut it off."

"Good," Jane said. "If you shut it off, you wouldn't be you."

A tingling wave rushed through her upper body as she watched Maria struggle through the blushing that forced its way out of her olive skin. Jane looked away, pretending to scan the crowd. "Is Kay coming?"

She turned back to Maria, finding her still slightly flushed and fidgeting with her white t-shirt. "No, he's performing tonight," she said, ceasing her restlessness and placing her hands in her jean pockets. "He can't wait to get into the dress your mother is making, by the way. She's going to come to the gala, right?"

"Oh!" Jane couldn't believe she hadn't thought of the possibility before. "I haven't asked her yet. I will, though." The future image of her mother out at a gay bar suddenly made her giggle.

Maria smiled, her eyes dancing with curiosity. "What?"

Jane shook her head. "My mother…at a drag show." She glanced up at Maria with her mouth agape. "I can't wait to see it."

Maria's smile widened. "Neither can I," she said. "And hey, if she gets nervous or stiff, there are ways to fix that." She shifted her hip slightly and snatched something from her back pocket. With the sly grin that always made Jane melt even deeper into the ground, Maria held out a perfectly rolled joint.

Jane smiled as Maria lit the weed with her chrome lighter, her confidence revealing she had returned to herself, free from the flushing. Jane enjoyed watching Maria like this, in her element, wrapped in a hazy plume, dark eyes searching the sky. She held out the burning dope. "No pressure," Maria said.

Jane knew there was no pressure. There were only possibilities.

It was a night of firsts, a night of flight and imagination. A night of men doing new things, extraordinary things, of rocketing to great heights.

She took the joint and inhaled.

It burned more than she expected it to, down her throat, deep in her chest. When she let the smoke out of her lungs, they spasmed, forcing her to cough. Maria was kind enough not to laugh too hard. "That means it worked," she said with a wink.

It didn't take long for the scent of marijuana to draw a few people in, and soon a small group had formed around them. Jane leaned into the conversation as the community joint made its rounds, trying to hold on to as many words as she could, though her building high proved retention difficult. She laughed at jokes she only half understood, and the usual stress that came with such clustered chatter dissipated like the smoke all around her. Standing next to Maria, she felt invincible, protected, seen. Always seen.

Jane thought she might as well have been stripped naked the way Maria looked at her through the haze, her deep eyes heavy and dark as Kalamata olives. She recognized that look although she had never been a recipient of it before. It was something one just understood, felt in the bones and guts, like guilt or intuition. Perhaps their encounter in her bedroom hadn't been as one-sided as Jane thought.

Her head buzzed with the high of weed and anticipation. Her limbs dissolved into dust, her entire body adopting an incredible lightness, as if she could float to the moon and join Neil Armstrong and Edwin Aldrin as they graced the lunar surface. She was brought back down to Earth with a light nudge of her shoulder.

"I hear you're going to Woodstock." Maria's friend Patrick was at her side, eyes alight with intrigue. "I'm going, too," he said. "And I hear Doug and Claire want to check it out."

"It's in Bethel now, by the way," Maria said, nodding at Jane. "Not far from where it was supposed to be."

"Yeah, apparently those stuffy asses upstate can't handle us freaks," Patrick said. "They're bouncing us around from town to town. They all act like we're invading them."

"Well, the festival already sold 50,000 tickets," Maria said.

"Fifty?" Jane startled at the sound of her own shout.

Maria laughed and took the first hit of another joint. "There's bound to be way more than that when all is said and done, I'm sure."

"An infestation," Patrick said, stealing the grass and shaking out his wavy brown hair.

"With our grass and our yoga and our exposed breasts, we will pummel Bethel with peace," Maria spat out like a Russian revolutionary.

"That's an oxymoron," Patrick said through tight teeth as vapor seethed out between them.

"So is bombing for peace, but no one questions that," Maria said, tilting her head.

"We question that," Patrick said. "But not at Woodstock, man. I don't want any bad vibes up there. No war talk, no politics. I just want groovy music, pretty girls, and good weed."

"I'm sure there will be plenty of that," Maria said.

Patrick lifted his joint along with his dark brows. "Shotgun?" He took a hit, and Jane watched in stunned fascination as he leaned into Maria, both of them parting their lips that nearly touched. He blew the smoke into her mouth, and Maria inhaled it, taking his high as her own. She backed away slowly, her eyes closed, before exhaling into the city. Patrick turned to Jane and lifted his chin. "You wanna give it a go?"

Jane felt plenty high already, but Maria took the joint from Patrick and held it to her lips, teasing, waiting, wondering.

She couldn't resist.

Jane nodded, stoned silent, and took a step forward. Maria met her in the middle and sucked on the weed. Jane placed a hand on the edge of the building, bracing herself as she leaned in, eyes focused on Maria's open lips. She inhaled so slowly she wondered if her lungs were even working. Her brain tingled at the closeness, at Maria's subtle gin breath, at the way she could feel it blanket over her tongue. She shut her eyes as she stole the last bits of smoke, pulling back after a few seconds with no sense of urgency. When she opened her eyes they met Maria's, so dark she could barely discern the pupil from the iris. It wasn't until a man's distant cheer shot out into the night that Jane remembered where she was, her mind liquid and lost. She turned to where the crowd had gathered in front of the screen with their mouths agape.

"He's steppin' out!" Patrick yelped as he jogged away.

Maria and Jane both cleared their throats and offered each other wary grins before they, too, joined the audience. They sat on a blanket while some sat in lawn chairs and others stood, all of them still and silent as gargoyles. The radio was off now, and the only sounds came from the static-stained NASA audio. The wind held its breath like everyone else. The world halted.

Jane steadied her vision as best as she could, forming clarity out of the snowy black and white footage streaming in front of her on the makeshift screen. She felt as if she were looking at a sonogram, and she supposed, in some ways, she was—the birth of a new era of exploration.

"Okay," a man from Mission Control in Houston said, his voice crackling behind Jane from the speaker near the projector. "Neil, we can see you coming down the ladder now."

A shadow moved out of the spacecraft, the sliver of it that could be seen. Neil Armstrong in his bulky white suit and bubble helmet came into view as he began descending the ladder, facing the door of the Lunar Module Eagle, each step measured and purposeful.

His left foot hit the white ground.

"That's one small step for man," he said, his voice casual yet firm, "one giant leap for mankind."

Jane shivered as the roof erupted with howling applause. The ruckus echoed from every corner of the illuminated city. She realized then that all over the world, millions of people shouted and celebrated in unison. For a moment, mankind truly was moving and living together.

She turned to Maria, who sat quietly, peacefully, shaking her head and smiling. Jane settled onto the screen again, of the footage of Neil walking across the plain of lunar dust. The crowd eventually simmered, and she listened in on the bits of conversation between the two parties located on two different celestial bodies.

"It has a stark beauty all its own," Armstrong said through the static. "It's like much of the high desert of the United States."

"Bullshit," Maria said. Jane turned and was flashed a sinister smile that made her float even higher.

Patrick turned over his shoulder from his seat in front of them. "You check out that desert on your way to Frisco and let me know," he said to Maria, who suddenly turned ghostly white.

"You're going to San Francisco?" Jane asked. "When?"

Maria seemed to freeze. She licked her lips as she turned to Jane. "I might go," she said. "In September."

"Might?" Patrick swiveled around again.

"Shhh." Maria shot him a hard glance that confused Jane's buzzed brain. Patrick rolled his eyes and returned to the screen.

Jane searched Maria's face for answers, for secrets, for explanations. She found none, and so she, too, refocused on the footage of two men solving their own far grander mysteries.

....

TWENTY-FIVE

MIDNIGHT, THE STARS, AND YOU

The crowd on the roof began to filter out, people fading through the fingers of smoke still drifting through the air. Maria closed her eyes and wished she could dissipate along with the haze, disappear into herself. From herself.

She shivered at the sight of Jane's questioning face, a face that glowed under the subtle pale moon, one that currently hosted two men from Earth. Each time Maria tried to focus on the magnificence of that moment, she only came back to the dread building inside her, back to the regret she hoped she could avoid.

She didn't want to ruin anything. She didn't want what she had with Jane, that nameless, frighteningly visceral thing, to be tainted. Lying, holding out further, would only do that.

Maria finished her cigarette, smashing it out along with her nerves, and turned to Jane as they sat on the blanket gazing up at the galaxy that suddenly didn't seem so out of reach anymore.

"I have to tell you something," she said, her throat parched. "What Patrick was talking about...I was offered a job in San

Francisco," she said. "It would start in September." She bit her lip, uncertain how to go on. When Jane's eyes lost nearly all their light, she truly froze.

Jane opened her mouth slowly. "Oh," she said, her brows tightening upward. "That's…great. Right?"

Maria could tell Jane was trying to force the light back into her eyes. It pained her to see how this had dulled her luminosity, the same luminosity that drew Maria in on the dark fire escape in June. That night felt like thousands of moons away now.

She shrugged. "It was," she said.

"Was?"

Maria took a breath. She glanced around the rooftop, grateful not many people remained. She wanted few witnesses to her exploration of the unknown—honesty.

"It pays more than both *The Torch* and Drip combined. I feel like it would be crazy for me not to take it." She bit her lip again, a reminder to work through the pain, even if she didn't understand it. She watched for Jane's reaction. She waited.

Jane cleared her throat and shifted in her seat on the blanket. "What's the job?"

"These guys opened a bookstore in San Francisco, and now they're starting their own publishing house. I'd be the editor of their journal. I'd get to bring in the best work by writers from all over the world."

Jane tightened her pale pink lips into a smile Maria couldn't decipher. "That all sounds very cool," she said. "And life-changing."

Maria nodded slowly. "Yes," she said. She inhaled deeply, her eyes swelling, her cheeks ballooning.

"What is it?" Jane asked, her galaxy eyes sucking Maria into their orbit.

She swallowed, unable to hear anything other than the blood pumping in her ears. She wanted to say it. She wanted to scream it.

You. You are it.

Instead, Maria only drilled her own eyes deeper into Jane's, saying everything she could without a single word. She watched those jade green irises bulge, then freeze over like a Siberian lake. Maria sighed, crumbling inside, unable to witness Jane soak in the unspoken truth without falling apart. Before Jane could even part her lips, her golden-locked friend Claire flung herself onto their blanket.

"Jane! Doug and I are going to Woodstock," she slurred. "You're coming." She turned to Maria and placed a hand on her shoulder. "You're both coming, right?"

Jane's wild eyes bounced from Claire to Maria, Maria to Claire. "Yes," she said, her voice scratched like old vinyl. "Stephen, too."

"Groovy." Claire settled deeper into her seat and cradled her beer.

A silence fell over the blanket, and even Claire, in her intoxication, seemed to notice the tense energy rippling between Jane and Maria. She narrowed her eyes, looking back and forth between the two of them as they floated in the excruciating unknown. Finally, she sighed, cutting the quiet, and took a sip of her drink. "I have a feeling it's going to be unlike anything anyone's ever seen," Claire said. "Once in a lifetime, baby."

Time. The concept itself took a strange shape in Maria's mind. In a mere handful of weeks, Jane had overwhelmed her life like a wildfire, scorching her heart open and exposed like the napalm-charred fields of Vietnam.

Yet she felt as if she had known Jane for years, with that night on the fire escape just below her now being the kindling for this inferno, one that had so clearly swelled beyond containment.

"Strange it is," Maria recalled from *The Well of Loneliness*, "but unforgettable moments are often connected with very small happenings, happenings that assume fictitious proportions."

She smiled to herself before turning to Jane and taking a hit of her cigarette. "Once in a lifetime."

Maria hoped the beams of light now reflecting off Jane's eyes weren't just from the moon, still radiant from its rare brush with intimacy. She glanced up at the glowing waxing crescent, offering it a silent show of solidarity.

TWENTY-SIX

I CAN'T EXPLAIN

The sound of Kay and her mother laughing upstairs was a torturous kind of delight to Jane. She sat by the windows reading yet another book, one of almost a dozen in the two weeks since she'd last seen Maria, since the world cheered as two of its own set foot on its sole moon. Since the earth came out from under her feet.

It was already August. Woodstock was just around the corner. Sarah Lawrence, down the bend. San Francisco…

Jane swallowed the lump building inside her throat. Sleepless nights had weighed heavy on her eyes and she struggled to keep them focused on the page. The epic of *War and Peace* was no match against the monsoon of Maria, who had surged into her life with great and sudden force and was apparently going to leave it just the same.

The sewing room door opened, pulling Jane back from the eye of the storm. Kay's bright laughter softened her face. She let herself breathe.

"Miss Jane," Kay said as he reached the bottom of the stairs, Rebecca just behind. "I've convinced your mother to come to the show. I'm counting on you to hold her pretty little feet to the fire." He lowered his head and raised one of his beautiful brows. Rebecca stood at his side, glaring at him lovingly, her hands at her hips.

"Will do," Jane said, closing Tolstoy and resting him on her lap. "How's the dress coming?"

"Just one more fitting," her mother said, placing a hand on Kay's shoulder before moving through the living room. She picked up an empty can of beer Stephen had left on the coffee table, clearing her throat as she fled to the kitchen to dispose of the evidence. Jane's tired eyes fell even heavier at the sight.

"You'll see me at least one more time before the show," Kay said with a wink. "Though I certainly hope I don't have to wait that long. Where have you been, girl?"

Jane fidgeted in her seat. She'd been avoiding Maria ever since she told her she'd likely be moving across the country in just a few weeks, dodging her calls, declining her invitations to parties and protests. Her impending departure shook Jane just as much as her arrival. Seeing Maria in the flesh would only remind her of how little time there was left to enjoy her, this woman whose presence was reshaping nearly everything Jane knew to be true about the world, and about herself.

"I'm sorry," she said, sighing. "The summer has been a bit…crazy. I guess I've just been recovering."

"Well, rest up and come to Coney Island with us this Saturday," Kay said as Rebecca walked back into the room. "I need some sun." He ran a hand over his long arm. "I'm getting pale."

Jane laughed, grateful for the reprieve from her self-pitying. "I'll think about it."

Kay pursed his lips and narrowed his eyes. "You better." He smiled, then turned to give Rebecca a kiss on the cheek. "Thank you, love," he said. "I'll see you soon, Jane!" He waved and swept across the wood floor into the kitchen.

As he descended the stairs, Rebecca sat in the chair across from Jane.

"Is everything okay?" she asked, folding her arms. "Kay's right. You haven't really left the apartment in almost two weeks, other than being down in the store."

"That counts as leaving," Jane said with a grin. Even she didn't buy it.

Rebecca lowered her chin, her brows drawing in for only a moment before softening. "Is it Stephen?"

Jane hesitated before sighing, her shoulders collapsing. "I'm fine, really," she said, though she knew her tired voice offered little reassurance. "What about you?"

"What about me?"

"How are you doing?" Jane asked. "I mean, with Stephen…"

Rebecca sighed and reclined further into her chair. She looked out the window, the mid-day sun highlighting the faint lines near her eyes. "I'm sure he just needs time," she said warily, "but I'm still worried." She turned back to Jane, her face gray just as it had been when Stephen was gone. "I've tried encouraging him to talk to me," she said. "I don't want him thinking he has to keep anything in. That's not good for anyone."

Even through her grief and fatigue, Jane could see the insinuating hint in her mother's eyes. She couldn't take the bait. Not yet. Not when she was still trying to navigate her new hunger. "I suppose he'll talk when he's ready," she said, shrugging. "Maybe he's still making sense of everything."

Rebecca leaked out an unconvincing smile. "You're probably right," she said. "I hope you know the same thing, Jane. You can talk to me anytime. About anything." Her grin widened.

Jane nodded. She truly wished she could divulge her despair, that she could form the words, but they clung to her raw throat and seeped into her bloodstream where they echoed throughout her veins:

I'm in love with Maria.

....

She stood on the roof. The moon was full this time, nearly blinding Jane as she gazed out across lower Manhattan. Maria was beside her, softly humming.

"Would you do it?" Jane asked. "Would you go into outer space?"

Maria ceased her wordless singing and turned to Jane. "Absolutely," she said, her kittenish eyes narrowed. "Would you?

Jane smiled. "Only if you went with me."

Maria smirked as always, lighting a cigarette. She took a hit and returned to her humming. Jane glanced up at the moon again. "Liar," she whispered.

She closed her eyes and prayed for Maria to be quiet. When she opened them, they landed on the midnight glow seeping through her bedroom window. The sound of humming made her wonder if she were still asleep. She sat up, ripping herself out of the dream, and crept into the hallway.

The bottom of the stairs was alight with the subtle glow of the living room lamp, and as Jane made her way down, she realized the humming was coming from the stereo spinning out a slow, twangy blues number. She turned the corner and found Stephen at the dining table, drink in one hand and a small shiny object in the other. He stared at it with hard brows.

Jane stepped closer. "I like this," she said, keeping her voice soft. Stephen flung his eyes up, and for a second she thought he might panic. But he merely looked back down at what Jane could now see was a bronze medal, held in its honorable place by green and white ribbon. Her heart sank.

"Fairport Convention," Stephen said, tucking the medal into his pocket as he stood and walked to the record player.

"What?" Jane wondered if her brother was sleepwalking, stuck in a dream just like the one she had just escaped.

He turned the volume down. "This band," he said, jutting his chin toward the large speaker. "Fairport Convention. You heard of them?"

"Oh," Jane said. "Yes." She watched, bewildered, as Stephen returned to his seat, leaning back and taking a casual sip of his whiskey.

"Was that yours?" Jane asked, joining him at the table. "The medal?"

Stephen's face withered. He stared into his glass for a few seconds before sipping it again.

"Stephen," Jane nudged. "Did you earn a medal and not tell us?"

He snickered. "Earn," he said, shaking his head. His eyes were weary, raw from insomnia.

"Stephen—"

"What do you want me to say?" His voice wasn't harsh. It was tired. He gazed back at Jane with tired anguish.

"Whatever you want to say," Jane said, leaning forward.

"I don't want to say anything," Stephen said. His eyes perked up as they hardened. "What I want is to forget why I got the fucking thing." He took another drink, setting the glass down after he emptied it. "And for someone to tell me why."

Jane sighed, partly with relief. Despite the knife twisting inside her stomach, she was happy her brother was sharing even a sliver of his pain.

"I wish I could do that," Jane said.

Stephen somehow let out a chuckle that pried at Jane's already tender heart. "Does Maria have any insight into the war she could share with me?"

Jane couldn't help but smile and shake her head at her brother's grin. She laughed. "I'm sure she would do that. Gladly," she said, allowing the image of Maria into her mind without chasing it away. Hiding and running suddenly seemed silly. She realized there were people out there with true woes, with real ghosts, real wounds. Grief over impending heartbreak was a luxury.

Stephen's face relaxed as he fiddled with his glass. "Sorry if I woke you up," he said.

"You really didn't," Jane said, swiping a hand through the air.

Stephen tilted his head. "Sounds like you may have something on your mind, too, huh?"

Jane shrugged. "It's nothing."

"Hey," he said, his eyes rigid again, "just because I'm fucked up doesn't mean your problems don't matter."

"Stephen—"

"I'm serious," he said. "You guys don't need to be walking on eggshells around me, okay?"

Jane's heart bulged. "I'm sorry," she said, barely above a whisper. "We're worried about you, that's all. Mom, especially."

"I know," Stephen said. He took a breath and looked away. "I know you want me to talk. I'm just not sure how I could explain," he said, turning back to Jane. His eyes appeared haunted. "And I don't want you to see any of the images I have in my head. Trust me, you don't want them, either."

Jane didn't doubt him. She'd avoided the footage of the war broadcasted for all to see over the years. The brutality cut too deep, and she wasn't even witnessing the atrocities herself. The weight of the memories her brother carried suddenly came fully into view. Her throat cracked as her eyes burned. Stephen, even in his ghostly state, noticed.

"Jane," he said softly. "Just…live your life. Okay? It's all you got."

She tried to smile, but Jane could only nod. She inhaled a deep breath, blinking out a tear, and stood.

She had the urge to hug Stephen, to tell him how proud she was of him and his honorable yet secretive bravery. Though she had a feeling he wouldn't appreciate the idea of pride being associated with his service.

"Don't hide," she said, forcing out a smile this time. "I don't want to have to come looking for you."

Stephen managed a chuckle. "I'll do my best."

....

TWENTY-SEVEN

LET THE SUNSHINE IN

Jane released herself from her self-confinement and entered the light of day, hazy and harsh like most August rays. Yet at Coney Island, the heavy heat clung to her skin with extra vigor among the swelling crowd on the boardwalk, their sweat slapping her arms as she wriggled through the fetid mass toward the pier.

She spotted Kay first, his black skin glistening as he leaned against the rail bordering the beach. Maria stood beside him, her tan arms exposed in her black, sleeveless tee. Jane almost gasped at the sight of her legs, uncharacteristically bare thanks to her cut-off jean shorts. She still wore her black combat-style boots, her whole appearance evoking that of the rebel she was. Michel ambled about beside them so unassumingly Jane didn't realize he was there until Kay grabbed his arm as she approached. "She made it!" he said with his giant smile.

Maria clung her fingers around the bottom straps of her leather bag. "That she did." She kicked the back of one boot against the other's toe. "I was about to put a search party out for you," she said with her foxlike grin.

"I'm sorry," Jane said, wincing.

Maria stepped forward and gave Jane's shoulder a light punch. "I'm just giving you shit, Red."

"You do love doing that," Jane said, suddenly grateful for the sun that had already turned her cheeks a generous shade of pink.

"It's one of her many talents," Kay said, lowering his sunglasses over his big, brown eyes. "Now, let's get baked."

They settled onto a blanket in the middle of the throng of half-naked bodies flopped upon the burning sand like fish. They barely sat down before Kay stripped down to his trunks, making Michel do the same, and the two took off for the water, just as crowded as the noisy shore. Jane draped her arms over her knees, scanning the sizzling scene, trying not to focus too much on the only person she truly cared to look at who sat so close she could feel the heat radiating from her skin. Her own flesh boiled when Maria ran a quick finger across her arm. "You burn quick, I bet," she said before digging into the large tote Kay had lugged. She pulled out a blue and white umbrella, popping it up in seconds and shoving it into the sand.

"I do," Jane said, chuckling. "Thank you."

Maria smiled as she settled back onto the now shaded blanket, her eyes barely visible behind her gold-rimmed sunglasses. "Well, you definitely need to protect that perfect skin," she said.

Jane blushed. Maria noticed but did the kind thing and pretended not to. "One good thing I got from my mother is her Sicilian blood," she said, lifting an arm. "Our skin is natural armor."

Jane relaxed, allowing herself to sink down into the blanket alongside the armored Italian. "I'm sure you can guess I'm Irish," she said. "Well, my mother is."

"I picked up on that," Maria said with a nod.

Jane laughed. Her stomach settled. A breeze swept up from the waves and brought with it the smell of salt. She watched Kay and Michel wade in the source. She felt calm.

A well-built man with dog tags dangling around his neck walked by their blanket, holding the hand of a small child. Jane wondered what stories he kept hidden from the world.

"Stephen got a medal," she suddenly said. "In Vietnam. He didn't tell us."

A flock of seagulls soared overhead, boisterous and bold. Maria's silence urged Jane on.

"I woke up the other night and found him looking at it in the living room. He was so…aloof," she said, turning to Maria, whose gaze was glued to Jane even through her shades. "He put it in his pocket and wouldn't talk about it."

Maria's face darkened as she let out a soft sigh. "I imagine whatever earned him that medal was the result of some pretty awful shit he wants to forget."

Jane pinched her mouth and shifted back to the sea. "Why does the army even give people those things if they only make things worse?"

Maria chortled. "You know what I'm going to say."

"Why does the army do anything?" Jane turned to Maria and smiled.

"You got it," Maria said with a wink. "But my anti-military views aside, my guess is those awards mean more to the families. Like yours."

Jane shook her head. "I feel like it can't mean anything if I don't even know what it's about."

Maria dug out her pack of cigarettes from her pocket. She lit one, blowing the smoke away from Jane into the rippling haze. "It means something if it means something to you," she said. "And it sounds like it does."

Jane let out a dramatic sigh and shot Maria a smirk she hoped she'd be proud of. "Must you always speak sense?"

Maria cackled. "I'm pretty sure sense is the last thing I have," she said, wiping away a strand of hair blowing across her face. "I guess…I just don't think you need to make yourself feel any worse than you do. It's okay to feel proud of your brother. It's okay to feel whatever you want."

What Jane felt and wanted was all wrapped up on their blanket on the sand. That was one thing she knew for certain, at least. She smiled. The sun made her bold.

"I feel happy that I met you," she said, plunging her eyes as deep into Maria's as she could through her black lenses. She wanted to be brave, in her own way. She wanted to face the light Maria brought to her life and enjoy it, no matter how fleeting.

It appeared to take Maria a few seconds to register what Jane had said. Then she smiled. "Me, too," she said. She leaned into Jane, nudging her elbow.

Kay and Michel crash landed onto the blanket then, soaked with sea as they collapsed onto their backs. Soon both Jane and Maria grew too hot for their clothes and joined their two friends in stripping to their swimsuits. Jane resisted the urge to study Maria's golden-brown body and instead buried her head into the pages of the latest Daphne du Maurier, though she did let her eyes wander occasionally, her own sunglasses offering her at least some camouflage. Maria was being slightly less cautious with her gazing. Jane didn't mind. She felt oddly comfortable lying so exposed next to her, and she let herself sink into the sand and sun.

She let herself feel.

....

The sunset fell, folding over into night, and the colorful carnival lights of Coney blew out the sky. As they walked through the loud, vibrant chaos, Maria felt like a child again. She gaped at the bumper cars with glee. She laughed at Michel's dry French humor with adoration. She looked at Jane with wonder.

They watched a snake charmer dance along to a guitar strummed by a red-bearded man. They rode the Cyclone and played "Knock Down the Cat" and ate hot dogs on their way down the pier. They stood at the edge, staring out at the Atlantic cloaked in indigo. Kay started singing Aretha Franklin, his arm draped around Michel, the two of them sharing an ice cream cone.

The seaside lamps offered just enough light for Maria to see the new patch of freckles that sprouted on Jane's nose since the afternoon. She didn't stop herself from admiring them.

Jane noticed and beamed. "What?" she said with a giggle.

Maria smiled and shrugged. She looked at Jane's lips, now dark red from the sun, before turning back to the waves. Kay and Michel spotted a few friends on the other end of the pier. They ran over to them, laughing and hollering, leaving Maria and Jane alone in their moonlit silence.

Jane leaned into the railing, her hair blowing slightly in beach-brewed waves. "You'll have an even more beautiful ocean over there in California," she said, turning over her shoulder. "I'd love to see the Pacific one day."

Maria bent down alongside Jane, grinning. "You're adventurous," she said. "I'm positive you'll get out there. Especially if I'm there." She bit her lip and nudged her elbow into Jane's. "You'll definitely have to visit me."

Jane smiled, but her eyes didn't flicker. She took a breath and nodded, glancing out to the black sea again. Maria couldn't bear the sight. "I know I need to go," she said softly. "Out west, I mean. The opportunity is too..." She paused and shook her head before turning to Jane, who stared back in sullen curiosity. Maria sighed. "Everything feels very bittersweet, I guess," she said, swallowing the lingering pieces of fright. "I just met you, and I don't find the timing to be very fair."

The light in Jane's eyes danced, but her face fell. That bittersweetness.

"Neither do I," she said, her voice resigned. "I'm happy you have this chance to do something so big. You deserve it." She took another breath, shaking her head slightly as she faced the ocean, vast and ghostly. "Any other thoughts I have are merely selfish ones," she said with a sad chuckle.

Maria bumped her arm again. "No, they're not," she said. "I have thoughts, too." Jane swiveled to Maria, her eyes scared yet optimistic. "One thing I know for sure," Maria said, lightening her tone, "is I really want to spend as much time with you as I can before September. Is that okay?" She nearly collapsed onto the pier at Jane's smile.

"I think that can be arranged," Jane said.

They stood at the edge of the sea, buoyed by the silent acknowledgment of a fate uncertain yet inescapable.

TWENTY-EIGHT

THE HILLS ARE ALIVE

It was unlike anything Jane had ever seen.

They had barely turned onto the tiny, two-lane 17B when the traffic appeared, tracing and winding like string lights through the hills of White Lake, the black night dotted with its bright, orderly chaos. Jane and Maria stuck their heads out the back windows, then their entire upper bodies, gazing out at the backcountry overrun with cars, some pulled off to the side and others still hanging on in the seemingly endless line toward Max Yasgur's farm.

It had been Maria's idea to leave the city when they did, to arrive at the site in the middle of the night to avoid the crowd. Jane's eyes swelled thinking of all the people who hadn't yet started their journeys to the festival. She had a strong feeling the organizers' original guess of 200,000 attendees would be proven laughable.

Stephen turned the radio off, the beautiful traffic jam offering a more than enjoyable soundtrack. Music blared from so many other cars anyway, all the songs weaving into a wild medley that somehow made sense. It echoed across the onyx fields that would turn green come morning, when daylight would reveal the true breadth of this mammoth affair.

Stephen finally pulled over to the side of the packed road, making an executive decision like a true platoon leader. "Looks like we made it to camp," he said.

Tents flanked the road, some tucked beside clusters of trees, others staked in right by the cars. Maria jumped out of Stephen's old Pontiac and practically howled with excitement. She threw her hands into the air and laughed. Jane admired her enthusiasm but couldn't replicate it; she was still stunned at the sight. Maria stood right in front of her and took her by the shoulders. "Jane! This is everything," she said, her eyes blazing despite the deep dusky hour. "This is history."

"And this is a tarp," Stephen said, tossing Maria the rolled-up black plastic from the trunk. She smiled and turned toward the line of shrubs next to the car. She leapt over it to where several other tents had already been erected. Communities sprouted along the rural route like weeds, settling in where they could, claiming their space. Jane realized that everyone might have been stuck, but no one was stranded. The fields were their home, at least for the weekend.

She was grateful for Stephen's time in Vietnam only as they set up their site. He'd learned from the monsoon jungle the proper, primal way of making camp, of preparing for the worst, of using what is available. He layered the ground with tarp, prepping for rain, and he brought food that would keep throughout the festival—jerky, oranges, canned peaches. He had lamps and knives and lighters, and he whipped their two tents up within fifteen minutes even in the dark. Both Jane and Maria stood in awe of his efficiency. Stephen looked at them as he shoved the tent bags back into the car and chuckled. "You learn a lot as a grunt," he said.

By the time they finished, the line of cars behind them had swelled, now slithering even further into the darkness through the poor usurped town. An older man in overalls had appeared just ahead of their new home, directing traffic and the people who meandered about it carrying guitars and babies, flashing peace signs with their free hands. He was a townie, no doubt, probably from the white house set back in the shadows just beyond their tents. He seemed at home there among the caravan, joking with the crowd, pretending to be grumpy but clearly loving every minute of the frenzy. Jane and Maria sat on the roof of the blue Pontiac, watching it all, while Stephen lounged on the hood drinking a beer from the cooler in the trunk. The night deepened and the hills throbbed as engines purred with anticipation. Jane felt sleep pulling at her eyelids, but her mind refused to succumb. When the blue hour breached the blackboard sky, she still sensed no fatigue, unlike the indigo that surrendered to the wispy layers of purple, then peach, then orange. As the sun lurked above the horizon, it began shedding slivers of red and gold onto the road continuing to flood with Mustangs and music and long-haired lovers.

Jane turned to Maria with stoned eyes after a group of young people in fringe and lace marched past, banging drums and chanting, the smiles on their faces seemingly as indestructible as the land that pulsed with life all around them. "I feel like I'm in the center of the universe," she said, almost chuckling out of ecstatic disorientation.

Maria's face glowed thanks to the encroaching daylight. She took a giant breath and let it out with a grin. "It's like a pilgrimage."

The seekers surged down the faintly wooded road, eventually swallowing Jane and her two companions into their tide toward the festival grounds, wherever they happened to be. They walked for over an hour, engulfed by the energy of thousands, until, finally, the route split and opened into a vast field swarming with even more people. Stephen with his large pack led the way as they humped through the chaos, passing food tents and drum circles and Volkswagen vans overflowing with beautiful women draped out the windows. Maria walked over to one of them, a beaming blonde handing out floral crowns for free. She snagged a yellow and white creation, radiant and earthy, and placed it around Jane's head.

"Queen Jane," Maria said as she adjusted the red locks around their new accessory. "Approximately." The Bob Dylan song reference made Jane's stomach flutter.

They crisscrossed the rippling green throughout the morning and afternoon, though the concept of time evaded Jane's mind. Nothing felt real, yet everything felt more alive than ever. When they finally breached the hill overlooking the stage placed within the base of its natural bowl, the out-of-body sensation exploded like the massive crowd spread before her.

Jane let out a single laugh, incapable of forming any other sound. Stephen whistled.

"Holy shit," Maria said. "This is…" She shook her head and placed a hand on Jane's shoulder.

"Yeah," Jane managed to say. No other words would do.

They somehow found an open pocket of grass on the hill choked by thousands of half-naked bodies. Jane planted herself in the earth, marveled at the breadth of the site. A great pond stretched out beside a grove of trees behind the stage, its blue-gray water dotted with swimmers, baptizing themselves in Bethel, the house of God.

As Richie Havens walked onto the open stage canopied in white drapes, his orange dashiki blazing like the hard rhythm he pounded out on his acoustic guitar, Jane couldn't deny anyone's belief in a higher power. The congregation roared, eager to praise, and she was eager to bathe in the groovy gospel.

She soaked in the contagious animation painted on Maria's face as the music swelled, drifting up from the immense wooden pulpit across the vibrating lawn. She couldn't believe she had truly considered remaining locked inside her apartment, avoiding the magic of moments with Maria, even if they would only be transitory. Wasn't everything ephemeral?

But she had realized they were both on shaky ground, erupted by the abruptness of San Francisco, even if neither of them would utter the words that swirled around and between them, tangling them up in a bind of their own making.

At least here, at Woodstock, Jane could let it all be. She could turn on, tune in, and drop out, as they all said.

She would simply deal with the parting later.

....

TWENTY-NINE

WE SHALL ALL BE FREE

By dusk the sky thickened, and as Ravi Shankar strummed his sitar, the notes wafted into a light, peppery drizzle, adding an even deeper layer of enchantment to the night. Maria closed her eyes and tilted her head to the black shroud. The hill continued to pulse even after the enlightening performance that yearned to open every blockage in Maria's body, a body burrowed into the earth beside Jane, a body that tingled at her slightest touch. An elbow. A shoulder.

Here among the greens and hollows of the Hudson River Valley, Jane's vibrancy seemed to glow even brighter, spread even wider. Maria observed her throughout the day and night and felt the dangerous tugging at her heart. The complete tearing and shredding of the muscle was approaching—she knew that—but it hurt so good to bleed, to drown in the ocean of Jane, to watch her place a reassuring hand on Stephen's shoulder as helicopters flew around the fields, transporting musicians from the blocked roads to the back of the stage. She rubbed his back, silent and steady. She flashed Maria her starwild eyes.

Maria was a goner, and she knew it. She sank into the feeling and into the damp earth.

Stephen sat quietly in the rain, pensive and sturdy. The night was calm despite the sky's tears. Or perhaps because of them. Puffs of smoke drifted through the air, among the black sea of bodies swaying within the languid tide. Bursts of light popped up here and there thanks to sporadic fire pits built within the hillside, the blazes orange but subtle. The crowd waited in silent earnest for Joan Baez to take over the glistening stage.

Stephen stood up, stretching his legs and back, the gentle rain sliding off his thick shoulders. A man, black and built, approached him, asking for a light. He wore loose fatigues and dog tags. And a stoned smile. "Thank you, brother," he said after Stephen stoked his weed.

Stephen nodded at the happy man. "Who were you with?"

"Charlie Company, 9th Infantry Division," he said, his tone dry. "You?"

"Third Brigade, 101st Airborne."

"Damn," the man said, wincing. "You need a hit of this more than me." He handed his joint over to Stephen, who took it gladly. "How long you been back?"

Stephen blew out a plume that quickly dissolved in the rain. "About a month." He lifted the joint, but the black soldier nodded at Maria and Jane.

"Give it to the sistas," he said with a squinty grin. Maria eagerly took the joint, hoping to calm Jane in the process, Jane who gaped at her brother with earnest confusion. He was talking about the war, willingly. Maria knew Jane was rattled.

She handed her the weed, happy that Jane accepted it with a smile.

The unknown soldier spoke on. "I was there in '66," he said, sitting down on the soggy earth, making himself at home. Stephen followed. "Already feels like it's a different war over there now."

Stephen chuckled. "Still a lot of the same shit," he said.

"No doubt, no doubt." The man looked out at the drenched crowd. "Look at all this crazy shit. All these people, searching."

Maria leaned in through the rain. "What do you mean?"

He turned back with his black brows raised. "You think we're all just here for music? Music's everywhere, man," he said. "We're all here searching for something, even if we don't know what yet."

He puffed out his lips, then smiled wide. "That's just my theory, anyway!" the bright stranger said while snatching the weed back from Stephen for a hefty hit. Everyone chuckled nervously. "Name's Goose, by the way," he said.

"Goose?" Jane's wet eyebrows shifted to the black, dripping sky.

The soldier grinned. "Was Quinton," he said. "Then I went to Nam, and now it's Goose. What about you, brother?" He nodded at Stephen. "What's your name now?"

Stephen smiled ever so slightly. "Radio," he said. "But Stephen's just fine."

Goose moaned. "I get it," he said. "Most men don't wanna bring anything back from over there." Stephen didn't deny it. "Me, though?" Goose went on, wrapping his arms around his knees. "I brought my name back. I saw it as a chance to start over here. Be someone different in a country that certainly didn't like Quinton the Negro. I thought maybe it would like Goose the soldier a little better."

Maria cleared her throat. "And how's that going?"

He smirked with a sparkle in his black olive eyes. "Funny enough, turns out Goose don't give a fuck about what anybody thinks about him," he said. "That's the real trick to freedom."

The sky kept crying. The ghosts of cigarettes drifted slightly before being swallowed by the rain.

"I can't lie, though," Goose said, his voice suddenly grave, "I've thought about re-upping a few times. Just here and there, you know?"

Maria held her breath. She couldn't believe he truly said he'd considered going back to Vietnam.

"Mostly when the nightmares get really bad," Goose said, defending himself, although he hadn't been challenged. "You don't have nightmares over there," he said with a textured chuckle.

"Because you don't sleep," Stephen said. Maria could feel Jane flinch.

"That's right." Goose laughed and gave Stephen a light nudge.

The rain picked up speed. Maria pulled the poncho draped across her and Jane up a little further.

"So, what are you looking for?" Jane asked Goose.

Goose squinted.

"You said we're all here searching for something," Jane reminded him.

Goose nodded a few times before facing the slippery slope of seekers. "I spent a year in a living hell," he said blandly. "I wanted to get a little taste of heaven."

By the time Joan Baez graced the stage, pregnant and perfectly content in the rain, Goose had left the nest and Jane had begun to shiver. Maria wrapped her arm around her throughout the acoustic set, and when Joan led the crowd in singing "We Shall Overcome," candles and lighters lit up the damp night, and Maria's heart nearly drowned in the sound of Jane sniffling through gentle tears.

....

THIRTY

YOU GOT ME FLOATIN'

The intrusive morning sun turned the tent into a greenhouse, the air inside thick and sticky like molasses. Jane rolled over on her sleeping bag, damp with sweat, and stared at the silhouettes of the raindrops still slipping off the sides of the tent from the evening's rain.

Beside her, Maria slept deeply. In the distance, a few songbirds sang unknown tunes to each other, continuing the concert from just hours earlier.

Jane appreciated the calm morning after a restless night of half-sleep. The combination of Maria lying so close and the realization that Stephen had contemplated signing up for another deployment invaded her bones, weighing her down into a heavy panic. She'd tossed and turned throughout most of the darkness, attempting to shake out the angst. Now, she simply yearned for clear, clean air.

She unzipped the tent flap and crawled into the day, already bright and muggy. Throngs of people still milled about the road, though they did so quietly, tiredly. But still smiling.

Jane found Stephen sitting by his own tent in a lawn chair, cigarette in hand, still in his white tee and blue jeans, just as she'd left him the night before. "Have you slept?" she asked, taking the chair beside him.

Stephen shrugged. "I dozed."

Jane recalled Goose mentioning nightmares and wondered if Stephen avoided sleep to avoid their haunting.

"What about you?" Stephen asked. "You sleep?"

Jane took a breath, sighing while bobbing her head from side to side. "Not really."

As they sat in silence watching the crowd march toward the festival site, Jane couldn't help but see the image of refugees traveling down a dirt road in Vietnam. She saw Stephen walking among them, an M-16 slung over his shoulder. She turned to face him as he existed now, sitting stoic yet peaceful with the sun dousing his sandy hair. She swallowed and steadied her breath.

"Have you really thought about going back to Vietnam?"

Stephen didn't say anything. He reached down and killed his cigarette in the dewy grass, then leaned back into the rickety chair. Finally, he let out a sigh and kicked out his feet.

"I thought about it before I even came home," he said. "They try to get you to re-up while you're there. They say they'll get you a nice, cushy job in the rear if you give them one more year, then another. Some guys were so desperate to get out of the fields they jumped at it." He bit his lip and stared out at a hoard of hippies prancing through the meadow across the road. "I took my chances and decided to ride it out."

"I'm glad you did," Jane said, smiling through the pain.

Stephen nodded slowly. "I understand why people go back," he said. "I lasted all of one day here before I lost it." He shook his head and chuckled.

Jane couldn't locate the humor.

"But you're safe now," she said, though she knew that wasn't how trauma worked. Demons certainly didn't care about coordinates.

"I don't know if there's any way I could put it that it would make any sense," Stephen said, his eyes distant. He still hadn't looked into Jane's. "Not to someone who hasn't been there."

Jane may not have been in the war, but she could empathize with the weight of confusion. Of trying to make sense out of chaos. That futile struggle.

"It's okay," she said. "Just promise me you won't go back. Promise me."

Stephen finally looked at her, truly, and smiled. "I can assure you all I'm thinking about right now is getting back to that stage," he said.

Jane relaxed slightly and leaned back, tilting her head toward the great blue bowl of a sky. The sound of music playing from someone's car drifted through the air. Jane brought her chin down and looked at her brother.

"Why did they call you Radio?"

Stephen smiled. "Because I listened to it every chance I got," he said.

Jane grinned at the thought that he at least had the comfort of music while in the thick of war. She nodded and returned to the sky.

....

The heat hung like a triple canopy jungle over the curves of Bethel. Stephen had learned how to handle it as a foot soldier, but Jane felt herself frying. So while he headed to the stage for Country Joe McDonald, she and Maria banked left for the water beyond the trees.

Jane had already seen quite a few naked bodies on the first day of the festival, yet the sight of hundreds of them all in one spot, floating and splashing about the large pond, gave her pause. She stood wide-eyed as she gazed across the reflective water soothing the sizzling flesh that dipped inside it. She marveled at the confidence, at the lightness. The unabashed joy.

Maria instantly flung off her tank, revealing a thin black bra. Jane's chest heaved with even more heat, and her tongue thickened.

"This is basically like a bikini," Maria said with a wink and shrug. Jane looked around and noticed several others in their makeshift swimwear. It wasn't so bad.

Maria wiggled out of her shorts, tossing them on the packed earth near a high, luscious bush along the water where a community pile of clothes had formed. Jane bit her lip as she slid out of her yellow dress. She watched Maria stand at the pond's edge with her hands on her hips. She swiveled around, one hand shielding her eyes from the unapologetic sun. "Oh, fuck it," she said. She walked toward Jane and the lump of fallen garments while reaching behind her back, untying her bra.

Jane felt her knees beg to buckle as Maria stripped down to her tanned flesh. She felt a lot of other bodily sensations, too, and hoped they weren't incredibly obvious. She laughed, praying it made up for her red face.

Maria never flinched, heading back to the pond. Jane held her breath as she watched the hourglass glide into the water. Maria turned over her shoulder, ripping Jane away from the view. "I don't have to look, if that will help," she said with a grin. "You can just tell me when you're in."

A swell of shame ripped through Jane's tingling bones. She was eighteen, for God's sake. She was a woman. She looked like one, and it was time for her to feel like one. Live like one. Forget the fear.

Jane took a breath and smiled through her disrobing. "It's okay," she said. "I may be sweet, but I'm not shy." Sure, it was a lie. But it gave her the confidence she craved to bring her closer to Maria, who bobbed in the natural bath, pretending not to watch as she descended the shoreline and slid into the chilled water. "This feels amazing," she said, plunging her entire body into the coolness.

Maria dipped her head back and threw her arms over her head, floating. Though they were surrounded by people, Jane couldn't see anyone else. She tried not to stare at the water lapping over Maria's breasts, the sight bringing a feeling of fullness to her own. She cleared her throat and glanced around the watering hole. A man stood shaving in the shallows, white cream slathered on his face. A border collie sprinted past him, diving into the deep. A group of happy hippies sat in a row on a surfboard, balancing and singing. The trees hummed with the vibrations pulsing from the nearby stage.

"I can't believe I've ever swam any other way," Maria said. Jane turned back, dancing through liquid. "It's so freeing!" She waded upright now, twirling in circles, laughing. Jane couldn't help but join her.

As their giggles faded, their eyes met. They studied each other now, gently, paddling. If it wasn't for the blond curly-haired teenage boy wading up to them and offering a joint, Jane would have exploded.

She and Maria each took one hit, both suffering laughable coughing fits from the oddly potent weed. "Groovy," the golden surfer boy said before slipping away. They bobbed, studying the pond's inhabitants, listening to the music play on in the distance.

Jane tried to focus on the festival, but her eyes always drew back to Maria. It seemed she wasn't alone.

Maria sank into the water up to her nose, peering at Jane with an invisible smirk.

"What?" Jane asked with a nervous, pot-fueled chuckle.

Maria grinned and lifted her mouth above the rippling surface. "You kissed me," she said, her grin widening, her dark eyes glistening.

Jane's jaw slackened, dropping her mouth open as she caught her breath. She shook her head, convinced she'd heard wrong. Her stoned silence sent Maria into a burst of laughter. Jane tried to hold back her smile, but soon she, too, howled along with her. She slapped water at Maria, who merely patted it away through her chuckling.

"I should've known you'd only let me go so long without bringing it up," Jane said, faking a pout. That marijuana nonchalance. Everything's groovy, even her embarrassing foibles.

Maria wiggled in the water, smiling at herself. "Listen," she said, "it's not like it wasn't enjoyable for me, obviously. I don't know if you've heard, but I *do* like kissing women."

Jane tried to laugh, but something choked it out of her. "Well," she said, her voice cracking, "I guess that's…good? You enjoying it, I mean." She felt her skin burning even while completely encased with coolness. Maria smirked. She was enjoying this. "Not that I wanted you to," Jane stumbled out, desperate to find ground somewhere as she floundered. "I don't…"

"What *did* you want?" Maria cocked her head slightly, her black hair dipping further into the water. Her eyes danced.

Jane shook her head as her eyes blew outward. "You're taking way too much pleasure in this," she said.

Maria cackled like the wild woman she was, yelping at the sun, basking in her glory. Jane was fine with it; Maria's glory was certainly worthy of indulgence.

The weed still poured through Jane's head, spreading downward and buttering her limbs and tongue. "Yes," she said, finally urging out the words. "I kissed you. I guess I just…wanted to."

Jane tightened her brows, then nodded slightly. It was as good as she could do. And as honest as she could be. All of her desires for Maria suddenly appeared that simple. They just were. They existed.

She knew there was no use in searching for better answers. Maybe sometimes there weren't any.

Maria pursed her lips, pushing out her dimples. Her eyes narrowed. "I like Jane with initiative," she said.

Then she floated away, winding her body through the water like a Sicilian mermaid. Just as unreal as she was beautiful.

....

THIRTY-ONE

DROWNING ON DRY LAND

Back on dry land, Maria still found it hard to steady herself. The high from the weed had faded, but the drug of Jane still purred through her veins.

They slipped back into their clothes, clinging to their damp flesh, and headed into the woods where a pathway was lined with tents and tables, pop-up vendors selling their homemade goods. And plenty of cigarettes.

The trees hung over them like a canopy, the sun filtering through their leaves shimmering onto Jane's face like a kaleidoscope as they browsed the wooded market. Maria smiled like a maniac watching her immense green eyes soak in the enchanted forest that smelled like pine and incense and marijuana. She watched them blow open when a familiar bright blonde screamed her name through the crowded pathway.

"Jane!" Claire barreled down the dirt lane and nearly jumped into Jane's arms. Doug followed behind, chilled and aloof, walking alongside Patrick, his eyes as wild as his hair.

"Hey!" Maria laughed, surprised to have stumbled upon the group among the nearly half million wanderers roaming the farm. "You made it!"

"Hell yeah, I made it," Patrick said, giving Maria's arm a light punch. "I hitched with these cats." He nodded toward Doug and Claire, who fawned over Jane in a drug-induced plague of affection.

"I've missed you," Maria heard Claire say while hanging on Jane's sun-pink shoulder. "I'm so happy I found you!"

Patrick buzzed with the electricity of the spirited woods. "Can you believe it?" he said, waving his arms around, his tie-dye shirt blowing and twisting around his torso. "Life, man. It's all happening, right here, right now."

Maria chuckled at his inebriated rambling. "You've clearly smoked more than me today."

Patrick waved it off. "I'm just feeling it," he said. "Aren't you? Tell me this isn't the perfect end to the summer."

"No, you're right," Maria said, watching Jane laugh along with Claire's exuberance out of the corner of her eye.

"It's a pretty good send-off to San Francisco, I'd say," Patrick said, lighting a cigarette. "Would you have believed three months ago that this is how the journey would begin?"

Maria smiled and shook her head. There were lots of things she would have never believed would happen.

"Three months?"

The slight surprise in Jane's voice ripped through Maria's chest. She winced internally, braving for Jane to realize what she had so conveniently left out when she'd told her about the job.

"Yeah," Patrick said through his cloud of Pall Mall. "Back in May, it was all just a tiny little embryo of a dream. Shit happens fast."

He pointed to a table behind Maria where two young men were selling records. "Oh, check it," he said before sliding past her, fleeing the scene of a fire he had unknowingly stoked.

Maria kept her face as relaxed as possible while Claire continued chatting and bouncing and insisting they all go check out John B. Sebastian's set. As they began twisting through the woods, Maria's stomach began twisting into knots as tangled as the roots all around her. She caught glimpses of Jane throughout the trek, one they both spent in strained silence, and wanted nothing but to soothe the tension working its way through the porcelain perfection. To reach out across the distance Jane had formed between them on the pathway. To touch her, let her know she didn't tell her about the possible move right away because she didn't expect their bond to grow as strong as it did. And by that point, it was too late. She was in too deep.

Maria had stumbled into a pond of circumstance and denial, and there had never been an escape. She'd merely just been treading water.

Now, the drowning began.

....

THIRTY-TWO

KOZMIC BLUES

Jane tried to sink into the magic of the late night, its star-soaked sky and musical vibrations that she imagined rippled across the highway. She wondered if her mother could feel them back home.

But mostly she wondered how to keep herself from falling into the dark depths the universe seemed to suck her into, the depths that told her Maria had known long before they met that she would likely be leaving. That Jane wasn't an option. That Jane had been a play thing.

She at least managed a chuckle when she realized this must be what Janis Joplin was singing about right then at the bottom of the hill, those great, consuming Kozmic Blues.

In between the raspy, whiskey-fueled songs, Jane tried to catch slivers of Stephen's conversation with the group of fellow soldiers he'd apparently stumbled upon earlier that day. All were friends of Goose. All had been in Vietnam. All wore either fatigues or dog tags, proudly. Jane watched them talk, sometimes low and deep, other times animated and rapturous, telling war stories among themselves because they couldn't tell them to anyone else.

They didn't have to explain them to each other; they could merely reflect, or grieve, or laugh if they felt like it.

As she studied her brother, relaxed and even jovial while shooting the shit with his army brothers, Jane felt it click. There were certain things one could only say to certain people. There were certain things one could barely say to themselves. Other things seemed impossible to explain at all.

Her sudden resentment toward Maria was one of them. And now, with Claire gone, her butterfly wings dragging Doug along to their next adventure, Jane had fewer places to focus her energy. Patrick had disappeared into the crowd as well, leaving Jane to burn alongside the one who held the torch.

As Janis left the stage, her echo practically embedded into the earth forever now, Maria leaned into Jane across the blanket, bringing her heat with her. "I'm getting kind of hungry," she said. "I hear some folks from the Hog Farm are handing out free food back at the concessions. Want to come with me?"

Want. Where did wanting ever get anyone?

Jane didn't want to be indignant. She certainly didn't want to give Maria a reason to abandon her more than it already felt like she was doing.

"Sure," Jane said, swallowing the bruised ego.

And so they left Stephen and his soldiers behind to secure their spot ("Looks like you're back on night watch again, Radio," Goose had said.) while they slithered through the crowd in search for food.

It was only the second night, yet it was clear the organizers never imagined just how many people would answer their call to create three days of peace, love, and music. Food had certainly become scarce, though it didn't seem to bother anybody. Even in the dead of night, that hour of ghosts, when drugs turned darkness into demons, the energy remained calm and free of ghouls. Jane's heart, however, continued to thrust itself into a frenzy.

Once she and Maria snagged their bowls of rice and vegetables, they took their time walking back to the stage where Sly and the Family Stone were bound to make everyone even higher. Jane yearned for it. She yearned to forget what day it was, how soon everything would change. How quickly so much already had. When a man in a ponytail and a southwest-inspired poncho walked up to her and offered a hit of his weed, Jane didn't think twice. She took one inhale, then reached to hand it back. She stopped herself and took three more hits, each longer than the last.

"Jane," Maria said, placing a hand on her shoulder, a forced chuckle under her breath. "This is a marathon, not a sprint."

The man laughed, a giant smile plastered on his tan face as Jane returned his joint. "I like you," he said.

Jane cleared her throat. "Thank you," she said, adjusting to the balloon swelling inside her head. "And thank you," she said again, pointing to the weed he inhaled with ease. "For that."

She felt Maria's eyes studying her as the three of them continued walking up the crowded hill toward the stage, but Jane merely took a bite of her food, pretending she felt nothing other than stoned.

"You have the most beautiful hair," the man said, running a hand through Jane's wavy tendrils. "I would bathe in it all day, mama."

Out of the corner of her eye, Jane saw Maria's head turn sharply. All Jane could do was laugh. "I don't think I've ever been called that," she said, tossing her already empty bowl into a trash can spilling over with the day's scraps, including hundreds of cigarette butts.

A tug on Jane's arm brought her attention back to Maria. "Hey, we should get back to Stephen," she said, nodding toward their spot within the hillside.

Jane freed her arm from Maria's grip, swiping a long lock of hair behind her ear. "Yeah, sure," she said.

"Mama," the tan hippie said, "where do you live? How can I see you again?"

Maria stepped closer to Jane, placing a hand at the small of her back. Jane felt an electric volt seize her already over-stimulated system. "New York City," she spit out, mostly out of a desperate need for distraction. "In Brooklyn."

"Far out," he said, nodding. "I'm in Chicago."

"Well, that's pretty far from New York," Maria said, tugging slightly at the back of Jane's dress now.

"That's true, that's true," the man said, then threw his hands in the air. "We are all just stardust though, am I right? I shall see you again someday." He blew a kiss at Jane as he spun away and as Maria led her away back to their haven on the hill.

"I was trying to save you from him," Maria said over her shoulder, chuckling.

"You didn't need to do that," Jane said, careful not to step on two lovers kissing on the ground.

"Well, you're pretty fucking high," Maria said with a laugh, hopping over another set of lounging bodies. "I was just looking out for you." She reached out a hand, offering it to Jane with a smile.

She ignored it, leaping over the roadblock on her own. "Well, you don't need to."

Jane pressed on down the hill, taking the lead, not bothering to look back for Maria's reaction. She wasn't sure she could handle it, and she didn't want to risk ruining the buzz returning to her brain as the music returned to the fields.

When they reached their blanket, where Goose and Stephen had sprawled out, Jane immediately snatched the joint from her brother's fingers. She opened her lungs and let herself fly.

She knew that soon she would fall. She wanted at least the chance to taste the sky before the soil.

....

THIRTY-THREE

TELL THE TRUTH

I t's a new dawn," the frizzy-haired Grace Slick declared to the sleepy, adrenaline-fueled crowd as she stepped onto the stage. The energy was still high even as pockets of people lay sleeping across the field. Jane was one of them. She had danced her high away during Sly and the Family Stone's electrifying set, sitting down with the intention to rest and falling asleep on her side within minutes.

The pastel morning sky hung behind a slight gray veil, just dark enough to soothe everyone's red eyes, bright enough to highlight the healthy pink glow of Jane's skin.

Maria had sat beside her once she fell asleep, partly to make sure no one trampled Jane during The Who's set, but mostly just to be close to her. Jane erected a wall between them ever since Patrick released the truth that now seemed to be devouring them both. It had pushed Jane away, Maria's biggest fear. Soon they would be apart, indefinitely and across several time zones.

All she had wanted was to enjoy the nearness of Jane for the short time the universe had given them. Now, she'd lost it.

Maria knew Jane wouldn't want to miss Jefferson Airplane and used the knowledge as an excuse to wake her from her obviously much needed sleep. "Jane," she said, shaking her shoulder gently from behind. "Jane, you're missing it."

Stephen, who sat on Jane's other side, took a bolder approach. "Jane!" he shouted into her face. She startled awake, sitting up slowly.

She smacked his knee and brushed her hair out of her face. "How long did I sleep?"

"Through The Who," Stephen said, taking a hit from the joint Goose had left him when he and his battalion humped away into the hazy twilight.

Jane glanced around the crowd swaying to the maniac music of the morning. She caught Maria's gaze.

"They were okay," Maria said with a shrug, not wanting Jane to feel she'd missed much.

Jane offered a meek smile and quickly refocused her eyes on the stage. She wrapped her arms around her knees, shrinking herself away from Maria. When Stephen offered her the joint, she happily accepted it, though she at least approached it with greater restraint than she had with the stranger who'd hit on her just hours before.

Maria knew she needed to talk to Jane. Too much resided unspoken in the wedge that Jane had created. Though Maria couldn't hide from the fact that she, too, had played her part. Even if Jane insisted on keeping herself distant, she at least needed the air between them to be clear.

She smiled when Jane passed her the weed, grateful she hadn't been completely shunned.

Maria drifted into the morning buzz along with the wooden ships Jefferson Airplane steered through the fields of Bethel.

Free and easy, she thought as the trio marched their way back to their tents after the pale dawn performance. That's how it was supposed to be.

She vowed to get her and Jane to that pitchblende night beyond the silver shoreline, even if she had to risk the humiliation of throwing herself overboard into the choppy waters.

·····························

After changing clothes, Maria and Jane sat in the lawn chairs outside their tent while Stephen went on the hunt for cigarettes. The air was thick, along with the clouds, though Maria knew it wasn't entirely the humidity's fault.

She watched the storm brewing behind Jane's eyes, their usual shine dulled like a rusted blade, thunderheads swirling inside them. The sight created a cyclone in Maria's guts. It was time to calm the tide.

She took a deep breath, hoping the height that came with it would give her some sense of strength. Before she could let it out, Jane rose from her chair.

"I think I might try to sleep a bit," she said. "At least for an hour or so. You okay here?"

"Oh," Maria said, gripping the arms of her chair. "Yeah, sure. Of course." She nodded and forced out a shrug. "That's a good idea."

Jane smiled half-heartedly as she turned and disappeared into their tent, the sound of the zipper separating them making Maria's skin itch and crawl.

Her knee bounced uncontrollably, and her craving for a cigarette spiked. She almost jumped up and ran off to find Stephen, but instead she jumped up and walked back to the tent, opening the flap and crawling inside.

Jane stirred only slightly, looking up for a mere second as Maria lie beside her on her side. They faced each other, an arm's distance away, just as they had been for almost a day. Jane's eyes were open and cautious. Her mermaid hair draped over the rest of her like a veil.

"I lied," Maria said, tucking a hand between her cheek and her pillow. "I'm not okay."

The little air that hung inside the overheated tent disappeared between Jane's lips as she sucked it out. Though the inhale was subtle, Maria felt it pull at her marrow.

"I'm sorry about last night," Jane said, her voice cloaked with shame. "I smoked too much, and I was rude—"

"No," Maria said, shaking her head. "Let me say this."

She chuckled and buried her face in her pillow for a moment. When she lifted her eyes, Jane's red brows were crumpled with concern. "Okay," she said with a wary, twitchy smile.

Maria grinned. The peace of Jane steadied her breath.

"I found out about Patrick's friends in San Francisco back in May," she said. "It was just a mere idea then, really. And I had nothing else to think about or consider..." She paused as she watched the pink of Jane's skin deepen. "I had no idea you would be coming into my life," she said, suddenly finding it difficult to breathe.

A layer of luster shimmered across Jane's eyes. "You don't have to explain anything," she said. "I'm not angry that you're leaving, I hope you know that."

"I know," Maria said. "I just don't want this...this barrier between us." She waved a hand within the space separating their bodies. "I hate it, and whatever you're thinking, I just don't want you to think it."

"What am I thinking?"

Maria smirked as she lowered her chin and hardened her brows. "You tell me."

Jane inhaled deeply, exhaling with a breathy laugh. She shielded her face with a hand briefly before resting it on her neck.

"I feel like a child," she said. "A selfish child who's acting out but doesn't know why. Except…I guess I know why. And it's silly."

"I doubt that," Maria said, softening her smile.

Jane sighed, and her eyes darkened enough shades to bruise Maria's heart. "I don't want to feel like a marionette," she said. "Like I'm this flailing, useless thing controlled by someone who knows all the moves, and soon I'm going to be dropped and sent crumbling."

Maria's stomach squeezed in on itself as Jane's eyes glistened brighter, the bubbles inside them threatening to burst.

"I have feelings for you," Jane said. "I wasn't expecting it. I'm not sure if I understand it, or if I need to. I just know I feel things I've never felt before, and I hate that those things might only be felt by me."

Maria's eyes flung open. "Is that what you think?"

Jane sniffled. "I don't know," she laughed, wiping a lone tear from her long lashes. "I don't know anything."

The sound of her laughter made Maria's brain tingle. "Neither do I," she said. "I can tell you, though, that I'm feeling things I've never felt before either."

Jane scrunched her face, its ornery doubt making Maria chuckle. "I mean, you know I like women," Maria said. "That's not the issue. It's just…*this*." She wagged a finger between herself and Jane. "This is new for me. Feelings…are new to me."

"Oh." Jane's freckled face unwound itself into a helpless heap. "I…"

Maria smiled. "Trust me, you definitely don't need to say anything back to that," she said. "I just need you to know that you're no marionette. I've never manipulated you or played you. I can barely control my damn self right now." She laughed, and her heart leapt when Jane joined in, her eyes no longer dewy.

"Maria!" Stephen's voice cut through the tent, making Jane jump. "I got smokes," he yelled.

"We're right here!" Jane hollered back through her giggles. "No need to scream."

"So, stop screaming!"

Jane shook her head and rolled her eyes, back to their valley green. Maria sat up and zipped open the tent. Stephen stood just outside, a cigarette already in his mouth. "Take one and let's go," he said, tossing her the pack.

"We just got back here," Jane said. "Weren't we going to sleep?"

"Joe Cocker's coming on soon," Stephen scoffed. "We're not missing that."

Jane hoisted herself up and stretched her neck outside the tent. "It looks like it's going to pour."

Stephen shrugged. "Better wrap up then, maggots."

THIRTY-FOUR

MASTERS OF WAR

After Joe Cocker heaved and roared and rattled a storm out of the sky, the festival came to a fierce halt. The winds blew against the massive pillars hoisting the speakers in the air. The rain poured sideways at times, whipping at scrunched faces.

Most of the crowd clung to the earth at the advice of the organizers belting through the microphone, some draping ponchos over their bodies, yet still others danced with the rain, drinking it as they twirled. Jane watched it all in awe from underneath the large poncho she shared with Maria. Beside her Stephen sat calmly, almost coldly, staring out across the muddy battlefield with his camera slung around his neck under his own poncho. Jane was happy he'd finally brought it out; she had planned to take pictures throughout the weekend but had been too busy living it.

"This is insane," Maria shouted over the lashing of the rain after what felt like hours but had probably only been thirty minutes.

"Hell, this is nothing," Stephen said. "I've slept in rain, I've eaten in rain, I've shit in rain…" He shook his head and grunted. "This is a holiday."

Jane embraced the downpour in her own way as it forced her and Maria closer. She'd felt an immense weight slide off her shoulders like the rain after they finally let their masks fall, and now, she could let herself lean in. And so she did, on Maria's shoulder, until it became clear their measly poncho was no match against the sky's tears. They flung off the useless piece of plastic, rousing a burst of applause from their fellow rain rebels who danced nearby leading the crowd in a chant. "No more rain! No more rain! No more rain!"

Whether by chance or by chant, soon the clouds thinned and brought a mere drizzle, and the trio slopped their way through the swampy field on a hunt for food that ended with Goose.

He stood at the top of a slick muddy hill where a large group had gathered, sliding and wrestling in the grassy waterfall. He wore a red headband around his subtle Afro and a wide grin on his animated face.

"Radio!"

Stephen looked up, shielding his eyes from the sunbeams begging to break through the gray. Goose howled and leapt down the hill, flying down the natural slide, mud sloshing up all around him until he reached the bottom near Stephen's feet. The crowd cheered, and it wasn't long before others followed the wild soldier's lead.

"Come on!" Maria tugged Jane's arm, pulling her toward the hill.

"What? No!" Jane laughed, yanking her arm away.

Maria put her hands on her hips and smirked. "You're coming up there with me," she said. "And we're sliding down this damn hill."

"It's a mess!" Jane said.

"Yes!" Maria said, her eyes bulging. "A beautiful mess!"

Her smirk widened, bending into a sharp crescent moon like the Cheshire Cat. She bent down and stuck her hands into the drenched mud, gathering two large clumps that leaked out through her fingers.

"Don't you dare," Jane threatened, but she knew she couldn't stop Maria.

There was never any stopping Maria.

She beamed as she slapped the mud across Jane's bare legs, her jean shorts, her peach top. Its coolness caught Jane off guard. She gasped through a stunned laugh while Maria waited for the counterattack with wild eyes that shook Jane to the bone.

And so the two tangoed, wrestling in the muddy benevolent brawl waging all around them as Stephen wandered through the red clay river taking photos of the jubilant clash. Jane surrendered to the sloppy, beautiful mess and wondered how she could have ever settled for anything less.

....

After diving into the pond to wash off the cake of battle as best as they could, the soaked soldiers gathered at Goose's battalion headquarters, a cluster of cars and vans amid the thousands of other clusters of cars and vans with tarps draped across them creating makeshift canopies. "Welcome to Hooch City," Goose said when they arrived, his arms spread as wide as his grin.

Maria glanced around at the men and women sprawled about the temporary commune, some smoking cigarettes on top of wooden pallets, others eating bowls of rice they quickly offered to the newcomers. She and Jane accepted the meal with ravenous glee and settled onto a blanketed pallet beside a large white van.

The woman with braided hair who gave them their bowls pointed at Goose, who grabbed a beer from a cooler and tossed it to Stephen. "You shouldn't say hooch, you know," she said.

"And why's that?" Goose cracked open his own beer and placed a foot on top of the cooler.

"It's racist," the woman said, sliding back into her lawn chair by the group's fire pit.

Goose let out a single guttural laugh in time with a sudden popping of the flames. Stephen flinched. "No offense, sis, but this is the goddamn U. S. of A. No one gets to tell me what is or isn't racist."

The woman threw her hands up, her long bell sleeves flapping in the petrichor air. "Fair enough," she said with a resigned smile.

"Besides," Goose said after a hefty sip, "racism is military training 101."

"Yikes," Maria said before she could stop herself.

Goose chuckled. "It's true."

"Oh, I know," Maria said, wiping her mouth. "I've just never heard anyone actually in the military admit it."

"Not any white soldiers," Goose said, his brows lifting. "Racism keeps soldiers sane out in the field. Without it, we'd be killing human beings, not gooks, and if that were the case, we wouldn't do any killing. Right, Radio?"

Stephen chuckled and kept his head low. "Something like that," he said.

Goose shook his head slowly and grunted. "Anything to justify a war." He took another sip and smacked his lips together. "But hey, they gave me a medal so I best be thankful."

Maria watched Jane's eyes snap up from her food and onto Goose before quickly shifting to Stephen. She glanced back down at her emptied bowl for a moment while Maria kept her gaze on her quiet brother, who cleared his throat and glanced around the commune.

"Why did you get the medal?" Jane asked, her mild eyes now back on Goose.

Goose chewed the inside of his cheeks and nodded several times. "I dragged the best soldier in my platoon down a hill away from enemy fire after he was shot three times," he said, his voice bland yet angry, full of charred coal. "I guess you could say I earned my medal by letting him have a long, painful death in the Dustoff chopper on his way to the hospital." He scrunched his lips and shrugged. "How very gallant of me."

At that moment one of the helicopters that had been soaring around the festival all weekend blew overhead, its rippling winds chucking and echoing as it buzzed toward the stage. Goose held up his can of beer and squinted at the sky. "To bravery!"

The woman with braids snickered and shook her head. "You're twisted, and that's why I love you," she said.

Maria grinned and turned to Jane, her own smile merely a sliver of what it usually was.

"What about you, Radio?" Goose slipped a cigarette out of his pocket and lit up. "Uncle Sam throw any jewelry around your neck to make it all seem worth it?"

Maria swallowed. She held her breath for Jane, who sat motionless now, her eyes glued on Stephen. He stood with one hand in his pocket, the other fidgeting with his beer.

He cleared his throat.

"They had us try to take this hill near Cambodia," he said. "We were told there were about a thousand Viet Cong on the other side. Turns out there were about three times that."

Goose whistled and took a seat on the cooler. "Been there," he said, shaking his head.

Stephen somehow managed a chuckle, though Maria wasn't sure how. Jane remained frozen in place on their pallet. The fire purred.

"Well, you know how it is," Stephen said. "We got ambushed. We couldn't stay where we were without getting pummeled with mortar shells, and we didn't have enough men to overrun them. Our second lieutenant went down first, then my sergeant got blown right through the head."

Stephen paused and scratched at his nose. He cleared his throat again and shifted his weight from one leg to the other. Maria watched Jane's face harden with horror with each word her brother spoke. She wanted to reach down and grab her hand but was worried it would startle Jane, who already looked like she would crack at the slightest movement.

"We called in for air support, but the fuckers kept getting closer so we couldn't use it," Stephen went on. "Our own fire still managed to hit us…Someone had to make a break for it. I didn't even think. Bravery sure as fuck wasn't on my mind. Nothing was on my mind except getting it all over with."

The deep pounding of the distant stage speakers coming to life again vibrated the earth. The image of bodies flying across a muddy hill, blown into bits from the relentless blasts, burst into Maria's mind. She could feel heat seeping out of Jane's skin beside her.

"I charged up the hill, and the rest of the guys followed me. We used hand grenades and just wiped out their bunkers one at a time. It still took an entire day before we hacked out the hill. By the time what was left of the VC fell back, we'd lost sixty-two guys. One of them had been my right-hand man for six months." Stephen sniffed and shook his head. "I watched his insides get blown right out of him."

He drank his brew as Maria winced inside. She glanced over at Jane, who pierced the ground with her glassy eyes. Maria suddenly ached all over.

Goose blew out a quick puff of air. "We lost eighty-five on our worst day," he said. "Our own tanks were rollin' over us. It was a fucking mess. I feel you, man."

The crowd beyond the hills cheered as the slide of a guitar echoed throughout the darkening sky. Maria shivered. She had always been happy her brother decided to flee the wrath of war. Now, as ghosts drifted behind Stephen's charcoal eyes, that happiness came with a sense of desperation, of gobsmacked gratitude. Coming home haunted was clearly the best-case scenario.

Stephen dug out a cigarette and lit it, letting the smoke leak out slowly, his cloudy, stoned gaze fixed on the fire.

"Only way to make sense out of something like that," Goose said, leaning over his knees, "is to stop rationalizing it. Stop analyzing it. Sometimes shit just is what it is." He shrugged, his white tee bunching up slightly on his thick shoulders. "No fate, no reason, no remedy. I went to war. I killed some people. Now, I lose my shit sometimes. Them's the facts. Anything else'll just drive you clear off the edge."

Stephen grunted slightly. "I hear that."

Maria wished she could see more than just the side of Jane's face. She longed to see what swam behind her eyes now, how her heart was handling the heat of her brother's pain.

"Know what also helps?" Goose rose from the cooler and reached into his front pocket, pulling out a small plastic bag of what looked like sugar cubes. "Tabs," he said with a sly grin, shaking the bag toward Jane and Maria. "Anyone want in? What better way to close out this grand occasion?"

Maria certainly didn't feel her mental state could handle an acid trip. She smiled and waved her hand. "I'll stick to weed and rice."

Jane shook her head, her eyes shadowed and heavy. "I'm actually thinking of going back to our site to try to get some sleep."

"Girl, don't walk all the way back there," the woman at the fire said, her feet hovering near the flames seeking their warmth. "Crash here for a bit. We've got plenty of room."

Goose pointed to the van just behind them. "It's all yours," he said, popping open his bag. He stood up and handed it to Stephen with a little shake.

Maria cleared her throat. "I'm tired, too," she said, turning to Jane. "I'll join you." She smiled and offered a wink that Jane accepted with a stale, sleepy grin.

Stephen reached into the bag and pulled out a tiny white cube. He inspected it as if it were a moon rock, holding it up to the waning light. "Well," he said with a shrug, "to bravery."

....

THIRTY-FIVE

THERE'S A LIGHT

Jane stretched out on her side with Maria just behind her, staring out the back windows at the blackening night, the blue velvet bed underneath them soft and somehow cool. She ran a hand across the plush upholstery, hoping to soak in its comfort.

The muffled sound of fireside laughter and chatter leaked through the van, its walls draped in tapestries and beads that shimmered within the dim cave on wheels. Jane wondered how long it took acid to kick in.

"Are you okay?" Maria's breath tingled the back of Jane's bare neck, her hair tossed into a massive bun at the crown of her head.

"Yeah," Jane said, her own voice sounding removed from her body. "Why?"

She felt Maria shift slightly in the bed. "It was a lot for me to hear those stories about the war," she said. "I imagine it was even harder for you."

Jane tried to block out the flashes of intestines flying through a jungle that radiated through her mind like mortar rounds. The cheers and shouts just outside the van turned into mangled screams of horror. She clamped her eyes shut for a moment, stomping out the picture she once so badly wanted Stephen to paint for her.

She took a breath, the air thick with patchouli, and let out a slow sigh. "At least he's talking," she said, tucking her hand under her chin. "Though I'm not sure I like him doing acid. I doubt his brain can handle that right now."

"I understand that," Maria said. "But he made it through war in one piece," she said. "He can handle anything now."

Jane struggled to keep the visions at bay, the sixty-two bodies blown to bits, every one of them a casualty of circumstances beyond their control. Goose was right—some things were best left unattended.

"Goose reminds me of you," she said.

Maria chuckled. "Really?"

Jane nodded toward the van's back door. "A bit," she said. "His take on life. His carefree attitude. Just taking things as they come and letting them go."

"Hmm." Maria sounded skeptical. "It's easier in certain situations than in others."

"When is it easy?"

The gentle crackling of the fire punctured the silence until Maria released a deflated laugh. "I guess I lied," she said. "Maybe it's never easy. Maybe you just get conditioned to it. Maybe it's all just…survival."

Jane listened to the steady, synced rhythms of their lungs for a few moments. Their harmony at least was one thing that didn't need to be questioned or doubted, even if the time it kept dwindled by the minute.

She shivered slightly.

"Are you cold?"

Maria didn't wait for Jane to answer before grabbing a blanket near their feet and draping it over both of them. She wrapped her arm around Jane, pulling her closer, their bodies cupped into each other's like two puzzle pieces.

Jane struggled to find her breath, the closeness stealing it all away. She allowed her arm to relax against Maria's engulfing her, their hands touching just enough to share their heat. She cleared her throat and closed her eyes. "Sorry, if my hair's in your face," she said, trying to laugh through her nerves that ricocheted off the walls of her stomach like a thousand Bouncing Betties.

"You're fine," Maria said, sparking up the back of Jane's neck once again. "You're perfect."

Jane wondered if Maria could hear her lips stretching into a smile, if she could feel her heart beating through her spine. The thought didn't linger long as she surrendered to the cocoon they'd created together and to the sleep that pulled her into the warming darkness.

....

Gray light poured onto Jane's face through the dusty windows. She shielded her eyes from its noise with one hand while sliding the other out from under the pillow and wiggling it back to life.

The concept of time couldn't find its place in the fog Jane worked to crawl out of from her blackout sleep. With Maria's tan, butter-smooth arm still wrapped around her waist, she wasn't sure she was ready to escape it. She closed her eyes again, shutting out the world to focus her senses on Maria, to bottle up her scent, embed the sensation of her body against her own into her skin like a sailor's tattoo. Jane had a feeling the phenomenon of Maria would reside in her forever anyway; she might as well seal it in ink.

She inched her way out from Maria's grasp to peer out the back window. "Maria," she whispered. "Maria, we slept all night."

She sat on her knees as Maria moaned and rolled onto her back, covering her face with both hands. "What?" The added gravel to her voice made Jane shiver.

She glanced back toward the daylight and nodded. "It's morning," she said.

"No, it's not." Maria flung her arms down and shot her eyes open. "Oh, my god," she said, sitting up. "How?"

Jane laughed. "Well, we hadn't slept in two days."

"Right," Maria said, squinting.

The intimacy of morning, of waking beside Maria in her natural state, made Jane feel stoned. Then her brother's face popped into her head.

"I'm going to check on Stephen," she said, opening the back door. The overcast glow hit her like a migraine, dull yet blinding. Maria groaned and flopped back onto the bed. Jane chuckled as she crawled out into the wreckage of the night. Beer cans riddled the swampy ground. A piercing, distant guitar echoed over the hills.

She scanned the sleeping soldiers wrapped around their lovers, tiptoeing around the site and peering into car windows. She circled back to the commune's center with a pit opening inside her stomach.

Jane walked over to the pallets near the van where Goose slept on his back with the braided woman draped over him. She leaned in and tapped his shoulder, whispering his name until he snorted awake.

"Goose, where's Stephen?" She hoped he would hear the urgency in her voice even through his half-sleep. "Goose—"

"He's sleeping," he said, rolling onto his side. "We all sleeping."

"He's not here, I looked." Jane sensed her pulse racing through her and wondered if that was how it felt to be on acid. The thought spiked her fears even higher.

Goose settled into the spooning his lover drew him into and grunted. "He's probably out there watching Jimi," he said. "Don't worry, girl."

"Don't worry?" she barely breathed out.

She took a few steps back until she felt a pair of hands on her shoulders. She whipped around, hoping to find Stephen but finding Maria instead.

"He's not here," Jane said, trying to keep her panic at bay. "Goose doesn't even know where he is."

Maria gazed up toward the hill that overlooked the main festival grounds. "Let's go find him," she said calmly. "He might just be at the stage."

Jane took a deep breath, wishing she shared the confidence. Maria took a step closer, her eyes serious, and grabbed her shoulders. "Like I said last night, your brother can do anything now." She smiled and gave Jane a light shake. "Let's go."

Though the crowd had dissipated on that final festival morning, Jane still couldn't fathom how she would spot Stephen among the thousands who remained. As they walked the pathway toward the muddy bluff, each passing face blurred into the next. None of them were Stephen's.

This wasn't the experience she'd wanted to have while witnessing Jimi Hendrix in the flesh. She pictured butterflies and zebras and moonbeams just like the poetic guitarist promised. She never imagined hunting for her brother who was quite possibly deep inside the claws of a flashback or in a horrid comedown or perhaps a venomous combination of both. She never imagined fear.

Jane stopped marching up the hill, letting the crowd sliver past her. She sensed invisible walls caving in on her and heat pressing down from some heavy, unknown source. Maria made it nearly to the top before she turned and spotted her frozen in panic. She ran back down and grabbed Jane's face with both hands. "Hey," she said, drilling her calm eyes into Jane's wild ones. "Breathe."

It was only one word, but it was enough for Jane to pause for a moment and gather her mind. She closed her eyes and inhaled deeply, exhaling along with Maria, who she could feel coming closer. Jane opened her eyes to find Maria's forehead resting on hers now. The nearness made her weak but calm. The peace of Maria despite her wildness was part of what made Jane drawn to her flame.

They took several more breaths together as Jimi's hectic energy dulled to a languid, marshy rhythm where he reigned alone, soothing Jane's ingrained impulse to fear the worst.

Maria pulled back slightly and smiled. "He's good," she said with a nod. "You're good."

Jane breathed out a much needed chuckle. "Yes," she said. "I will be."

The subtle breeze suddenly carried a familiar-sounding melody. Maria pulled back further as her eyes lit up like the rockets' red glare. It seemed Jane wasn't the only one to detect the national anthem wailing into the sky.

"Uncle Sam is calling," Maria said, wiggling her eyebrows. Jane spit out a laugh and let Maria grab her arm. She led her to the top of the hill where they overlooked the mighty morning crowd that stood and sat and smoked in awe of Jimi's instrumental warped spin on "The Star-Spangled Banner." He looked like Goose, a red scarf tied around his slightly more voluminous hair. The fringe on his white gypsy blouse dangled like wind chimes as he worked his guitar and the crowd into a beautiful frenzy.

Jane shook her head slowly, mesmerized by the song's mad beauty, the violent splendor. She scanned the crowd, soaking in all the marvelous reactions of amazement, and spotted a gentle mop of sandy brown that caught her eye. She yelped.

"Stephen!"

Down the hill he stood, straight and sturdy, gaze stuck on the stage. Jane grabbed Maria's hand and set off through the maze of bodies, practically floating with relief along the mud-soaked grass. She grabbed Stephen's shoulder as they reached his side. "Hey! You okay?"

Stephen stared forward, his eyes alert, his lips slightly open as if he yearned to speak but couldn't find the words. Jane leaned in to ask him again before she spotted the dog tags draped around his neck. "Martin" the first line read, and the second "Stephen R."

She studied his face. She saw him. At least part of him.

Jane found a speck of light in his hazel eyes she hadn't seen since he came home. She didn't know how long it would last, when it would come again, if at all. She knew it wouldn't be easy, but Goose was living proof that it could be done. It was possible.

It was always possible. She hoped Stephen saw that, too.

As the stunning anthem ended in a sea of applause and melted into the wild rock and roll of "Purple Haze," Stephen threw his hands into the air and howled. Jane instantly turned to Maria and laughed before watching her, too, belt into the sky. Stephen ran a few more feet down the hill for a closer view while Jane joined Maria and the surrounding herd of strangers in dancing to the Hendrix groove, its chaos controlled and tight.

Jane let her limbs finally shake off the weight of worry. Her state of wonder made her feel oblivious to the world until the sensation of Maria gripping her waist pulled her back into being.

She closed her eyes, certain she was dreaming, as Maria drew her in with a hand behind her neck. When their lips touched, they did so without hesitation or shame, and Jane instantly understood how it would feel to kiss the sky just as Jimi sang of just a few feet away from where she floated. Her head begged to explode as Maria slid a subtle tongue across her own before pulling away. Jane opened her eyes and looked directly into Maria's. She searched the wild, brazen thickets of her mind for something to say before realizing it was pointless. It was another one of those things best left unattended.

Instead, she smiled. Maria smirked. The music breathed. And they danced one last time in the name of love and peace.

....

THIRTY-SIX

TIME IS TIGHT

Jane stared at the empty boxes piled up in the corner of her room. She didn't have much to pack; that certainly wasn't the cause of delay. It was the next phase of her life that began the moment she placed the first piece of clothing inside the box. It was the bittersweet aroma of change, of impending heartache. It was the end of a summer she was certain she could have never predicted. She focused instead on getting ready for the gala.

She studied herself in the mirror, surprised at how pink her skin had gotten at Woodstock. The freckles on her nose had multiplied, along with the size of her hips, it seemed. Jane turned to the side, gazing at a body she only partly recognized as her own. It was softer here and edgier there, golden all over. Her lips looked the same to the naked eye but they hadn't felt the same since Maria graced them with her own, pressing with purpose, with passionate tenderness. They tingled and swelled at the mere memory.

She placed her fingertips on her warm lips and sighed.

A knock at the door startled Jane out of the fiery fog. Her mother stood just outside the bedroom in a sleek, classic navy dress, her auburn hair free of its low bun and draped along her shoulders. "Honey, could you zip me up?"

She stepped into the room as Jane struggled to find her voice. "Mom, you…you never wear your hair down," she said with a smile. She tried to keep her eyes from bulging out of her head over her mother's beauty.

Rebecca turned her back to Jane, who slid the gold zipper up her mother's spine. "Does it look silly?"

Jane laughed. "Are you serious? You look amazing."

Her mother faced her and ran her hands down her fitted dress that Jane couldn't remember ever seeing her wear. "I certainly have no idea what to wear to something like this," she said with a nervous laugh.

She reminded Jane of herself back in June when she had panicked over her outfit before going to Spin City with Maria. The image made her smile.

"You look beautiful," Rebecca said, running a finger down Jane's arm.

Jane glanced in the mirror on the other side of the room. Her mustard yellow dress brought out her sun-kissed skin. She wondered if Maria would like it.

Rebecca sighed and shook her head as she softened her gaze and folded her arms. "Where does the time go?"

Her voice was weary but sweet, her eyes soft and light yet full of longing. Of memory.

Jane wished she had the answer.

Rebecca tucked a piece of Jane's hair behind her ear. "I'm proud of you, by the way," she said.

"For what?"

"For everything," she said nonchalantly. "I'm proud of the woman you're becoming, the woman you already are."

Jane huffed out a laugh. Rebecca flashed a curious smile and tilted her head, her eyes sparkling. "What is it?"

Jane shook her head and tightened her lips. She wasn't even entirely certain she knew the woman who looked back at her in the mirror, not that it was a bad thing. There was a sense of familiar newness, that same sensation she felt pulling at her the moment she laid eyes on Maria all those moons ago.

"Nothing," Jane said with a half-smile, the horns and howls of the Village swirling all around her as if she were right back on that fire escape. "You're right. Time has a mind of its own."

Her mother glanced around the room and pointed at the empty boxes. "You better get started," she said, giving Jane a gentle poke. "You leave in a few days."

Jane bit her lip and nodded. "That I do." She tried to laugh but it came out like a sigh of defeat. She sat on the bed and wondered exactly how many miles stretched between New York and San Francisco.

Rebecca joined her at the bed's edge. "Kay mentioned to me that Maria's heading out west." She cleared her throat and placed her hands in her lap. "That's exciting for her, of course, but I'm so sorry she won't be around."

A balloon began swelling inside Jane's throat. She swallowed it away, not ready for the burst. Not yet.

"So am I," she said, and she could tell her mother was watching the large bubble building over her eyes, willing Jane to go on.

She couldn't. There was nothing more than those facts, stubborn but solid. Something to hold onto in a world where ground was nearly impossible to find. Not everything had the luxury of being wrapped up in a perfect bow. Not the idea of self. Not sex. Certainly not war. Never loss. Closure was a myth, she realized, though one of honest intention. She thought perhaps closure wasn't quite the right term, or the right goal. Maybe all anyone could get was some peace. And what was so wrong with that?

. . . .

Maria had been to the underground bar a thousand times before. She'd danced in its heated shadows, made out with nameless girls in the hallway, hiding. Running. Yet tonight, as she leaned against the bar stool nursing a beer while waiting for Jane and her mother, Maria felt a wave of nerves surge through her, sweeping her into a nostalgic tide of schoolgirl flirtation, of newness. She chuckled to herself as she gazed out at the packed crowd and saw herself and Jane in the center of them all dancing, sweating, falling.

It had been almost two months since that night when the heat that pulsed between their two bodies told Maria all she needed to know. The dust-covered wick had been struck; a small happening, perhaps, but one with the consequences of a wildfire.

She spotted the flames of red blazing in the doorway and nearly jumped at Jane's glow. It was magnified by the rays emitting from Rebecca, who walked in beside Jane looking ten years younger and several inches taller. They threaded through the masses, two electrical currents giving light to the darkness, and met Maria at the crowded bar.

"You two clean up nice," Maria said, too stunned to work anything else out of her parted lips, too embarrassed to go bolder. Another sign of that new softness, that malleable mold.

Jane smiled and looked lovingly at her mother, who clutched her pearl handbag near her navel and glanced around the loud cellar sparkling with sweat and glitter. "Well, I assumed the bar would be quite high," she said.

Maria nodded. "Oh, it is." She grinned and took a sip of her lukewarm beer. "I saw Kay's dress," she said with a wink. "You've set the standard."

"I can't wait to see it," Jane said, her green lagoon eyes shimmering like the purple shadow Kay painted onto his hooded lids a few hours earlier. She tapped her mother's arm and smirked. "She barely let me have a peek."

Maria's heart swelled for Jane, her lightness leaping from her vanilla cream skin like Goose diving down the red-clay hill. She had her mother back, and it showed.

The dim room suddenly blackened over, an eclipse cloaking the cramped space save for the tiny stage lights that flashed upon a drag king in a tuxedo, his thick brown hair slicked back, his feminine brows penciled and impeccable, breasts bound beneath a silky black vest.

"Ladies and not-so-gentle ladies," the Romeo shouted, sending a wave of hoots and hollers rippling across the eccentric crowd of queens and other royalty, of young misfits and classic Geralds, of two glowing redheads and a Sicilian. Smoke drifted over their heads like the morning fog clinging to the trees of Bethel. "Tonight, we bring you the queens of the Village, a court of the finest kind, from the busty bitches of the Bowery to the great women of the Wild West. As we celebrate them on this annual evening of pomp and powder, let us remember it is ours and ours alone! We fought for this, we bled for this, and by God, we have earned it!"

Maria laughed through her howling and imagined Brian and his beloved megaphone, loud and imposing but not nearly as magnanimous or charming as the crisp king on stage now. She smiled at Jane's billowing, bright eyes glued to the gender-bending glamour, at her mother's peach blush that bloomed red now. It was a show all in itself.

They watched Ella Titzgerald and Grace Slicker and Patsy Divine shake and sing and swoon their way across the low platform backdropped against blinding tinsel curtains. The intoxicated audience sucked it up like drunk leeches. By the time Kay graced the stage, they were itching for the heart.

Maria roared when her dazzling roommate burst through the dangling silver streams to the punchy horns of "Lavender Coffin," her tone, shadowed arms spread wide. She wore her handmade slim cocktail dress like a layer of her own flesh, cinched at the waist with a draped front overskirt, shimmering with lavender and plum iridescence. Maria was happy to see Kay donning her classic black wig with the short tapered back; it was both of their favorites.

She prayed to God, just as Kay sang out to St. Peter, that she would remember all of this—Rebecca's prideful yet bashful smile, Jane's youthful amazement at the scene, Kay in all her purple triumph, Manhattan nights that bled into Manhattan mornings. The best of New York City, this accidental home that had wrapped its metal wings around Maria, offering her a concrete nest in which to grow and one day leave. That moment would come in mere days when she would barrel out west, keep flying, stretching wider. And Jane would be doing the same, growing smarter and richer and brighter than she already was, her own flight in a different direction a four-year journey Maria prayed would lift her even higher. To the moon, maybe, to the heights Jane deserved.

For now, Maria watched her in the dark with sharp eyes, sketching and embedding her into memory, her colors, her caramel freckles that formed constellations that were all her own. Jane turned and caught her staring, but Maria didn't flinch away. Their lips curved upward together, two crescent moon smiles that knew anything was possible despite the chaos that came with life's unpredictable currents. Joy, beauty, peace, growth. They came in moments like these, hot, surprising summers, smoke breaks on fire escapes, darkrooms and muddy fields, a brick through a window. Spontaneous kisses. Unspoken love.

Maybe moments were enough. Maybe they were more than enough.

THIRTY-SEVEN

NO REGRETS

They lay on Maria's bed, face to face, still in their clothes. The night was still. Kay had ventured to another bar after walking Rebecca to the subway, the apartment ghost-quiet now without him. Maria seized the silence and listened to Jane's breath, memorizing its rhythm.

"What will you miss most about New York?" Jane asked.

It was so strangely mute that Maria could hear the distant rumble of the subway deep inside the city's belly. Train cars of memories from the last six years flew by, though there was only one that mattered now. She smiled. "The possibilities."

Jane grinned back, her pale lips plumping. "I'm sure the west coast is full of those."

Maria felt her eyes sadden. She forced some life back into them by looking deeper into Jane's. "Yeah, but they won't be the same."

Nothing would be the same in San Francisco. The air would smell of sea instead of trash, the summer would taste like crab, not concrete. There would be friends she would make, but they wouldn't be Kay. And, sure, there would be women. None of them would be Jane. None of them would look like a Celtic princess in the middle of the night as the window's white sheer curtains blew behind her long sheets of red, like Queen Boudicca on her chariot with the Roman winds whipping past her in battle. Lilith the temptress and her rebellious heart bursting into flames.

Temptation certainly clawed at Maria's warm flesh as Jane lay before her in her golden crochet dress, only one layer away from her own skin. But something akin to guilt bit back, or some sense of sisterly protection. Maria was five years older, and though not necessarily wiser she still couldn't bring herself to go under those sheets, make those moves, take that step. It would be a big one for Jane as it was for many, one that shouldn't be followed by a goodbye that may or may not be for now or for forever. Maria glanced at her mother's candle over Jane's shoulder and prayed it wouldn't be the latter.

She sat up and slid over Jane onto the floor, crossing the hardwood to her desk where she brought Mary's virgin wick to life. She held the tall glass container in her hand, its surface painted with the blessed mother's solemn, serene face looking down at her hands in prayer. The subtle click and crackle of the lighter purred within the dim room. Maria smiled as she set the candle back down.

Back in bed, she stared at the small shadow of the holy flame dancing on the cream-white wall.

"Is there anything in your life you would do differently?" Jane asked after a short stretch of quiet. "Do you have any regrets?"

Maria smiled when she realized the question didn't make her nauseous. "I used to wonder if I should have tried harder to get my mother to talk to me," she finally said. "Then I realized I don't think there was anything I could have done. When someone doesn't want to see something, nothing will make them see it."

"That's not your job, anyway," Jane said, her voice soft as silk yet firm as Maria's mattress. "Kids shouldn't have to make their parents be parents."

Maria shrugged. "What about you? Any regrets?"

Jane puffed out a laugh. "I don't think I've lived enough yet to have any."

"Of course you have!" Maria tapped Jane's arm. "Look at everything you did this summer."

She was thankful Jane didn't say she regretted the two of them meeting. She couldn't have imagined her life any other way.

"Who was your first kiss?" Jane asked, tucking deeper into her pillow.

"Who do you think?" Maria smirked. "Theresa."

"It wasn't a boy?"

Maria shook her head violently and laughed. "Absolutely not. I've never kissed a guy, other than Kay, of course." Jane's beautiful eyes swelled, making Maria chuckle even more. "What? Is that surprising?"

Jane sighed, then shrugged. "Oh, I guess not," she said with a nervous laugh. "I suppose you would have been my first if Joey didn't shove his tongue at me after prom."

Maria scrunched her face at the repulsive image. "I'm so sorry."

Jane cackled, bending her head back, giving Maria a clear view of her neck. She swallowed back her own tongue that longed to run itself along the long, elegant canvas toward Jane's lips.

As they settled back into their silence, two heated bodies separated by mere inches and two layers of clothing, Maria saw in Jane's eyes what she felt in her own veins—longing restrained, but barely, by sadness and grief, by the sense of urgency that told them to bare their histories to each other instead of their flesh. They ran through their lives like slideshows, desperate to make up for time the universe hadn't granted them. Maria showed Jane the diamond-shaped scar on her elbow that she'd earned at the previous year's disastrous Democratic National Convention. She'd also earned her second arrest during the riot, along with a black eye from a cop with a southern drawl to his spit-sputtered bark. Jane blushed when she recalled the time at eight or nine years old when she decided to count all of her freckles and moles one night but fell asleep before she made it to one hundred. Maria had to keep her own flushing at bay as the thought of running her fingers across every mark on Jane's body rushed through her like a napalm cloud. She cooled down by refocusing on the facts: three days, Sarah Lawrence, San Francisco. Everything else was too slippery.

They finally stopped their storytelling when the sun began to seep in through the window. The light shone onto their weary eyes, red and raw. They lingered in each other's until the bittersweet wakeful night swept over them, and they fell asleep to the sounds of Manhattan moving on all around them.

....

THIRTY-EIGHT

LOVE IS A BURNING THING

Claire's eyes were wide behind her sunglasses, almost as wide as her smile. "Really?"

Jane smiled, hiding behind her ice cream cone. The two of them sat on Doug's apartment stoop in the late afternoon sun that burned off the concrete back onto their faces. Despite the heat, Jane felt a weight melt off her shoulders like the chocolate dessert melting in her mouth as she finally told her best friend about the other special woman in her life, one who was leaving it just as quickly as she entered it.

"Why didn't you tell me?" Claire nudged Jane's elbow, nearly knocking her own cone out of her hand.

Jane looked down and shook her head. "I didn't know what I was feeling at first," she said. "Then I found out Maria was leaving…I guess I didn't think it mattered at that point."

"Of course it matters!" Claire's high-pitched shout made Jane laugh, a welcome reprieve from the agony of impending goodbyes.

"Well, I'm sorry I didn't tell you earlier," she said. "I was kind of a mess."

Claire moved in closer to Jane, shimmying up against her arm. "Now, you're just like the rest of us," she said with a wink.

Jane smiled but buried her head, finishing off the last of her cone before tossing the napkin into the trash can on the sidewalk. She wiped her hands and sighed, glancing out at the busy Village street.

Claire put her chin on Jane's bare shoulder. "Love is a burning thing," she said.

Jane managed a light laugh through a moan. "I'm learning." She recalled the burning from just two nights earlier when she lay beside Maria in her bed, desirous and dizzy. Neither of them made the move, an unspoken decision they'd made together. Jane wouldn't have known what to do anyway. Though she certainly had ideas.

Claire stood and threw out her vanilla treat before settling back onto the searing steps. "Have you told your mom?"

Jane shook her head. "No, but I think she knows something's going on."

"Well, I'm honored you told me," Claire said, beaming. "And I'm sorry."

"About what?"

"About what you're going through." Claire slipped her sunglasses to the top of her head, her blue eyes soft and sincere.

Jane smiled. "I'm not."

She turned back to the street before glancing up at the fire escape above her. She thought of that sticky night in June, how she could have never predicted where it would lead, what it would bring, who it would embed into her skin. There was never any knowing.

She smiled again as Claire wrapped her sweaty arm around her. "You'll be okay," she said, pulling Jane in tighter.

For once, Jane didn't doubt her.

Because regardless of the muddiness of love and heartbreak, of fate and coincidence, the facts, at least, would always be the facts. They never changed, and there was a calm that came with their consistency.

She met Maria. She knew Maria. She loved Maria. Them's were the facts, as Goose would say.

And there was beauty in every one.

....

THIRTY-NINE

FARE THEE WELL

The meadow was soft and hazy as the sun dipped behind the metal horizon. The light poured over Jane like liquid gold. Maria wanted to bathe in it.

She watched Jane shake the bag Maria handed her when they arrived at their spot on the lawn, one that they now viewed as their own private lot in Manhattan. Jane's eyes lit up when she pulled out the record, "Sweet Jane" by The Velvet Underground. She turned it over and laughed. "Maria!" She looked up from the gift with a pouty smile. "How appropriate," she said with a chuckle that made Maria's stomach flutter.

Jane shook her head and sighed. "I didn't get you anything," she said, her eyes sullen.

"Oh," Maria said, knowing full well her face was brazen red. "You did." She nodded and smiled, happy to see she wasn't the only one with a crimson coat. Jane smoldered.

They sat in silence in the afterglow of day, watching the city fall into shadow. When the moon finally sponged its way through the blue, they folded their blanket and walked back to Columbus Circle.

They stood at the edge of the park, and at the edge of something much greater, Maria knew. The aching, beautiful uncertainty stretched out before them like the traffic in Bethel. They stood at the entrance, hesitant, as bodies whizzed by them, eager to get on with their days and their lives.

Maria pulled out a piece of paper from her back pocket and placed it in Jane's palm, closing her hand over it. "I'll be staying with Patrick's friends for a while until I get my own place," she said. "That's the address and phone number."

Jane smiled and offered a single, solid nod. Her glistening eyes made Maria's burn.

"When you become a literary critic or a famous photographer, you better not forget me," she said, sliding a finger down Jane's arm.

Jane laughed, and it nearly echoed around the concrete circle. "And you better not forget me when you're a famous writer. Make sure to invite me to your debut book release." She winked.

Maria couldn't imagine remembering anyone else.

She pulled Jane in, melting into her body, hoping the grip around her waist would leave indents in her skin like train tracks. She closed her eyes and smiled as vanilla drifted into her nose. "Goodbye's too good a word, babe," she tried to sing, but it came out like a cracked whisper. "So I'll just say fare thee well." She finished the Dylan lyric and pulled back as Jane palmed her cheek, kissing it just long enough to make Maria's head spin.

Jane tucked a piece of her mermaid hair behind her ear and smiled. "I'd stick to writing," she said.

Maria's mouth fell open as Jane tightened her lips. They drifted in the teasing silence until they both finally broke out in laughter. The streetlamps above them flickered on, dusk descending like a cloud.

Jane edged away toward the sidewalk, swinging her record bag. Maria waited for the light to turn green. "I'll see you, Red," she said with a nod.

She watched Jane all the way to the subway steps, holding her breath at the sight. As the red queen disappeared beneath the city, Maria turned on her heels and smiled. "I'm not that horrible of a singer," she said aloud.

She shook her head and lit a cigarette, chuckling to herself as she ventured back to her apartment where Kay and her two packed bags awaited. The midnight train was coming soon.

But until then it was just her and Manhattan, and the scent of Jane that lingered on her collar.

....

FORTY

EVERYTHING'S GONNA BE ALRIGHT

Jane stood in the middle of her bedroom that smelled like cardboard even after Stephen had taken all of the boxes out to the car. She took a breath and scanned the empty space. When she landed on her bed, which her mother refused to strip just in case Jane found her way home on weekends, the scent of Maria suddenly drifted into her nose. Smoke and gin, earth and spice. Her lips of rouge cream.

She smiled as sat down in the same place where she had kissed Maria all those weeks ago, weeks that felt equally distant yet close now. She could touch them if she wanted, but through a thin veil of glass. They were delicate memories. She wondered how tightly she could hold them without breaking them into pieces.

A knock at her open door pried her out of the bittersweet pang of nostalgia.

"You almost ready?" Stephen hung in the doorway, his slightly shaggy hair catching the early sun drenching the hallway.

"As ready as I will be." Jane smiled before blowing out a sigh.

Stephen folded his arms and smirked. "You're taking my camera, right?"

"I will if you want me to," Jane said. "It's yours, though."

Stephen shook his head vigorously. "You've proven that to not be the case," he said, chuckling. "You have a talent. Please use it."

Jane felt her face slacken. "What about you? What are you going to do?"

He took a breath, his vast chest expanding even wider. He let it out and walked over to Jane, joining her on the bed. "I'm technically still on active duty," he said. "I'll finish up here in a few months, then I'll keep helping Mom with the store. Everything else will just…come when it comes, I guess."

"Hmm." Jane smiled and nodded.

"By the way," Stephen said, reaching into his back pocket and pulling out a small envelope, "I got the few photos we took at the festival printed. I wanted to give you this." Jane took the envelope, her eyebrows peaking. Stephen stood and headed for the door, stopping just as he got to the hall. He turned and said, "I'll see you outside," before vanishing down the stairs.

Jane smiled and looked down at the surprise envelope. She opened the unglued flap and pulled out the black and white photo with gentle fingers.

Her heart swelled.

She and Maria wrestled in the mud bath of Bethel, baptizing themselves through the brawl, slathered in sticky brown clay and joy. Their smiles nearly blew out the image, blinding in breadth and brilliance. Their arms wrapped around each other, holding themselves down to the sodden earth, legs intertwined.

Jane chuckled, covering her mouth with her hand that clammed up almost on instinct at the image. The effect of Maria.

She shook her head and felt her lips twitch, unable to sustain their smile any longer. A tear fell without warning, dropping onto her lap. She laughed again, wiping her lashes as she took a deep breath.

She glanced down at her leather bag at the foot of the bed, the only thing left for her to load into the car, where inside were a few books and her favorite records, one of which she'd received just the day before in the dusky haze of Manhattan. A gift no one could replicate, from a woman no words could ever do justice, at the end of what felt like a feverish dream.

Slinging the bag over her shoulder, she went down to the living room and grabbed an envelope and stamp from her mother's desk. She'd already memorized the address. As she wrote it, the zip code felt foreign to her pen stroke: 94117. The distance was palpable. But so was the bliss in the photograph she slid into the envelope and carried outside to the mailbox on the corner.

An army of butterflies surged through her belly as she walked back to the packed car where her mother and Stephen waited to take her to the next stage of her life. She smiled knowing the gift of memory would be awaiting Maria as she moved into her own in the hills of San Francisco.

Sitting in the back of the Pontiac, Stephen at the wheel, her mother in the passenger seat, Jane watched the city disappear behind her as they flew across the Whitestone Bridge, the powder-blue sky opening around the East River as if in heat. She could almost feel Maria's head on her shoulder just as they had slept on the drive home from Woodstock only days earlier.

She glanced up and caught Stephen's eye in the rearview mirror. He winked, offering a subtle smirk in its wake. Jane smiled and leaned her head against the window.

Everything will come when it comes.

ACKNOWLEDGMENTS

This novel came to me in a manic wave this past spring, even though it includes many of the things I've always wanted to write about. The universe channeled the story of Jane and Maria through me, and I am so happy to have been the recipient.

I have to thank my beta readers, Tessa Markle and Jessica Semler, who read this so quickly even as they juggled their own hectic schedules as creatives. You two are amazing, and your insight and eyes are more than appreciated.

I also have to thank my co-worker and writing mentor, Barbara White Stack, who edited this novel in mere days. Your red pen may be scary at times, but I know it will always help me improve my skills.

To all of my other co-workers and friends who are the victims of my dribble before anyone else sees it and who are forced to hear my creative ramblings and rantings—you're godsends. Truly, truly godsends.

I also want to acknowledge the activists who ignited the Stonewall riots and the movement that followed, the activists who are no longer with us and whose stories deserve to be told— Marsha P. (Pay It No Mind) Johnson, Sylvia Ray Rivera, and Stormé DeLarverie, along with so many unknown others who lit the flames of resistance. Because of their bravery and endurance, those of us in the queer community today have a platform and a purpose. And a shit ton of Pride.

To my teachers and mentors throughout the years, from elementary school to university—you lit the fire in me that fueled my creative pursuits, and I owe a great deal of gratitude to you all.

And, of course, thank you to my family for accepting me as I am and for supporting all of my endeavors and adventures, no matter how strange they may be. I love you.

ABOUT THE AUTHOR

Chelsey Engel is a writer and labor activist based in Pittsburgh, Pennsylvania. She earned her bachelor's degree in photojournalism from Point Park University in 2011 and began working for the United Steelworkers (USW) union in 2012.

www.chelseyengel.com

www.ingramcontent.com/pod-product-compliance
Lightning Source LLC
Chambersburg PA
CBHW021118110726
47900CB00007B/2238